Every Storm

Also by Lori Wick in Large Print:

Bamboo & Lace
The Proposal
The Pursuit
The Rescue
The Visitor
Beyond the Picket Fence and Other Stories
City Girl
Every Little Thing About You
A Gathering of Memories
The Knight and the Dove
A Place Called Home
A Song for Silas
A Texas Sky
Who Brings Forth the Wind
Wings of the Morning

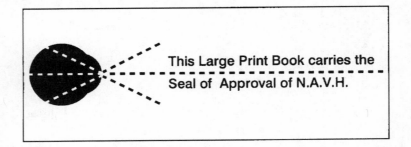

This Large Print Book carries the
Seal of Approval of N.A.V.H.

Every Storm

Lori Wick

Thorndike Press • Waterville, Maine

Published in 2004 by arrangement with Harvest House Publishers.

Thorndike Press® Large Print Christian Romance.

The tree indicium is a trademark of Thorndike Press.

The text of this Large Print edition is unabridged.
Other aspects of the book may vary from the original edition.

Set in 16 pt. Plantin by Christina S. Huff.

Printed in the United States on permanent paper.

Library of Congress Cataloging-in-Publication Data

Wick, Lori.
    Every storm / Lori Wick.
        p. cm.
    ISBN 0-7862-7057-8 (lg. print : hc : alk. paper)
    ISBN 1-59415-055-9 (lg. print : sc : alk. paper)
    1. Survival after airplane accidents, shipwrecks, etc. — Fiction.   2. World War, 1939–1945 — Naval operations, American — Fiction.   3. World War, 1939–1945 — Oceania — Fiction.   4. Americans — Oceania — Fiction.   5. Oceania — Fiction.   6. Large type books.   I. Title.
PS3573.I237E93 2004b
813′.54—dc22   2004059549

This book has been in my heart for more years than I can remember. It needed a war setting as a catalyst for the relationships involved. The history buff and readers who enjoy very accurate details will find much to forgive. But at no time in this fictitious account did my heart lose track of the sacrifice that took place at sea, on land, in the air, and on the home front — not just in WWII, but in every war.

I wish to dedicate this book to the men and women who gave up much — sometimes everything — for the freedoms I enjoy each day.

As the Founder/CEO of NAVH, the only national health agency solely devoted to those who, although not totally blind, have an eye disease which could lead to serious visual impairment, I am pleased to recognize Thorndike Press★ as one of the leading publishers in the large print field.

Founded in 1954 in San Francisco to prepare large print textbooks for partially seeing children, NAVH became the pioneer and standard setting agency in the preparation of large type.

Today, those publishers who meet our standards carry the prestigious "Seal of Approval" indicating high quality large print. We are delighted that Thorndike Press is one of the publishers whose titles meet these standards. We are also pleased to recognize the significant contribution Thorndike Press is making in this important and growing field.

Lorraine H. Marchi, L.H.D.
Founder/CEO
NAVH

★ Thorndike Press encompasses the following imprints: Thorndike, Wheeler, Walker and Large Print Press.

Special People to Thank . . .

Lorri Bauer, a friend from long years past. You always told me two *r*'s are better than one. My sweet memories from that time made me want to use the spelling of your name over my own. It was so special for me to share a name with you. Thank you for your love and kindness over the years.

Matt and Abby, precious son and daughter. You were real troupers. When this story arrived, it came in a rush. Thanks for all your efforts and great attitudes. Some days it's the laughter that keeps us going.

Julie Koehn, my niece, for your wonderfully creative mind and marvelous suggestion. And **Jessica Taylor,** another niece. I don't think I could mention Julie and not also remember what great listeners the two of you were. Lazy days at Fish Lake where you listened to my plans and dreams and laughed in all the right places. My deepest love and thanks to both of you.

Ian and Colin. I used your names for my Australian rancher. Bob and I look forward to seeing you each summer. Thank you for all your support and kindness year after year.

Bob Wick. The motto of the Marines is *Semper Fi.* Always faithful. Is there a better way to describe you? Thank you for always being there, not only leading the chase but enjoying the ride with us. There is not enough paper in the house to write down how often you have been my rescuer.

One

Carson Point, Australia
April 1945

"Miss Josie," the little girl said, tugging at the hem of her teacher's dress. Josephine Archer looked down, her face patient and calm.

"Yes, Norma?"

"I finished my picture."

Josie suppressed a sigh. Her sister, Lorraine, who taught with her, had just given the assignment before leaving to run an errand. Josie knew that if she looked at eight-year-old Norma's paper right now, it would be a mass of scribbles that went far beyond the bounds of the page.

"Thank you for telling me, Norma. Go back to your seat, and I'll come and see your picture in a moment."

The little girl started away, but Josie's voice stopped her.

"Norma."

The little girl turned.

"If you used only one color, I want you to add at least two more colors before you show the picture to me. Can you do that for me?"

"Yes, Miss Josie."

"Do your best," Josie encouraged with a gentle smile that the little girl returned.

After making sure that Norma headed in the direction of her desk, Josie returned to the large desk that sat at the front of the room and sat down to look at the papers piled there. She was just beginning to read, when Lorraine — Lorri — slipped into the room and came directly toward her.

"Mail," she said quietly, her excitement showing in her eyes and nowhere else. Josie's gaze scanned the room to see that all was in order and then followed her younger sister out the door.

Stationing themselves by the window so they could still see their students, they each took one letter.

"Mine's from Mother," Lorri said.

"Then mine must be from Max."

Silence fell and smiles emerged as the two women read the words that came from so very far away.

Dear Jo and Raine, Maxine's letter began. *I hope this gets there soon, or there won't be any use in sending it. I have a huge test coming up in chemistry. I've studied until my brain is soggy, but I still fear failing. You've got to pray for my brain! It's preoccupied these days with a cute boy who sits two rows over. In church, he's always behind me, but in chemistry, he's in view the whole time. Isn't that rotten luck?*

Well, enough about me. How are the kids doing these days? Is Philip still biting? I think I'd be tempted to bite back. Tell Norma I received the picture she drew for me. I couldn't tell what it was, but I guess she doesn't need to know that.

Josie's shoulders shook with laughter as she read this fun letter from her youngest sister. Max had been slightly boy crazy from the time she was three years old. She didn't do anything to encourage the boys — their mother and grandfather would never have allowed that — but her dreamy, romantic heart was often smitten with someone new.

Wanting to laugh much louder than she should, Josie glanced up to find students moving around the room. She poked her head back through the door long enough to tell two boys to sit back down in their seats. Waiting only for them to obey, she returned to her letter.

Lorri, a smile pulling at the corners of her mouth, completely missed her sister's reprimand of the children. Fully ensconced in the letter from her mother, her heart was thousands of miles away.

I've decided to put hostas on the north side of the house, Ruth Archer wrote. *They do well in shade, and that flower bed has needed some sprucing up for too many years. Also, I can weed over there when the weather gets warm and makes the backyard unbearable. I could go with ferns but thought hostas would be more fun.*

Max wants to repaint her room. The admiral was amenable to the suggestion, but I'm still thinking about it. With the two of you gone, your grandfather has no one to spoil but your sister. He didn't even blink when she suggested purple walls and a lavender ceiling. I'm still discussing it with her and telling her not to get her hopes very high.

"Oh, no!" Josie suddenly said, bringing Lorri's head up. The women looked through the window to see that a fight had broken out between two little girls. For the moment letters were put away. It was time to return to work.

Because of a family connection, the Archer sisters had landed wonderful jobs as governesses. They had good hours, long holidays, decent pay, and the respect of their employer. The only drawback was the location: Burra Hills, in Carson Point, Australia, was over 7500 miles from their home in southern California.

Ian Colins, a successful cattle rancher in a remote area of the country, had set up a school for his children and the children of his employees. He had hired the Archer sisters in the fall of 1940, and they had come to Australia in late January of 1941 to begin teaching.

They hadn't been home to see their mother and sister since they arrived. Their grandfather, a U.S. naval officer, had been to see them about six months after they arrived. He had stayed for three days, but it hadn't taken long for that visit to feel like a long-ago dream. Letters and boxes were wonderful, but sometimes the girls wondered if it was worth it, especially after news of the attack reached them.

It had been horrible to be so far from home when Pearl Harbor was bombed. As with most Americans, the women were in shock for many days. Then fear set in, fear they knew they must fight. God was working His plan for their family — they were sure of this — but trust came hard.

Then months turned into years, and at times news of the war, ashamed as they were to admit it, became routine. They corresponded as much as possible through the mail, and even though information was delayed at times, it was always a relief to know all was well at home. Letters that spoke of new paint in a bedroom, flower gardens, and upcoming tests, helped them to feel as though some portion of their world was normal.

For the most part, life on the ranch was insulated from the fighting going on around them, but the radio and weekly newspaper delivery helped to keep them informed of the situation. Both girls would have given much for a visit home, but such trips were very expensive and simply not an option.

In the room the sisters shared, family photos were always in sight. They kept a basket with the latest letters available and did everything they could to make their space feel like home. It wasn't the home they were accustomed to, but they had each other and knew that someday they would be back in California again.

Josephine Archer was in love. First Lieutenant Kenneth Showers of the United States Army was stationed in England. He had asked Josie to marry him before she had left for Australia. A ring didn't follow for almost a year, and a date for the wedding was contingent on the war, but their love was very real.

Josie stretched out on her bed that night, a stack of Ken's letters in her hand. It had been wonderful to hear from Mother and Max, but Josie naturally yearned for a recent letter from the man she loved. She reread his last one, trying to imagine him in combat and then deciding it was best not to think about it. In the midst of these speculations, Lorri returned from the bathroom.

"Let me guess. You're reading Ken's letters."

Josie only smiled.

"I can't think why you need to do that," Lorri teased her, hair-brush in hand, "when I'm such charming company."

A pillow flew through the air. Lorri settled on her own bed, her eyes on the ceiling. If the truth be told, she envied her sister. Hard as it would be to be separated, Lorri thought it would be wonderful to have someone like Ken Showers love you enough to ask for your hand. She sighed a little just thinking about it.

"What was that sigh for?" Josie asked.

"Did you hear that?" Lorri asked, surprised.

"Yes."

The younger woman was silent.

"Are you going to tell me?" Josie prodded.

"I was just thinking about Ken."

"You're not supposed to be sighing over my fiancé," her sister teased.

"It wasn't specifically about him — just about being in love and knowing someone is waiting for you."

The yearning she heard in her sister's voice brought Josie up on one elbow to look across at the other bed.

"I didn't know you felt that way, Lorri. You've never given any hint of wanting a man in your life right now."

"Really, Josie!" Lorri's voice held a measure of mild disgust. "Just because I don't swoon and carry on the way Max does, doesn't mean I don't have any interest."

"What type of man would you want?" Josie asked, her voice tender, which was her way.

"Someone like Ken." Lorri's eyes were still on the ceiling. "Someone who shared our faith and was so sweet and capable all at the same time. It also wouldn't hurt if he was as dreamy as Ken."

"He is good-looking, isn't he?"

"Um hm. Is that the first thing you noticed, Jo?" Lorri finally looked at her sister.

"It probably was, but it didn't take long for that to be of little importance."

"What did you notice in its place?"

"Just what you said: his sweetness. He's the kindest man I know. When he goes out to fight, he has to be tough and brave, but he couldn't be more gentle with me."

"How often do you think about him fighting?"

"Not very much. I wouldn't be able to concentrate on anything else."

For a time the room was quiet. Both women lay looking at the ceiling. It didn't matter that it was a Friday night and at home there would have been countless things to do. They lived in a small cabin on a cattle ranch, and most evenings of the year there was next to nothing going on.

It certainly helped that they enjoyed each other's company and never ran out of things to talk about, but on Friday nights, when they dreamed of going for a drive on the California coast or popping corn and listening to records at home, it was especially difficult to be away from family.

"Who's going to start tonight?" Josie asked.

"I will," Lorri volunteered.

And with that, she began to pray. They had made a commitment to pray together every night before they fell asleep in their room. And so far, they had kept their word.

This night — even being a Friday and a little bit disappointing — would be no different.

Admiral Dean Archer was headed to see his oldest granddaughters. They didn't know of his arrival, but that made it all the more fun.

Their father — his son, Tom Archer — had been dead for more than 12 years, but Dean still thought about him often and knew that he would really come to mind when he saw Josie. They didn't look alike, but her mannerisms were most like his.

All three girls took after their mother with their dark hair and skin like fresh cream, but Josie always reminded him of Tom. Not that she wasn't attractive — she was really quite lovely — but he never looked at her hazel eyes without seeing his son.

Lorrie was the most like Ruth. Slightly more petite, she was swift to smile, and her eyes were large and deep brown. Max looked like a younger version of Josie, but for some reason, never reminded Dean of his son.

Dean thought about how different Josie and Lorri would look. He tried to prepare himself for anything, but his mind wandered to the years apart. What a time it had been! Seeing his granddaughters had been almost impossible, and he knew their mother and sister missed them terribly. They might have surprised the girls with money for a trip home, but not after the war started. It was all too long and unpredictable.

For the moment Dean forced such thoughts from his mind. He would be seeing his granddaughters in less than an hour, and he wanted this to be a happy visit. Only God knew when he would see them again, and he had very little time — less than 48 hours — to spend time with them.

He made himself a little more comfortable in the staff car and thought about how surprised they were going to be.

"All right, children," Lorri said with a laugh in her voice. "We've been silly long enough, and now we need to get back to our studies. Paul," she called on a boy whose hand was in the air.

"Miss Lorri, I can't remember the last continent."

Lorri handled the request in short order and drew the children back to the statement she'd written on the board up front. She could tell that the day was almost over because they were all getting antsy.

Not taking too much time with any one point, Lorri made herself clear and assigned homework for the next day. This was met with groans and long faces, but she stood firm.

"I'm not happy with the way you're struggling with this, so we'll take a little time at home to get it settled in our minds."

And that was the final word of the day. Lorri dismissed the children and worked with her sister to straighten the room, glad that the next day was Friday.

"My feet hurt," Josie commented as the women exited the schoolroom.

"Do they?" Lorri looked down. "Why did you wear those shoes?"

"I always wear these shoes."

"No, you don't. You wear the black ones."

Josie looked at her own feet and giggled a little. She had been tired that morning but hadn't realized how much.

Lorri laughed as she watched her, so neither woman was looking ahead. Dean had come around the corner of the building and simply stood, waiting to be noticed. Just seeing the girls had brought tears to his eyes, but he still knew the moment they saw him.

"Grandpa!" Josie was first, running like a five-year-old, Lorri close behind her, to be caught in the arms of the man who had been both father and grandfather to them for more than ten years.

"When did you get here?"

"We had no idea!"

"How's Mother?"

"How long can you stay?"

The words tumbled from both women as their grandfather kissed them and hugged them again and again. Everyone cried, and after some moments they grew quiet and just looked at each other, drinking in every detail.

"Where can we talk?" Dean asked as he finally found his voice, emotion still filling him.

Josie led the way back to the schoolroom, and the three of them grew comfortable on the seats there, sitting close, needing to be near.

"First of all, your mother and Max send their love."

Lorri didn't think she would cry again, but tears flooded her eyes. Her little sister would be so grown up by now, and they had missed so much.

"They miss you but love your letters."

"We love theirs too," Josie put in, her voice thick with tears.

"You both look wonderful," Dean suddenly said. "Oh," he continued as he reached for his case. "I have a few things for you."

The women took the small packages and letters but didn't open them. Such things could wait; getting to look at their grandfather could not.

The admiral was older — very tan and fit — but a few extra lines had inched their way around his eyes. His mouth was a bit drawn when he wasn't smiling.

"I spoke to Ian Colins when I arrived. I asked if I could steal you for the next day and a half, and he agreed."

"He said we could cancel the children's lessons?"

"Yes. Now what would you like to do?"

"It doesn't matter," the women laughed and told him, "as long as we can be with you."

"In that case," Dean took delight in answering, "we're going into town."

"We can't," Lorri said, her voice almost sad.

"Why not?" Dean asked, both family members looking at her.

"Josie's feet hurt."

Both Dean and Josie laughed at this, just as Lorri hoped they would. Her brand of humor was always dry and subtle, and it set the tone for the next 36 hours. Dean, feeling like a king with his granddaughters at his side, took them away from the ranch, not willing to waste a single moment.

"What looks good?" Dean asked, his menu open as the three of them sat in a restaurant that evening in downtown Carson Point.

"The chicken," Josie decided. Lorri wanted the same.

"I, on the other hand," Dean teased a little, "will have the beef, since I don't have the pleasure of living on a cattle ranch."

"The beef is good," Lorri agreed, gaining a wink from her grandfather that made her smile to herself at what joy one could have over simple things. They had not done anything special that afternoon — a little shopping and now a meal in a small café — but it was more than that. She had been with people that she loved and cherished, and every act made it the most special.

"So tell me," Dean prompted when the order had been taken, "are you enjoying the job?"

"Yes." Josie was the one to speak up. "The children are wonderful, and so are the parents. We are treated well."

"Very well," Lorri added. "In fact, there's

a birthday party tomorrow night, and we're invited. Just like family."

Dean stared at them.

"You both have accents. Do you know that?"

"We do not," Josie argued on a laugh.

"Yes," he was adamant, "you do. It's subtle, but it's there."

The girls exchanged a look, smiling in surprise.

"Now tell me," Dean pressed, feeling the hours running fast, "when do you go to Hoyt for vacation?"

"Next month."

"Are you looking forward to it?"

"Yes, we'll have almost a week to ourselves here and then follow the family in a separate plane."

"We're both ready for the change. And the children need this as much as we do," Lorri offered.

"Tell us more about Mother and Max," Josie suddenly put in.

"I will, Jo, but you must understand that Ruth and Maxine are going to ask about you. I can't go home with no information."

"When will you be home again?"

"Possibly in July." He shrugged. "It all depends on this war."

The very word caused silence to fall on

their little table. The food was delivered to this silent group, but Dean was not going to let them be sad. As soon as he prayed, he began to tell them more about home.

In short order the three were laughing and sharing, holding nothing back. If there was a feeling of desperation in each heart, well, that was to be expected. These few precious hours were to be treasured, and treasure them they did.

The Saturday morning goodbye was one of the most painful they could remember. For a time after the admiral left, both Josie and Lorri were inconsolable with tears.

"This is silly!" Lorri declared, working to dry up. "We should be thankful that he came and not bawling like children."

Josie looked at her, eyes still swimming. Lorri looked back. It was no use. They both cried until they had headaches.

June

"Of all the times to break my heel!" Lorri said with disgust, taking a seat inside the small building where they waited for word from the pilot.

"Let me see it." Josie put her hand out and waited for the shoe. She examined it just long enough to see that her sister was right and then tried to hand it back. She found her sister opening her suitcase and searching along the edge.

"All I've got in this bag is a pair of saddle shoes. I'm going to look like a bobby-soxer!"

"Don't wear socks with them. That will help."

"That's true, but the backs of these will scrape my heel if I do that," Lorri answered, even as she pulled on a pair of white socks, slipped on the shoes, and tucked the broken-heeled pumps into her case.

This accomplished, the sisters settled themselves a little more in the seats, their eyes going to the windows.

Crossing the tarmac, Josie and Lorri squinted against the wind outside the small airport. With one hand they each held a suitcase, and with the other, they attempted to keep the hats on their heads.

Walking in front of them, confident and all business, was their pilot, Clarence Fuller. He worked for the Colins family, and if Lorri's guess was right, he was sweet on Josie. He never did or said anything improper, but she was always given preference in the plane, and when he had a question or statement to make, it was directed at Josie.

As if to confirm this belief, they arrived at

the plane, and Lorri watched Clarence settle Josie with the utmost care in the front next to him. He was kind to Lorri, but in a rather impersonal way.

Lorri wondered whether she should ask Josie if she'd gotten a recent letter from Ken but decided that was mean. Her sister was all grown up and able to handle her own affairs. It was also true that she never did anything to encourage Clarence. However, she was lovely and sweet, and Lorri couldn't say she blamed the man.

"Are you comfortable, Lorri?" Josie asked.

"Yes, Jo, thanks. How about you?"

Something in Lorri's voice made Josie turn and give her a stern look. Lorri's eyes danced with silent laughter — she'd teased Josie about Clarence's interest in the past — but both women remained silent as their pilot chose that moment to join them.

"All set?" he asked.

"I think so." Josie did the honors.

Clarence nodded, checked a few more dials and switches, and just minutes later, the plane and its three occupants were airborne.

Two

**The South Pacific
July 1945**

Lieutenant Donovan Riggs stared down at the pieces of radio that lay on the desk in the small radio room of the PT boat, *Every Storm.* Click, his radio operator, said something under his breath, frustration evident, but Rigg, as he was known to most, remained silent. A patient man, he was used to things going wrong aboard his boat and took this latest setback in stride.

Before moving down to check with Click, Rigg had been on deck where he had stood and looked at miles of endless, calm sea. It was not a peaceful scene because the enemy loomed constantly, but Rigg had peace within — even though he knew they were sitting ducks when their boat acted up.

"Rigg?" Ensign Hugh Westland, his second-in-command, suddenly appeared.

"What is it?" Rigg asked, turning to him.

"Quinn says we've got to make land for repairs. He's been down three times and can't get the hole sealed."

"All right. I'll be up in a minute." Rigg turned back to Click. "I'll be back."

A grunt was all he received in reply, and Rigg knew that his good-natured radio man was "at the end of his rope," a term that could have been applied to most of his men.

He didn't know what had gone on the day they commissioned this vessel, but in the last few months anything that could go wrong, did. The radio was unreliable, and they had sprung a few leaks. They were due into port in Seaford, Australia, at the end of the week, but they would only make that if repairs were successful.

"We've got to make land," Quinn wasted no time telling his skipper.

"There's the Knot Islands," Hugh suggested.

"Too far," Rigg said, shaking his head, his mind working as his eyes scanned the charts. "Let's head toward Cooley. There are some small islands there, and hopefully we can get in unnoticed."

The decision made, they limped along. The men fell to daily tasks, and Rigg left them to it. Inside, however, his mind was busy. He was asking God for wisdom and to get this boat safely to shore.

A group of ten made the beach about noon the next day. The lifeboat went smoothly up onto the sand, and the men wasted no time getting it and themselves out of sight. There were no guarantees that this island was unoccupied. Three and four to a group, they spread out, armed and ready to scout the area.

Lionel Pauley and Quinn were with Rigg. Taking the center of the island, the three men moved silently through the trees and brush of a rather dense forest. Light flickered through the trees occasionally. The day was sunny and warm, but everything smelled like fresh rain.

The further they walked, the more Rigg began to relax. He had had a sense that this island was occupied, and not by anyone they wished to meet, but clearly he'd been wrong. He brought up the rear but stopped when Lionel and Quinn did, all three men hearing it at the same time. From somewhere ahead of them — not very far, he would guess — a woman was singing "Deep in the Heart of Texas."

As soon as that song ended, another began. They stood stock still as the sweet words from the first verse of "Amazing Grace" came gently with the breeze.

Hearing it, Lionel and Quinn moved for the first time. They turned to look at their commanding officer and found him looking as stunned as they felt.

The woman had just started "Oh, What a Beautiful Mornin' " when Rigg moved past his men and took the lead. They moved toward the voice quietly, but not quietly enough. They were very close when the song cut off and they heard rapid movement and then complete silence.

Rigg, ready with his rifle, stepped into a small clearing to find the wreckage of an airplane. His eyes scanned the area swiftly, taking in the makeshift camp and debris. He stopped before intruding on what felt like private space and spoke.

"You can come out," he called, his voice sounding deeper than usual amid the thick foliage.

Quinn had moved under cover, but Lionel stood just a few feet away and watched with Rigg as a thin face appeared in the window of the wrecked cockpit. A pair of huge, surprised eyes looked out at them.

"You're not Japanese," Lorri Archer said with relief.

"No, we're not. You can come out."

Moving slowly, Lorri stepped down from the plane and stood looking at them, completely unaware of the picture she presented. Rigg was still taking in the bone-thin woman in a skirt and blouse that had seen better days when she spoke again.

"Do you have a ship? Can you take me off this island?"

"Yes," Rigg answered, his mind snapping back to duty. "What's your name?"

"Lorraine Archer."

"What happened?"

"Our plane crashed."

"Where are the others?"

Rigg watched her shake her head, her eyes like those of an injured animal. He knew better than to question her right then and started forward, only to stop when she stepped back in fear.

Quinn had suddenly come from the bushes, and one of the other scout teams had joined them. Rigg only glanced at them before speaking to Lorri again.

"I'm Lieutenant Riggs. These are my men. No one will harm you."

Rigg had come close enough now to see the pulse beating at the base of her throat. She was so gaunt that the throb stood out in an unnatural way. He looked into her eyes and read a mixture of fear and hope.

For Lorri's part, she could barely think at all. She knew she couldn't last out here forever, not with so little to eat. Her mind had become a little less clear every day, but today was a good day. Today she had remembered some songs and some verses from her Bible.

"How long have you been here?"

Rigg's question brought her back to reality, and she looked up at him.

"How long have you been here?" he repeated.

"I don't know. Our plane left on June 1."

"That's more than six weeks ago," Rigg told her.

"Is it?" Lorri tried to take it in.

"Where are you from?"

"Can you take me off this island?" Lorri asked again, not having listened to his question.

"Yes, but not just now. We need to make some repairs to our boat. When we go we'll take you with us."

The word "boat" seemed to get through.

"What have you got — a destroyer, a cruiser?"

"A PT boat."

Lorri blinked up at him. "They're not very big."

Watching her, Rigg wanted to laugh for

the first time, but as he watched, she suddenly sat down. She glanced up at him, even that costing her, and spoke quietly.

"I don't have much energy."

Rigg didn't know when he'd felt such pity.

"We'll get you something to eat."

Lorri nodded a little before she heard him turn and speak to his men, but she didn't listen very well. She was talking to the Lord, hoping that she was making some sense.

I know I might be dreaming again, but this feels more real. I think I could smell shaving soap, and I've never done that in a dream. Please, Lord, she begged in her heart. *Please let me see Mother and Max again. Please let me go home this time and not wake up on the ground.*

"This is Lionel Pauley." Rigg broke into her thoughts, and Lorri tried to pay attention. "He's going to take care of you for the next few hours."

A sailor hunkered down in front of her and made eye contact.

"Did I hear you say your name was Archer?"

"Yes."

"Miss or Mrs.?"

"The children call me Miss Lorri."

"Are you a teacher?"

"Yes. On a cattle ranch. Is it true that President Roosevelt died?"

"Yes, I'm afraid it is."

Lorri nodded. "I couldn't remember if I dreamt that or not."

"Tell me, Miss Lorri," he said, working gently to draw her back. "What have you been eating and drinking on the island?"

"Mostly leaves and water. Some berries." Lorri made a little face. "They don't taste very good."

"One of the men will bring you some crackers. I think we'll start there."

"I love crackers."

Lionel smiled at her, feeling the same pity that Rigg had known. He was a married man with two little daughters. If his Alma or one of his girls was ever alone and starving, he would want someone to treat them with all the care and respect he could muster.

"Do you suppose you're in my dream?" Lorri suddenly asked.

"Not unless I'm having the same dream."

Lorri couldn't process that comment. She looked off into the distance and tried to work it out.

Not sure what to say to her next, Lionel stood to his feet to watch for Cliff, willing the man to hurry with that food.

★ ★ ★

"You find a way to make it more than clear, Hugh," Rigg said sternly to the other officer. "She might not be what they've been dreaming about for weeks, but she's still a woman. If anyone lays a hand on her, I'll have them in the nearest brig before they can state their full rank."

"I'll see to it," Hugh assured him, looking up at the man he admired like no other. "It's not going to be fun once we're back at sea."

"I know that better than anyone. I just want to be sure that the men know there's no fun to be had here."

Hugh smiled a little.

"She's certainly a surprise."

"She is that." Rigg shook his head in wonder. "First those songs and then that dazed expression that tell me she can barely think straight."

"What songs?"

Rigg told him how they found her, and Hugh almost laughed. It was nothing short of amazing.

"Oh, and make sure Lionel keeps her comfortable here on the island tonight. There's no point in having her on board until we have to."

"Aye, Lieutenant."

The men parted company, Rigg to check on the boat's repairs and Hugh to organize a meeting and make a few announcements.

"We'll have a guest aboard ship for some days, men. I can't say how many," Hugh stated plainly at the end of his speech. "She's off limits in every way, shape, and form. I don't even want you to speak to her unless you have business with her, and you only have business with her when I or Lieutenant Riggs say you do. Do I make myself clear?"

"Yes, sir!"

Hugh looked along the line of men at attention on the beach and wondered if this was going to work. It was true that their guest was not in the best of shape, but the lieutenant was right: She was female, and for some of the men that was all that mattered.

"Dismissed," he finally told the men, hoping he'd been clear enough. He knew Rigg meant what he said about arresting anyone who stepped out of line, but in the end, the rest was in the hands of the men.

Harlan Ellis, cook on the *Every Storm*, did not allow Cliff to return alone with the crackers. He was fit to be tied to learn that a woman would be on his boat, and only grudgingly did he prepare something for her to eat. When the food was ready, he followed the other sailor off the boat and onto the beach, trailing him through the trees until he reached Lionel's side.

His heart softened a bit when he saw Lorri. He didn't know what he was expecting, but it wasn't to see a woman truly in need of sustenance. He had taken fresh crackers and knew the broth was tasty, but something inside of him wished he'd done more.

He returned to the *Every Storm*, already working out what he could make her for supper that night.

"Here you go," Lionel said, handing a cracker to Lorri. She smiled and thanked him, but she didn't put it in her mouth.

"Go ahead and eat," he urged her and watched her put it in her mouth.

"That's good," she said around the crumbs, needing no further urging. Lionel handed her four more crackers and stepped back to give her some space.

It was a funny thing in Lorri's mind. She'd thought about how much she would enjoy food if she got it again, but when he'd handed her the first cracker, she couldn't make herself eat it. Memories having little to do with food had suddenly assailed her, and her mouth had gone dry.

"How were those crackers?" Lionel asked, noticing how slowly she chewed.

"They were good."

"I've got some beef broth here for you now. Do you think you can manage it?"

"I think so."

She drank slowly and gratefully, smiling at him often. Lionel just smiled back and kept his hand ready as hers seemed to be shaking all of a sudden. The warm broth gone, she thanked him one last time and moved a little to let her head fall against the side of the plane.

"Don't forget me," she said at one point, her eyes closed.

Lionel didn't answer. She was already asleep.

"What's the news, Quinn?" Rigg asked him on the beach, the boat in sight.

"I can get to that hole now, but it's going to take more hours of daylight than we have left."

Rigg's head went back as he studied the sky. He knew they would be spending the night here, but he had hoped to be on his way in the morning. It wasn't going to happen.

"Get back to it at first light."

"Will do."

Rigg turned up the beach then and made his way back into the interior of the island. He hadn't checked on Lionel and his charge all afternoon. He could fill a book with questions he had for the woman but was quite certain they would all have to wait. Some questions he was sure never to have answers for, but maybe Lionel had learned some things.

He found that man on the edge of the clearing but no sign of Lorri.

"She slept all afternoon," Lionel told the lieutenant.

"Where is she now?"

"I suspect she needed a few minutes of privacy."

"Is she any more lucid?"

"About the same as before she slept, and very groggy when she woke."

"When is her supper coming?"

"I expect Ellis any moment."

"Head back to the *Storm* and gather some things to make her a little more comfortable for the night. I'll stay here until you get back."

"Yes, sir."

Rigg looked around while Lionel was away. He took in the wreckage and shook his head that anyone had lived to tell about it. It crossed his mind that she was more than starved, that her brain had been affected in some other way because of the crash, and he found himself praying it wasn't so.

Rigg was still taking it in, inspecting the damage and the small ways she tried to establish some comfort. Not until he'd nearly cut himself on a piece of sharp metal did he realize he was being watched.

Lorri had come back from relieving herself and stood watching the man she had spoken with earlier. He was looking around, and she couldn't understand why.

"Did you lose something?" she asked in all sincerity.

"No, nothing like that. How are you doing?"

Lorri came forward, thinking about his question. She felt a little better but was very thirsty and realized that she hadn't had salt in all this time.

"I think I might go and have a drink. I'm thirsty."

"Your supper will be coming soon."

"I won't be long."

Rigg almost stopped her but changed his mind. Instead he followed her. She didn't move very fast but clearly knew where she was headed. If she knew he was behind her, she gave no indication but followed a well-worn path to a rocky area. She stepped around a very small pond to where water trickled from the rocks. Here she went to her knees and drank for a long time. When she sat back, Rigg questioned her.

"How long was it before you found this?"

"Not long." She remembered this part well. "I was so thirsty the first day that I could smell the water. I think it might be the only reason I'm alive."

Without comment, Rigg stepped around to help her to her feet. The bones in her arm felt as though they would break in his hand, but none of his feelings showed on his face. "I'll let you lead the way back," he said.

"All right."

They stepped back into the clearing to see that Ellis had arrived with the food. He didn't speak but set the food down, dipped his head a little, and went on his way. Rigg took Lorri's arm.

"Here you go. Let's see what Ellis brought for you."

One look at the plate and Rigg's heart sank. The man had outdone himself, but Rigg wasn't sure Lorri was ready for this type of food. Lorri had sat down and reached for the plate. It took all Rigg's will, but he made himself take it from her. The hunger and confusion in her eyes were almost too much for him, but he sat near her to try to explain.

"I think you need to take very small bites of this, Miss Archer. I don't know if your stomach is ready for gravy and beef yet."

"Oh."

Rigg gave her the plate and hoped she understood.

Lorri looked at it, her mouth watering, but didn't know what to do. Rigg watched her, feeling his helplessness grow. Trying to remember commonsense eating guidelines, he searched the plate.

"Why don't you take some potato from right here," he pointed, "without too much gravy."

Lorri used the fork and took some, but it didn't make it to her mouth.

"I forgot to pray," she said quietly, surprised at her own thoughts.

"Would you like me to?"

"Please."

She looked so grateful that Rigg was glad for a reason to close his eyes.

"Gracious Father in heaven, thank You for leading us to Miss Archer. Please help her to grow strong. Help her stomach to handle the food. Help us to get her home safely. And please end this war swiftly. In Christ's name and for Your glory I pray. Amen."

"Thank you," Lorri said, hearing his words in her head as she put the food into her mouth. She hadn't heard anyone pray for a very long time. It had sounded so nice. And his prayer had reminded her of her grandfather.

"He's probably wondering where I am," Lorri said suddenly, thinking she'd never tasted anything so delicious.

"Who is?"

"My grandpa."

Rigg knew nothing but relief to see Lionel returning. He stood to his feet and warned him about letting Lorri eat all that was on the plate. With a word to her to rest well, he took his leave.

Working his way back through the foliage to the beach, Rigg thought about his ideals as he entered this war. He'd told the Lord he was up for anything. He told God and his family that if he had to lay down his life for his country, he was willing.

What he hadn't banked on was an island in the middle of the South Pacific and a woman almost starved to death. He was supposed to be working alongside men. He was supposed to be commanding them, getting this war fought, and sending them all home if he had any say in the matter.

What he hadn't figured on was a woman

with huge brown eyes, probably close to his own age, whose family must be sick with worry for her and whose vulnerability was almost more than his heart could take.

Three

Rigg lay in his bunk early the next morning and knew it would be the last time for some days. He shared a cabin with Hugh Westland. Hugh's bunk was built into the wall. Hugh would completely vacate for their guest. Rigg would take Hugh's bunk and hang a blanket in the middle of the room. It wasn't the most convenient, but it was unavoidable as the rest of the sleeping bunks on board were not in private cabins. Hopefully it would only be a matter of days before Miss Archer could be delivered to the base at Seaford. As soon as the radio was back in order, they would send word that she was coming. In the meantime, they would all have to learn to coexist.

"There's something you might want to see," Hugh said as he snagged Rigg the moment his feet hit the beach. "This way."

Hugh led Rigg toward an area not far off the clearing where they had found Lorri. She was separated from them by thick trees and bushes. After working their way through the foliage, Hugh stopped and Rigg found himself at the edge of a smaller clearing. He looked at the ground and knew he was staring at the graves of the other people who had been on the plane.

"Just the two, do you think?" Rigg asked Hugh, his eyes scanning beyond.

"As far as I can tell. It wasn't a large plane, but maybe she put more than one person in each grave."

Rigg shook his head, trying to imagine Lorri Archer having to complete such a task. He hoped for her sake that the folks in these graves were strangers but wasn't sure that would have made it any easier.

"Do you want me to question her?" Hugh asked.

"No, I'll put as much as I know in my report, and when she's ready to talk about it, she can tell us."

"And if she's never ready?"

"Right now I can't worry about that."

Hugh nodded and Rigg went on his way. The second-in-command stood for a time after the lieutenant left, his eyes strangely riveted to the fresh mounds of dirt, his concentration on the churning in his gut.

Lorri woke up in a way she hadn't in over six weeks: She was warm and under a blanket; she had a pillow; and there was no headache or stiff neck. But it was more than that. She wanted to think about things. It didn't take long for the terrifying plane crash to come rushing back to her, an event she forced from her mind, but it didn't matter because other things began crowding into its place.

She could see the children's faces at the ranch. For days now, maybe even weeks, they had slipped from her mind. She could come up with a name but not a face, or a face that she could not label. Today she could do both.

The next thing she wanted was to bathe. She rose with just that in mind, only to see Lionel as soon as she stepped from the interior of the plane.

"Good morning," he greeted her, looking very fresh and put together, not in the least as though he'd spent the night in the jungle.

"Good morning."

"How are you feeling?"

"Better, thank you."

"I'm headed back to the boat, but Donald will stay with you."

For the first time Lorri noticed the other man. He was younger than Lionel, and he dipped his head nervously in her direction before looking away.

"Thank you for your concern, but I'll be fine on my own."

"It's no trouble," Lionel assured her as he went on his way.

Lorri watched him leave and then looked to the other man, who was still looking everywhere but at her.

"If you'll just excuse me a moment," she started to say, moving away from him.

"I think I'm supposed to go with you."

"I'll just be a moment, really."

"I'll come with you."

Does this man not need to relieve himself when he first wakes up? Lorri wondered but stood silent. She had given up on washing herself, but the other would not wait. She thought fast, not wanting to make trouble but sensing a very real need.

"You may tell Lionel or whoever asks that I am to blame."

At first Donald was too surprised by this statement to act. He watched this emaciated woman slip into the trees, following a little too late. He went after her but soon realized she was not to be found.

Just managing to retrace his steps, he

went back to the clearing in time to see the lieutenant arrive. He saluted, mentally cursing the woman for the trouble he was sure to be in.

"At ease, sailor," Rigg said calmly. "Where is Miss Archer?"

"She slipped into the trees, sir, and I can't locate her."

The newest man to the crew, Donald should still have known Rigg well enough by now to understand that he didn't overreact, but he was surprised when the man only nodded.

"Are you not afraid she'll be lost, sir?" The question popped out before he could stop it.

The officer's brows rose. "She's lived here for six weeks. She's not going to get lost on this island." Rigg glanced around. "We'll just assume that she'll be back when she's ready."

As though just saying the words caused them to be true, Lorri stepped into the clearing. She was moving slowly, a look of concentration on her face, and for a moment she didn't see the men.

"Miss Archer?" Rigg spoke to her.

Lorri looked up at him and asked, "Why are you on this island?"

Rigg felt a measure of relief flood through

him. Her voice was stronger, her eyes a little clearer.

"We had to make repairs to our boat. We'll probably leave here in the next few hours."

"And you'll take me with you?"

Rigg nodded and said, "Yes, we will."

Something in his voice made Lorri uncomfortable. She ducked her head before saying, "I know you have things on your mind."

And you're one of them, Rigg thought, but he only assured her again that they wouldn't forget and went on his way. He passed Lionel, who was on his way back to see Lorri, his arms full of clothes.

"Good," Rigg said when he saw the pants and shirts. "She can't possibly be aboard the *Storm* in that skirt."

"I thought as much."

"And from where did you get these?"

"Several of the smaller men."

"Clean?"

"Yes."

"She keeps asking me not to forget her, but other than that, she seems a little more lucid."

"All right. I'll keep her here until we're ready to shove off."

Rigg began to agree and move away but stopped short.

"No, get her ready with about half an hour to spare."

Lionel didn't question or delay him, but all the way to the clearing he wondered what the lieutenant had in mind.

"What'd Lionel get from you?"

"Nothing. Did he take some of your clothes?"

"A shirt and a pair of socks."

"A shirt? You lucky dog."

Harlan Ellis looked up from the pot he was stirring, his gaze stern on the grinning men.

"What's your problem, Ellis?" the younger of the two asked.

But Cook's only response was to turn his back on the two sailors. This had little effect. As their eyes met, they shrugged and went on their way.

Ellis turned long enough to scowl at the place they'd been standing. He wasn't that much older than the men who'd been talking, but in his mind, he was certainly old enough to know when someone needed pity and not to be lusted after.

"All right, gentlemen," Rigg said softly, knowing he had the attention of every man. "I know you've heard that we're going to have a guest on board. I'll be leaving in a matter of seconds to bring Miss Archer onto the boat. You're going to meet her. After that you're not going to do anything. You're not going to speak to her, look at her, or even think about her."

With those words still hanging in the air, Rigg turned and made his way off the boat. He moved calmly onto shore, a few men in his wake, only to have Lionel coming toward him at a fast pace.

"She's gone."

"She's what?"

"Gone, sir," he repeated reluctantly. "I can't find her anywhere."

Rigg stared at Lionel for a moment in disbelief. *What could she have been thinking? She was so worried about being left, and now she's disappeared! Or was it not her fault? Was she harmed or suddenly sick?*

Rigg's eyes scanned the tree line, his mind reeling with several possibilities.

"Let's look for her," he said grimly, knowing what this delay might cost them even as he moved toward the trees. Rigg, Lionel, Cliff, and Donald were halfway there when she suddenly emerged from the thick foliage. Rigg covered the distance alone.

"Where have you been?" Rigg's tone demanded an answer.

"I had to do something."

"What?" he asked. He was not yelling, but there was an edge to his voice.

Lorri looked up at him, trembling a little under his stern gaze.

Rigg gave her a few moments, but when she said nothing, he started in.

"I realize this has been a harrowing experience for you, Miss Archer, but in case you have forgotten, we are at war!"

"Yes, sir," Lorri whispered, not able to take her eyes from his.

"I have a PT boat full of men waiting to get underway. No area of the Pacific is safe. We could be under attack at any moment."

Lorri nodded but didn't try to speak or explain.

When Rigg saw that he would get no explanation from her, he gave up.

"Come on," he ordered shortly, not having noticed that she was dressed in jeans and a shirt that were a bit too large but covered her well compared to the skirt and blouse. At the last minute, he saw that she carried a small tied bundle.

"Let me take that for you."

Lorri surrendered the extra clothing she'd been given and trudged across the beach behind this angry officer. She hadn't come to the beach much. The trees, even with the bugs and reptiles, had felt safer.

Not even noticing the ship they were headed toward, Lorri climbed into the lifeboat and sat down, her heart thundering. A moment of panic filled her and she looked back at the island. She moved a little and found her wrist manacled in the lieutenant's hand. Looking from her wrist to his face, she didn't realize that he'd been watching her closely.

"We have to go to the boat now." His voice was calm again.

Lorri nodded but couldn't control the trembling that had started. She reclaimed her wrist and folded her arms tightly over her chest. It was a hot day, almost noon, but she felt so cold inside that her teeth chattered. And again, her eyes went to the island. She wasn't going to jump in the water and swim back, but for more reasons than she could name, she couldn't take her eyes from that small strip of land.

And small it was! The farther the raft went from shore, the more she realized how tiny it was. It had become her world. She knew every inch of it. It had never felt small to her until this very moment.

"All right, Miss Archer," Rigg was saying. "Do you think you can manage this ladder?"

They were at the boat! Lorri was so startled that for a moment she only stared at it. If she had thought the island tiny, she knew not what to think of this PT boat. It was one of the smallest crafts in the war, and she couldn't help but wonder where everyone lived and slept.

"Can you manage it?" The question was asked again, and Lorri mentally shook herself.

"Yes," she whispered, hoping it was true. She did not wish to be carried on board.

She was given no time to think or look around. She climbed the ladder, only glad she was able to accomplish it, and then found her upper arm in the lieutenant's grasp as she was led to an open space on the deck. The men were lined up.

"Miss Archer," he began. "The men are lined up to meet you. They will step forward and introduce themselves."

Lorri looked at each man as he stepped out of formation, stated his name and rank, and then moved back into line. Lorri had met a few of them already, and even though she concentrated on each one, she knew she would never remember all the names she'd just heard.

"Thank you, gentlemen." Rigg's voice was at its most commanding. "Now I'll remind you again. For however many days Miss Archer is with us, you will keep your distance. Some of you will have business with her; most of you will not. Any man caught fraternizing with our guest will answer to me. Dismissed to get underway."

The men fell instantly out of formation to scatter in all directions, and Lionel was suddenly there.

"I'll show you below, Miss Lorri."

"Thank you." She almost smiled at his familiar face, but feeling as though she'd just been swept from one surreal world to the next, Lorri only followed him down the narrow steps to the passage below.

"This is the galley," Lionel said from the incredibly tight space of the passageway, the throb of the engines all around them, as he forced himself not to look at Lorri's vulnerable face. "You'll take your meals in here in the officer's mess." Lionel indicated the table. "Ellis will tell you when."

Lorri looked up at the cook, who nodded at her, his expression open.

"Right this way is your cabin. Lieutenant Riggs will be in here with you, but you'll have privacy behind this sheet. Ensign Westland may need to stop in now and again to retrieve something, but they'll both give you as much privacy as you need."

"Thank you." Lorri uttered the first words that had come from her mouth since boarding the vessel.

Rigg chose that moment to see how the tour was going, and as he did, put Lorri's small bundle of clothes on his bed in his cabin. His bed was not built into the wall but was actually in the room, next to a small desk. He then moved into the passageway where he listened to Lionel.

"And right here is the officer's head."

Lionel opened the door, and Lorri looked in to see a toilet, sink, and an area to hang wet things.

Rigg had come upon them and just stood listening as Lionel finished explaining. He'd no more stopped speaking than two enlisted men chose the moment to come through the passage. The men backed up to give them room, as did Lorri, but it wasn't remotely the same. Rigg watched the men's chests as they passed Lorri's front and was strongly reminded that this boat was not meant to be shared by men and women.

"Miss Archer." Rigg got her attention. "Whenever you can step out of the passageway for the men to pass, that's going to be best. Do you know what I'm talking about?"

Lorri nodded. The men hadn't touched

her, but small as she was, it had still been a tight squeeze.

"Yes, sir."

"Did you want to rest now?" Rigg offered, wanting her out of the way as much as possible.

"Thank you."

"I've got lunch ready for Miss Archer."

The three in the passage turned to find Ellis addressing them. Rigg turned back to Lorri.

"It looks like you can rest or eat, Miss Archer. Your call."

Lorri looked into Rigg's face. Some corner of her brain registered the fact that she shouldn't be on this vessel. It was nothing but trouble having a woman on board; she knew that. And besides, she had already gotten in trouble for not being ready to leave on time. For all those reasons she wanted Lieutenant Riggs to tell her what to do, but he was waiting on her.

"I'll eat, thank you."

Ellis disappeared back into the galley, and Lorri went to the door she thought Lionel said was the officer's mess. She slipped in, sat at the table, and saw the galley beyond. The boat vibrated all around her. She wasn't afraid of sea travel, but this was a new experience. She couldn't see out. The rooms were well lit, but not with sunshine.

Suddenly she was tired. Food was placed in front of her. She thanked Ellis without looking up and began to eat. She didn't get very far. Only halfway through the meal of soup and crackers, she found herself too weary to continue. She was getting ready to lay her head back and sleep, but Rigg had come from the cabin and spotted her. He went directly to her.

Lorri never knew a thing. Rigg lifted her and took her across the passageway to his own cabin and the bunk that would be hers. He laid her down, covered her with a sheet, attached the sheet overhead that would give her privacy, and went out and shut the door.

Topside he found Lionel and told him to check on her in a few hours. From that point, he went in search of Click. That radio had to be repaired and soon. A PT boat was no place for Lorri Archer or any woman.

Four

Lorri couldn't remember which door led to the toilet and which door was the storage area. She stood in the passageway, making it harder than it was. She gave a knock on the first door and got no answer. A swift peek told her that no one was using the room, and it was the head. She slipped inside with a sigh of relief.

Once inside, she found that the door locked. She secured this, checked it twice, and then turned to take care of herself.

It had not occurred to her before. The most basic of facilities, when one was asked to go without them, suddenly became wondrous. Toilet paper. A seat. They had been the least of her worries on the island, but here they became luxuries of untold worth.

She heard a voice in the passageway and remembered that she was not alone. Finishing swiftly, but taking time to enjoy the soap and running water at the sink, she slipped back out and shut the door. The passage was quiet again.

Lorri didn't know how long she'd slept but felt almost desperate to see the sunlight. She walked back to the cabin, intending to straighten the bunk. She felt as though she'd already been too much trouble and didn't want to do anything to get in anyone's way.

Suddenly Lorri's thoughts stopped. She remembered coming on board and eating, but then she was in the bunk waking up. Moving slowly, she turned the light off in the cabin and went across to the officer's mess. Ellis was there.

"Hello," Lorri greeted.

Ellis turned in surprise.

"Did you sleep?" he asked after a moment.

"I must have. I don't remember."

His eyes having returned to the pan he was drying, Ellis spoke, seeing her in his mind. She had some new color in her face, but her cheeks were too thin, causing her lips and eyes to stand out.

"It'll take some time to feel like yourself again," he said.

"Did you give me some soup?"

"That I did."

"I'm sorry I left without thanking you."

"It doesn't matter."

"It matters to me."

Ellis finally looked over at her.

"Would you like a cup of coffee?"

"Oh, that sounds wonderful."

"Sit yourself down."

The table was more of a booth with benches than an actual table with chairs. Lorri made herself comfortable and looked around. There wasn't a lot to see, but she was taking in a chart on the wall when Ellis approached.

"Sugar?" he asked as he placed a steaming cup and saucer in front of her.

"Yes, please."

At home she would have had cream as well but didn't expect that here. Not a minute later she took her first sip, her eyes closing in satisfaction. Right now she couldn't remember the other foods Ellis had made for her. Her mind was solely on this coffee and the wonderful flavor in her mouth.

Ellis watched her a moment and then, remembering the lieutenant's admonition from that morning, he got her a few crackers and some more broth. He arranged things on a plate and set them beside her.

"Thank you," Lorri said, still enjoying the coffee.

"You're welcome."

Lorri proceeded to eat every bite. It wasn't a lot of food, but she found herself very full in little time at all. Picking up her plate and cup, she thanked Ellis and made her way along the passage, finding it odd that she hadn't seen anyone. She was nearly to the stairs that led up when a door opened and two men entered.

That they didn't expect to find her was obvious. They stopped, stared for a moment, and then moved past her. Lorri tried to get flat against the wall, but the men were still very close as they inched past her. Both turned to look at her, and Lorri smiled a little.

As they moved out of sight, Lorri heard, "She smiled at me."

"No, she didn't. She smiled at me."

"That's a joke."

The rest of the words were lost on her, but for the first time in a long while, Lorri wanted to laugh. With a small shake of her head, she made for the deck.

Once topside, Lorri stood and let the wind hit her full in the face. The *Every Storm* was moving at a good pace but not a hurried one. Men moved here and there, but no one seemed to notice her. She felt her hair whip into her face and reached up to pull it back with her hands.

"Did you need something, Miss Lorri?" Lionel asked, coming from nowhere to stand in front of her.

"No, I just wanted to see the sun."

"You can't be up here without a life jacket."

Lionel saw the "Oh" that formed on Lorri's mouth, but he never heard it. Without warning, the skies filled with the sound of aircraft, men yelling, and gunfire exploding the calm world around them. Lionel all but shoved Lorri back through the door that had brought her topside, only to have men coming up so fast behind her that she was shoved out again. Rigg was suddenly in front of her, eyes ablaze.

"Get below!"

Lorri didn't argue. She scurried as fast as she could but was thrown around on the stairway and again when she reached the passage. She was knocked to her knees twice in her attempt to gain the cabin. Finally there, she curled in a corner of the bunk, listening to the world explode around her.

What irony was all she could think. *To be rescued off an island only to die at sea. Who will there be to tell my mother what's happened? How will Max and Grandpa know?*

A sudden lurch of the boat forced her to brace herself with her hand and foot against the wall. She wasn't very strong, but fear gave her a measure of strength she didn't know existed.

Cannon fire, men shouting, and what seemed to be many low-flying planes filled her ears for long minutes. All the while the boat bounced and turned its way through the water like a thing possessed. Lorri prayed and held on for dear life.

It took some time, but things eventually calmed. Even then, Lorri held tight to her spot and stared out the open door of the cabin. She hadn't bothered with the light in the room, but the light from the passageway gave her some comfort. She was staring straight at it when it was blocked out by a tall, broad figure.

"Miss Archer?" Rigg called her name as he flipped on the light.

Lorri scrambled from the bed.

"Is everyone all right. Is anyone hurt?"

"No, we're fine. Are you all right?"

The moment she had seen him, Lorri had started to shake and couldn't stop. She noticed that his face and the front of the life jacket that was secured tightly to his person were both wet. She wondered absently if anyone ever fell overboard and was lost.

"Miss Archer?" Rigg tried again.

Lorri looked into his eyes.

"Was it the Japanese?" she asked, sure of the answer.

"Yes."

For a moment, Lorri could only stare at him.

"It's like this for you all the time, isn't it?" she finally asked in a small voice. "They come and try to shoot you out of the water, and you have to fight back."

Rigg could see that this sudden introduction to the war had upset her. He could only imagine how it seemed from her point of view, but it was their job. He did his best to explain.

"We're all trained to do multiple tasks. And every man on this boat wants to win this war and go home. We're doing our jobs, and we're good at them."

"I didn't want anyone to be hurt."

"We're fine. But you didn't tell me if you were all right?"

"Yes, I think so. I didn't do anything."

"Yes, you did," he surprised her by saying. "You did your job, which is to land yourself in that bunk and hang on for all you're worth."

Lorri couldn't stop the smile that came to her mouth. She felt so relieved and safe all at the same time.

Watching it, Rigg smiled as well.

"We'll make a soldier out of you yet."

It was there again: She wanted to laugh. But before she could do that, Rigg had nodded and gone on his way. He'd shut the door on his way out, and Lorri, weary once again, sat back down on the bunk. She remained there until Ellis told her it was time for dinner.

The next morning Lorri found herself trembling all over again, but this time for a very different reason. She didn't want to make any mistakes or be a bother. She stood in the small head, undressed and poised before the sink, washcloth in hand, knowing she had very little time with the water — Lionel had explained this — and very little energy to spare.

What she hadn't counted on was how cold the water would make her. She shivered all the way through soaping and rinsing. Nevertheless, she felt cleaner. Her skin smelled of soap, and she'd even managed to wash her hair. She thought she might have taken a little longer than allowed but hoped she would be forgiven this one time.

Without warning "White Christmas" came to her mind. Even though she was still chilled, she hummed as she dried herself — words weren't long in coming. She sang, softly at first, and then with a little more volume, completely unaware of the effect it had on every man within hearing.

Sailors came from their rooms, men stopped in the passage, and even Ellis walked from the galley. They stood frozen, their eyes on nothing, and listened to Lorri's soft, clear soprano voice singing about home.

Rigg heard it as well. He had been at the desk in his cabin and stepped into the passageway. His men didn't even notice him. They all stood until the song came to a quiet end. Not until the soft strains died away did the men notice their commanding officer. Rigg didn't need to say a word. Each man went back to his business, as did Rigg, but each and every sailor could still hear the song in his head.

Her stomach full of the soup Ellis had made for lunch, Lorri felt as though she could take another nap. She wanted to resist but wasn't sure she should. Just in case, she decided to use the officer's head before returning to the cabin. She had been keeping very much to herself, wanting to be out of the way. Her need had not been urgent, but she was weary of being weary and of the officer's cabin as well.

The bright red spot on the tissue, however, shocked all vestiges of lethargy from her brain.

"Oh, no," she whispered. "Please, no, Lord. Anything but that."

Not in all these weeks had she had a period. It wasn't any wonder, considering the trauma she'd been through, but to have her body shift gears on this boat full of men had been the last thing on her mind.

She tried to be calm, but long moments of panic filled her. The very thought of telling anyone on board about her need caused her to flush painfully with embarrassment. She was going to have to deal with this on her own, but she couldn't calm down enough to think straight for some time.

Pacing a bit in the very small space — little more than turning in circles — she knew she couldn't stay in the bathroom forever.

"Socks!" she said out loud, the thought coming from she knew not where. Scrambling to open the door and rushing back to the officer's cabin, she tore through her small cache of clothing and found a thick sock. She returned to the head, glad that no one had slipped in during her absence. She took care of things as best she could, and finally left the small room behind, willing her body to go easy on her but fearing that too much time had passed.

She looked at her clothing again and found all the socks she could. There weren't many. Lorri began to pray for calm, even as she panicked more and told God she couldn't do it. Lionel had been beyond kind to her, but not in a million years could she tell that man the exact reason she needed more socks.

"You must have been praying," Click teased the lieutenant a little.

Rigg couldn't stop his smile. They were having engine trouble again but were also within an hour of a small island where they'd stopped before.

"Find Quinn," he ordered, not feeling it necessary to tell his radio man that he *had* been praying; he prayed all the time.

As was becoming a pattern, Lorri found herself waking from yet another nap, this time to find the boat rocking gently, no throb of the engine. Trying to wipe the cobs from her brain, she stood and walked to the door and looked into the passage. All was very quiet. She slipped into the head long enough to see that things were still manageable. With a prayer of thanks, she exited back into the passage and stood thinking.

She wasn't supposed to be topside without a life jacket, she remembered that much, but no one was about as she decided to go up the stairs. Figuring they would have a life jacket for her when she got up there, she headed out into the sunlight.

She was frozen with surprise to see that they had come to another island. There was no need to anchor out from shore, they were "parked" next to the beach, which held an impressive stretch of white sand.

"Miss Archer." A sailor had approached from behind her.

Lorri turned, a little startled.

"I'm Jack. Lieutenant Riggs and some men have gone ashore. He said that I could escort you ashore if you wish."

"Oh. Thank you."

"Can you manage the ladder?"

"Yes."

She was on the beach a short minute later, looking around at the trees and the sand. She turned and finally saw men working on the boat. She assumed the others were patrolling to see if the island was safe.

She watched the men work for a time, taking note of the fact that the sailor assigned to her was staying close by but not speaking. Lorri thought about walking up the beach and was about to do so when she saw Rigg heading from the trees and coming her way. She waited for him to approach.

"How are you?" he asked.

"I'm fine. Are we broken?"

"A little. It shouldn't take long to fix."

Lorri nodded.

"Stay close."

Lorri was about to agree when her eyes caught sight of the PT boat's name. She'd not seen it before.

"*Every Storm*?" she questioned before the lieutenant could move away. "Why *Every Storm*?"

Rigg's mouth quirked a bit.

"Because every storm in the Pacific finds this little boat. We seem to draw them like magnets."

Lorri's eyes had grown a little with this statement, but Rigg did not take time to reassure her. Someone called his name, and he turned away to go toward the working men.

Lorri began to walk slowly, hoping the sailor would stay put, but soon seeing that he was going to be on her heels. She felt bad about being a bother, but the thought did not have long to linger. As if waiting for her to be in a place of inconvenience, she sud-

73

denly felt as if the floodgates of her body opened wide. Without warning, she began to flow heavily. At the same moment, her eyes clapped onto the ocean. She moved that way, ignoring the man behind her.

"Miss Archer," she heard Jack say.

"I'm going to take a little swim," she said over her shoulder, not stopping or slowing in the least, barely even pausing as she kicked her shoes from her bare feet.

"I don't think that's such a good idea."

But Lorri was desperate. At the moment she'd forgotten that she didn't want to be any trouble. She didn't consider how weak she might be, or how taxing swimming could be on the body. Right now she was desperate to stop the flow, if only for a few minutes.

Jack could hardly believe his eyes. One moment she was walking along the beach, the next she was in the ocean. He didn't go in after her but stood on the beach and tried to reason with her.

"I need you to come out, Miss Archer."

"I'll just be a moment," she called to him, moving around a bit, and trying not to think about sharks.

"I'd rather you came now."

"All right," she agreed, but made no move for the shore. She was already tired but willing to buy every moment she could manage.

"Miss Archer."

The voice had changed. Lorri looked to see Rigg on the beach, Jack headed back to the boat.

"Hello, Lieutenant," Lorri called, able to see his anger from the water.

"I need you to come from the water," Rigg said, his tone measured. "I need to speak with you."

Lorri couldn't take her eyes from him. He was livid, and his anger propelled her from the sea. She found her footing and trudged out of the surf and up onto the sand, her clothes clinging from neck to ankle. She tried to pull the wet shirt away from her shrunken chest but looked up to see that Rigg only had eyes for her face. Furious eyes.

"What are you doing?" he asked.

"I took a little swim."

"Why?"

Lorri licked her lips, tasting salt and sea.

"I'm waiting for an answer."

"I just needed to swim for a moment."

Rigg's brows rose to an amazing height, and he looked as if he was going to blast her with his anger. Lorri disarmed him by showing some anger of her own.

"Are you married?" she snapped.

Rigg actually started over the question.

"No," he said quietly, his voice calming as he realized she had lost all reason.

"Are any of your men married?" she said, her anger now fully showing in the lowering of her brows and the stubborn tilt of her chin.

"Several."

"Well, maybe one of them can explain it to you!"

With that curt word of advice, she moved around the man in charge, picked up her shoes, and made for the boat. Not looking at any of the men she passed, she made for the ladder and took herself on board.

The men hadn't missed a thing, but not a word was spoken, especially when the lieutenant came behind her not five minutes later and followed her on board.

Lorri came from the head where she had changed her clothes to find Rigg in the cabin. She was already ashamed of the way she'd acted, but he gave her no time to apologize.

"Have a seat." He directed her to the desk chair, shutting the door as soon as she was inside.

Lorri did as she was told.

"I don't have time for embarrassment and blushing, I just need to know right now what you're using to take care of your needs."

Lorri couldn't look at him. He might command that she not blush, but it wasn't that simple.

"Tell me now."

His voice was all business but not unkind. Lorri didn't look at him to answer.

"Socks."

If Lorri had been looking at Rigg, she would have laughed. His mouth had opened a little, and for a moment he was surprised speechless. Lorri missed all of this. She heard him move just before he placed several pairs of socks in her lap.

Surprise brought her eyes to his.

"If you need more, tell me."

Lorri just looked at him.

"Do you understand?"

Lorri managed a nod.

Rigg exited without another word.

Five

"What do you mean she stood up to the lieu-tenant? What did she say?"

"I couldn't hear; they were down the beach. But she went swimming and he got mad. It looked as though she put him in his place."

"But you didn't hear it?"

"No."

"Did she sing again?"

"Not that I've heard."

The men were silent until the guy in the top bunk wanted more.

"What'd she wear swimming?"

"Her clothes."

"Did you see her wet?"

"Yep." The word was said with pride.

"You dog."

The occupant of the lower bunk was laughing softly when they were joined by two other men. Both men fell asleep happily but silently breaking the order not to think about their guest.

Lorri couldn't remember where she was. She woke knowing that someone was in her bedroom and that it wasn't Josie or Max. She gasped in fright, wanting to call for her grandpa.

"Miss Archer?" Rigg's voice came from the darkness.

"Oh, Lieutenant, it's you." She breathed heavily with relief, coming back to the boat in a rush.

"Are you all right?"

"Yes. I'm sorry I woke you."

"Don't worry about it," Rigg told her, not elaborating on the fact that he was just now coming to bed.

As swiftly and as quietly as he could, he climbed into Hugh's bunk and willed sleep to come. He battled worry over the repairs that didn't get done and his desire to land Lorri Archer safely at Seaford.

"Lieutenant?"

"Yes."

"I'm sorry about earlier today."

"Don't trouble yourself over it."

"I shouldn't have said those things."

"It's all right."

Lorri heard a thump and started a little.

"Are we moving?" she asked.

"No. I think we'll be underway about midmorning."

Silence fell in the cabin. Lorri thought the lieutenant might say more, but he didn't. She didn't feel reassured about her apology. She wanted to say she was sorry again, but too much time had passed. He might be sleeping.

Making herself more comfortable, she forced herself to go back to sleep. It wasn't that easy, but about ten minutes later she lost consciousness.

Not at any time did she suspect that Lieutenant Riggs was wide awake for a good deal longer.

With no idea as to when she might be on dry ground again, Lorri was up early, washed, dressed, and on the beach. Her monthly situation was well in hand for the moment, and if that status changed, she would simply return to the boat and remain in the officer's cabin.

Not worrying about an escort — no one had been waiting for her — she hit the sand and strolled along between the waves and the line of trees. She'd seen other men moving about and figured if she remained in sight, she was plenty safe.

What she hadn't figured on was the way the island made her feel. Memories of the accident and the burials came flooding back to her. Her steps slowed and her mind wandered. Lorri saw images in her mind that made her shudder, and she suddenly wished she had stayed on board.

"Well, well. What do we have here?"

Lorri stopped her walk and looked up to see a sailor she hadn't met before. He was not alone, but it still took Lorri a moment to realize these men were from another crew. She had stopped in her tracks, but the men were approaching, boldness written on every move.

"What's your name, pretty lady?"

Lorri took one step back and then another.

"Don't be afraid," one of them said. "We just want to talk."

"Speak for yourself," another put in, and Lorri felt a jolt of fear. She glanced behind her and wondered how she could have gotten so far down the beach.

"You're on the skinny side, but we like skinny women," one foolish man said, his smile very wide, his eyes studying her body in the baggy men's clothing.

"I have to get back to the boat," she told them, but one was already close enough to touch her.

He reached up and stroked down the side of her hair. That was all Lorri needed. Bringing herself painfully erect, she reached up and pushed his hand away with as much force as she could find.

"Do not touch me," she ordered in her teacher's voice.

"Ooh," several men said from behind him, "she's a feisty one."

Lorri turned and started away, but the man grabbed her hand and held it.

"Let go of me," she ordered, but trembling had come over her, and her voice lacked conviction.

"You heard the lady," Jack said, suddenly appearing, Donald and Cliff behind him.

"Well, now," the physical sailor started in, his hands going up in innocence. "This must be the lucky crew who has a woman on board. Must be nice."

"Shut your mouth!" Jack told him.

"I'd be happy to shut my mouth as soon as you open yours. Where'd you find her?"

"Can we have one?" another of the strangers asked, bringing a lot of unpleasant words from the three sailors off the *Storm*.

Lorri didn't wait around to see if the words would lead to blows. She turned and moved up the beach as fast as her legs could carry her. Up the ladder she went without talking to anyone. She sank into the first alcove she came to and curled into a ball.

Lionel had seen her come aboard and gone to check on her, but her face was buried against her bent knees. He kept his distance, but he could see on the beach that word was spreading over something that had happened. Not sure what she'd done this time, he knew it would only be a matter of time before Hugh or the lieutenant came looking for her.

It was Rigg. Not 20 minutes had passed before the encounter reached his ears. Lionel watched him come on board but didn't speak to him. Not until he'd disappeared below deck and returned did Lionel catch his eye and nod in Lorri's direction.

Rigg came around the wheelhouse and found her curled into a ball, her body rocking slightly.

"Miss Archer," Rigg said after he'd hunkered down in front of her, but she shook her head against her knees.

Rigg let his eyes roam over the island and then out to sea, debating what to do. He thought they might be underway in less than an hour. Did he let the incident go or find the other commander and tell him what he thought of his men? And could he really do that if he didn't find out from Lorri Archer exactly what had happened?

He looked down at Lorri's bent head, knowing only one thing was important.

"Are you hurt, Miss Archer? I need to know that."

Again the shake of her head against her knees. He'd hoped for more. Rigg suspected that she'd been through things on the other island that would devastate many. And now an encounter with hormonal, foolish sailors. How much more could she take? He stood to his feet with no answers.

"Stay close," he said quietly to Lionel, and then he strode back onto the beach.

The *Every Storm* was back at sea when Ellis served lunch. Lorri still hadn't spoken to anyone about the incident on the beach, but she went to the officer's mess when she was beckoned and found Hugh already eating.

"Have a seat, Miss Archer."

"Thank you."

Lorri thanked Ellis when he put food in front of her, and without praying, she began to eat. Hugh didn't try to speak to her for a time but waited until she'd had some food.

"Are you feeling better?"

Lorri had almost forgotten his presence.

"Yes, thank you."

"Not all sailors are honorable men, I'm afraid to say."

Lorri looked at him, her mind working on a question.

"You have something on your mind."

Lorri nodded and hoped he wouldn't press her.

"You can voice it."

Lorri tore a piece from the small biscuit she'd been given and tried to put her thoughts into words.

"Would the men aboard this boat have been rude to me had we met in the same way?"

"The same way as the men on the beach?"

"Yes."

"I don't think so. I can think of a few who might get out of hand, but be bold enough to touch you? No."

"How do you know I was touched?"

"Jack reported what he saw."

Lorri felt cold. She reached for her mug of coffee and wrapped her hands around it.

"I want to go home, Ensign," Lorri said quietly. "I want it more than I can say."

"We'll do our best, Miss Archer."

Lorri looked at him.

"How selfish of me. You all want to go home."

"We're doing our best with that too."

Lorri smiled a little and went back to her food. Hugh studied the top of her head, taking in the dark hair that looked so soft. He knew how wrong it was for those men to have taken such liberties but could see how tempting it would be.

Lorri stared down at the book on the desk, her eyes not believing what they were seeing. A Bible. A Bible sat in the middle of the desk. It had a black cover and looked as if it had been well read.

She had not touched anything on board. She had been careful to keep to herself and to the few belongings she'd been given, but this was more temptation than she could handle.

She pulled the chair out and took a seat. Her hands gentle, she opened to the middle and began reading in Psalms.

With a deep hunger and an ache for the words, she read slowly from chapter 52. The first verses were about an unrighteous man and his choices, but starting at verse 7, the psalmist summed up and determined not to follow the wicked man's path.

She read, "Lo, this is the man who made not God his strength, but trusted in the abundance of his riches, and strengthened himself in his wickedness. But I am like a green olive tree in the house of God; I trust in the mercy of God forever and ever. I will praise thee forever, because thou hast done it; and I will wait on thy name; for it is good before thy saints."

The word *saints* took Lorri back to her home church in southern California. She could see the building, the pews and pulpit, and then the people of her church family who filled those pews.

She didn't want to cry, so she went back to verse 7. Again, she read, "Lo, this is the man who made not God his strength, but trusted in the abundance of his riches, and strengthened himself in his wickedness."

Please don't let me trust in anything but you, Lord, she prayed, her heart and mind wanting to honor. *I don't think clearly right now. I fear and don't trust anyone or anything. I want to recover from this time, Lord, knowing You had a plan. Please help me in the days to come. Help me to go home to Mother.*

Lorri could say nothing more. She was breathless with the pain in her heart. The thought of her mother was enough to make her sob with despair and longing. The things she was going to have to tell her, the ache to see her and know her touch.

Lorri suddenly stood, still breathing

hard. She needed to get out of this cabin and get some air. She moved from the room, planning to go topside and ask for a life jacket.

"Find the lieutenant," Click told the first man who walked past the control room. The radio had been unreliable for weeks, but word was now coming through. Click listened to the message, his heart beating painfully in his chest.

Having written it all down, he glanced at the door. He'd give the sailor about two more minutes and then look for the lieutenant himself.

The sun was dropping fast, but there was still plenty of light. It hadn't started out as a time for visiting, but it ended up that way.

Lionel had found Lorri on the deck, a life jacket nearly swallowing her thin frame. He sat down to talk with her, well remembering the incident that morning. She seemed in better spirits, and it wasn't long before Jack and Cliff joined them.

"You should sing," Jack told her.

It took a moment for Lorri to realize he was talking to her.

"I should sing?" she questioned him.

"Yes. It sounds nice."

"How do you know the way my voice sounds?"

Not wanting her to know they'd heard her in the officer's head, Lionel reminded her of the island.

"That's how we found you, remember?"

Lorri nodded as it came back to her.

"So will you sing?" Cliff asked this time.

"I don't know what to sing," Lorri admitted, feeling more than a little self-conscious, her eyes going to the front of the vest.

"Anything."

Lorri's mind was blank until Jack hummed, "I'll Be Seeing You." Lorri was immediately caught up with the melody in her mind. She hummed a little with him, and then launched into the words. Every man who could move from his station came near to her voice. They stood very still as she started another song — a hymn this time — even knowing that if the lieutenant found them, they'd all be in trouble. At the moment no one cared.

The sounds of a third song were dying away before anyone noticed Rigg. How long he'd been standing there was anyone's guess, but they took their cue and moved on. Darkness was coming in fast, but Rigg decided to talk to Lorri where she was.

"Miss Archer, I need to ask you some things."

"All right."

"I don't know if anyone has explained to you, but our communication systems have been unreliable lately. I've only just now gotten word about your being reported missing."

Lorri blinked. "You got word about me?"

"I believe so. Are you Admiral Archer's granddaughter?"

"Yes." Lorri perked up as she said this, her whole body moving toward Rigg. She completely missed the way every man within hearing snapped around to stare at their commanding officer.

"My grandfather is looking for me?" Lorri asked.

"Yes, for you and your sister. Can you tell me where Josephine is? Did she fly with you?"

The change in her was visible. Lorri bit her lip, her brow furrowing with pain. "I have to tell him about that," she said softly.

"Whom do you need to tell?"

"Grandpa. He'll want to know."

"What do you need to tell him?" Rigg asked, even as he watched her shake her head, tears filling her eyes.

"She didn't make it," Lorri whispered

now. "I tried to talk to her — I tried to get her to wake up — but she wouldn't. I don't know how I'm going to tell him, Lieutenant. I don't know how I'm going to explain to Grandpa. He'll be so sad.

"And Clarence Fuller's family!" The words burst out of her, almost as though she'd been desperate to talk for years. "I have to tell them that he tried. He was always a little sweet on Josie. He did everything he could to get us there, but the storm . . ." She was gasping now. "The winds and rain were so hard. We couldn't see a thing! The trees rushed up at us and then nothing but darkness and rain. I was so scared. Josie wouldn't answer."

Her hand was over her mouth now, her eyes telling the horror of it all, but Rigg could still hear her words. He thought about stopping her, wishing he knew what was best.

"I didn't die. I thought I would." Lorri breathed heavily, her eyes pleading with him to understand, but her voice had almost returned to normal. She talked as though she were alone on the deck.

"It took me days to dig those holes. I buried Clarence first, but I couldn't make myself put Josie in the dirt. I took her locket." As if to prove the point, Lorri reached to her neck and pulled out a gold chain, a locket on the end.

"It's from Ken. He loves her. How will I tell him? I didn't have anyone. It should have been me. I should have died!"

The tears were coming again, and this time all calmness left her voice.

"How will I ever tell my mother?" Lorri begged the lieutenant. "I'll never be able to explain to Mother and Max!"

Rigg didn't wait any longer. He moved forward, scooped Lorri into his arms and moved for the stairs. Men were there ahead of him, holding the door and making the way clear. Lorri sobbed into her hands, saying words that no one could understand.

Someone had turned the light on in the cabin. He went to the bunk he'd given Lorri — his bunk — and laid her down. She tried to curl into a ball, but he stopped her while he worked the buckles of the life jacket, not wanting her to sleep in something so constricting. He tossed it aside and pulled the desk chair close. He sat down and pulled a sheet over her already-curled-up body. At that point, he sat helplessly and listened as she cried herself into exhaustion. Had she cried since it happened? How long had she been holding it all in? So many questions raced through Rigg's mind that he almost forgot to pray.

Not until she slept soundly did Rigg move from her side. He went directly to Click in the control room. His orders were to keep it simple. The message read:

```
Attention Admiral Archer, U.S.
Navy — Have found Lorraine Ar-
cher — Will deliver her to Sea-
ford ASAP — Josephine Archer
and pilot Clarence Fuller, de-
ceased.
```

Six

"She buried her sister on that island?"

"Yeah, and the pilot who flew the plane."

As with all PT boats, crews were small and word traveled fast. *Every Storm* had 12 men and 2 officers. It didn't take long for those who missed Lorri's firsthand account on the island to hear every word.

Ellis had a few words of his own. Anyone who spoke to him about it also got a tongue lashing: "You lusted after that poor girl and she's been through all of *that!* You ought to be ashamed!"

And in truth, some of them were. Almost to a man they envied Lionel's and Rigg's contact with her, but their dreams weren't as risqué as Ellis claimed. Every man longed for a little touch of home. Lorri Archer might have been one of the girls from high school or someone who lived down the street.

Of course, that was easier to imagine before they remembered the identity of her grandfather. Admiral Archer! He was one of the toughest men in the navy and a man who hadn't been many years from retirement when the war broke out. He had stayed on, seemingly stronger than ever, ready for battle at a moment's notice. No one even suspected. And as far as they knew, the woman herself hadn't said a word about their connection.

Every Storm moved swiftly toward the base at Seaford, but not a man forgot about their valuable cargo. They would patrol their way to base, eyes more watchful than ever, probably arriving the next afternoon. What none of them bargained for was a storm that moved in sometime after midnight and more than managed to force their boat to live up to its name.

Lorri woke suddenly, not certain if it was her stomach or the boat that was rolling. She felt her body tipping out of bed and just managed to catch herself before tumbling to the floor. Her stomach lurched again, along with the boat, and Lorri wondered how long she could take such movement.

She found out a moment later. With no choice but to stumble out of bed and find the head, she scrambled out of the cabin and just made it. It was hard to lose what little she had inside, but the rocking of the craft was more than she could take.

Not sure she could stay on her feet for the trip back, Lorri forced herself to leave the officer's head. She ran into Rigg in the passageway.

"I'm sorry," she mumbled, barely aware of the way his arm kept her from hitting her head when they stumbled with the motion. The boat rocked like a child's hobby horse.

"Are you sick?"

"Yes."

"I think you'd better go right back to bed."

Rigg's hand to her arm kept her on her feet, and when she'd lain down, he found a basin and put it by the bed.

"Don't try to go out into the passage. I've put a container here if you need it."

"I'll do anything," she said cryptically when he stopped talking and stood looking down at her.

"What do you mean?"

"I won't disappear when you're trying to leave." The words were whispered. "I won't go swimming. I'll let you have your bed back. Please just put me off this boat, Lieutenant. Please make the rocking stop."

Rigg couldn't hold his smile. He thought she would have felt seasickness before and was quite impressed at how well she'd done to this point. He would tell her that, but not now. Now she thought she was going to die from the rolling in her gut, and there was little he could do about that.

"I'll send Ellis to check on you. He might have a little something that will help you keep things down."

Rigg braced himself when the boat rocked mightily and reached for Lorri when she rolled toward the edge. As soon as he had his footing, he found a strap and made short work of tying her into the bed. With the strap secure around her waist, he took her hand and guided it over the edge of the thin mattress.

"Here's the basin. Do you feel it?"

"Yes."

"Don't get up. Just reach for it right there."

"Okay," Lorri agreed, but there was no time. She needed it so swiftly that Rigg held it for her. She finished and apologized in a tortured whisper that he ignored. Such things were never a problem for him.

When she lay back, pale and breathing hard, Rigg put one hand on her arm and one out to brace himself on the wall.

"I'll send Ellis to you," he said.

"I'm going to die, aren't I?" She sounded beyond miserable. "Such irony. I've made it off the island just to die at sea."

Rigg fought the smile that threatened to peek through, gave her a little pat, and went in search of Ellis.

Lorri watched him leave, certain she had her answer.

He left without a word. That can only mean one thing: He's too kindhearted to tell me I'm going to die.

She'd been singing in the head again. Rigg didn't have the heart to send the men to their duties with a harsh word, but as soon as he arrived in the passageway, they scattered.

Just two hours now. They were limping along, needing more repairs and communications on the fritz again, but they were going to get to Seaford and deliver the woman that had affected every man on the boat.

It was easy to sit in the middle of the Pacific and forget for whom you were fighting. At times it became personal, and thoughts of home and family were very far away. Lorri Archer had changed all of that. She was worth fighting for. An all-American girl, most would have called her. She sang like a bird, was sweet and uncomplaining, and had experienced the tortures of this war the way few women had.

Rigg knew it wasn't easy to sit at home; that was its own form of torture. But Lorri Archer didn't have to imagine any longer what battle looked like. She had become an eyewitness. She had ridden the waves of a PT boat under attack, both from the enemy and the elements. She had tasted the death of a loved one, much the same way any of these men might be asked to part with a fellow sailor.

And not a word out of her. Other than feeling as though she needed a bath at an inopportune time, she had been almost invisible. Not in the physical sense, of course — every man was aware of her — but she made no demands and was thankful for the smallest act of kindness.

Rigg's mind ran with all of these thoughts as he waited for her to come from the officer's head. He knew his pride was on the line this day and would have freely admitted to anyone that he planned to deliver the admiral's granddaughter in the best shape he could. Just last night she had spent the night losing what little she held, and today he wanted her strong enough to walk off his boat.

Rigg was suddenly aware that the singing had stopped. He stood ready, his eyes on the door. Sure enough, she came out a few seconds later.

"Did I take too long?" were the first words from Lorri's mouth.

"No, but I wanted to make sure you're all right."

"I'm a little tired is all."

She was more than that, but Rigg didn't comment out loud. She was pale and still painfully thin, her eyes standing out like a frightened doe's.

"Ellis has made a good breakfast for you. We should be in port in about two hours, and I want you to be at your best."

"My grandfather will be there?"

"I'm not sure about that."

"You didn't get word to him?"

"We did send word, and maybe it reached him. But then the storm hit, and we haven't heard back."

"That's right," Lorri said, speaking her thoughts. "You don't know where he is, do you?"

Rigg smiled before saying, "Navy admirals don't usually check in with me."

Lorri smiled as well. She felt hungry and a little lightheaded, but she was close now — closer than she ever hoped to be.

"Go ahead and eat," Rigg urged her.

"I need to wash the fatigues I used."

"Don't worry about that right now."

"I'll take care of it after I eat."

Rigg didn't comment on this, but he planned to let her do no such thing. It was the least of their worries.

Seaford Naval Station

Dean Archer paced the confines of Captain Dunlap's office, thinking he might lose his mind if he had to wait any longer. He didn't let himself think about how close the call had been. Within the hour he'd been scheduled to head back out to sea. He'd been headed home to see Ruth and Max, knowing they needed him close. But then word had come. Lorraine was alive. Josephine was not returning.

It had never once occurred to him that only one of the girls would come home. In his mind he welcomed or mourned them both. That the pilot had died as well was almost more than his heart could take. What had Lorri been through? What had she survived? Would she ever be the same again?

"I'm going for a walk, Captain," Dean said abruptly, desperate to divert his thoughts.

"Yes, sir."

"I'll be in plain sight and not far away."

"I'll find you, sir."

Halfway hoping the other man would tell him it would be better to stay, Dean made himself walk out the door.

Every Storm was headed to dock in an out-of-the-way spot. All the men had come topside and were lined up, ready to speak with Lorri. She moved carefully on the shifting deck, Rigg and Lionel nearby.

"Thank you, Ellis," she told the cook. "Everything you did — it was so kind. I can't thank you enough."

"It was nothing, Miss Archer. You just get home and have a good life."

Lorri smiled at him and moved on. She shook the hand of each man, thanked each one, but took extra time with the men she knew a little better.

"One last picture?" Click asked, holding his Brownie in place, unaware that Lorri had not noticed how often he used it.

"Sure," she said with a smile, and Click made a few of the men laugh with his enthusiasm. He took great delight in lining everyone up, positioning people just so, and making them stand there for at least five takes.

They were docking by the time he was

done, but Lorri didn't hurry. She took time to thank the rest of the crew, with special words for Lionel, Jack, and Hugh, and then turned to accompany Lieutenant Riggs ashore.

"Are you all right?" Rigg asked as soon as he could.

"Just a little shaky all of a sudden."

"Ellis tells me you didn't eat much."

"I tried," Lorri said apologetically.

She was pale, her dark hair accenting that fact, but Rigg decided not to worry about it. Her grandfather wasn't going to care how she looked, and Rigg had only one goal at the moment: to see her safely to that man. Even if the admiral wasn't there, he still knew she would be safer at Seaford than on the boat.

Lorri was vaguely aware of the eyes that watched them. Rigg walked her onto the dock and then toward a building and an office. He held the door for her to go inside and waited for her to precede him. The sailor inside had heard about the admiral's situation, and he was swift to make a call to his superior. More calls were made, and in moments Captain Dunlap and an aide were running for a jeep, intent on finding the admiral on his walk.

Lorri sat inside the office and looked out

the window. She didn't want to cry but felt tears threatening nonetheless. She had made it. She had made it safely to land where telephones worked and the world didn't rock with every whim of the sea.

She was trying not to think about all that had brought her here when her grandfather walked past. Lorri came to her feet, swaying a little.

"Are you all right?" Rigg asked.

"That was my grandfather," she got out just before her eyes rolled back in her head.

"Go after him!" Rigg barked to the sailor and gathered Lorri in his arms to lower her back onto the chair. He thought it might be best if she lay down but wasn't about to put her on the floor.

"Miss Archer," Rigg called as he tried to revive her. "Can you hear me?"

Lorri started, her body jolting back to consciousness. She looked into Rigg's face, sure she was still on the boat, her heart sinking with dread.

"Is the storm over? I don't want to be sick again."

"We're at the base," Rigg told her quietly, holding her shoulder against the seat back until she was ready to sit up a little more. She had just managed that action when Dean Archer's frame filled the doorway.

"Grandpa," Lorri said, her voice sounding as though she'd been rehearsing for weeks. "I didn't do a good job."

"I'm sure you did very well, Lorri," he said calmly, going slowly and hiding his concern and shock over her appearance and the strange tenor of her voice.

"I couldn't bring Josie home, Grandpa. I wanted to, but I couldn't."

"It's all right, honey. Don't you worry about it anymore."

"I don't know how I'm going to tell Mother and Max."

"I'll tell them. You can just rest."

He was in front of her chair now, a sob breaking in the back of his throat. With that, Dean waited no longer. He bent and took her tenderly into his arms, his own tears coming in a rush. Lorri clung to the man who had been more of a father than a grandfather and sobbed like a child. Rigg made his exit on that note.

He gave the sailor information about where he would be, with plans to return to his boat and crew. They wouldn't be leaving anytime soon, not with so many needed repairs. And anyway, right now it was best to occupy his thoughts with those duties — anything to get the reunion scene from his mind.

★ ★ ★

Dean sat on the room's one chair and watched his granddaughter sleep on one of the twin beds. On the floor by the bed were her saddle shoes, filthy and worn, but nothing else she wore was hers. This came to Dean slowly, after 30 minutes of studying her face, more tears trickling down his cheeks.

He would have to get word to Ruth and Maxine, but not just yet. Right now he was still taking it in. Almost seven weeks missing. He had started to give up hope. A small plane going down in these waters would certainly disappear without a trace. That the plane hit land was nothing short of a miracle.

The sailor had told him where Lieutenant Riggs would be. This was important to the admiral. He had questions for that man. Not right now, but eventually.

"Grandpa," Lorri suddenly asked. Dean had not seen that her eyes were open. "Do you have any water?"

"Right here." He went to the small bathroom and filled the glass provided. Their quarters weren't fancy or large, but they were one of several available to officers. Thankfully a room with two beds had been vacant, because Dean had no plans to let Lorri out of his sight.

Lorri sat up and drained the glass of water. Dean refilled it, and she drank half of it. He then sat down on the opposite bed and stared at her. Lorri looked back.

"I hope you're really sitting there and I'm not dreaming."

"I'm here, honey."

"Where are we?" She frowned a little, not sure if someone had said.

"We're at Seaford, a naval base in Australia."

Lorri showed a little panic over this.

"Grandpa," her voice pleaded, "I wish to go home. I don't think I can stay here and teach without Josie. I need to see Mother and . . ."

"Lorraine," her grandfather cut in, reaching for her hand and waiting for her to focus on him. "We're going home just as soon as I can arrange it. You're going back to California, and you're staying there."

Lorri nodded, her eyes closing in relief. She had been close to panic. This was almost worse than the island or the boat. She wished she could think a little more clearly, but she found herself ready to cry again. Never had she wanted to see her mother so much.

"Do you want to sleep a little more, or shall we find you something to eat?"

"Oh, food sounds good. Is there some place nearby?"

"You leave it to me."

Lorri nodded, feeling safe, and went into the bathroom. She used the commode and then moved to the sink to wash her hands. She ran the water but forgot to get her hands wet.

Had there been mirrors on the boat? Lorri couldn't remember having seen one. Right now she stood frozen as a stranger looked back at her from the vanity mirror. Who was this person whose cheeks were sunken and pale, whose eyes stood out unnaturally? There was a scar on her forehead. Lorri couldn't remember when she got that. Was it new, or did it happen during the crash?

"Lorri?" her grandfather called anxiously from outside the door. "Are you all right?"

"Yes, I'll be with you in a moment."

Just remembering she wanted to wash her hands, Lorri made herself look down and get the job done.

I'm alive, she said to herself, enjoying the cool water and the white sink. *Nothing else matters.* Her mother came to mind, but Lorri had no worries on her account. Her mother wouldn't care how she looked as long as she was alive.

Following Dean as he led her to the mess hall, Lorri could tell that her energy was low. The thought of food, however, was worth the effort of staying awake. They exited the barracks, not seeing anyone else around, and walked a short distance to another building, one full of tables and benches.

No one was eating, but Dean saw Lorri to a table and then went toward the galley. He wasn't long returning with a tray of food.

The meal was simple fare, bread and meat with some dessert on the side. Lorri built a sandwich and took sips of the coffee her grandfather had brought her. She was about halfway done when they were joined by another officer.

"This is Commander Tyler," Dean explained. "He's a doctor. I've asked him to examine you when you're done with your food."

"I'm all right," Lorri wasted no time in saying, her eyes direct as they met those of the other man.

Dean looked as if he would argue, but the doctor cut in.

"I'm just going to take your pulse, listen to your heart, and ask you some questions."

Lorri nodded, still not thrilled with the idea, but telling herself to be calm.

"If you want, we can even cover the questions right here."

"All right," Lorri agreed. No one was around, and she didn't think he was going to get overly personal.

"What day did you fly away from Carson Point?"

"The first of June."

"And what day did the PT crew find you?"

Lorri didn't know. Her brow furrowed as she tried to remember.

"Was it a week ago or a few days?" Dean prompted.

Could she have been through all she'd been through with the lieutenant and his men in less than a week? Or was it longer?

"A week, I think," Lorri guessed. "I'm not sure."

"Okay." The doctor kept his voice casual. She had stopped eating to concentrate, and he didn't want that. "What did you eat on the island?"

"Leaves and berries."

The doctor had not been taking notes, but Lorri suddenly realized that he watched her very closely.

"Why don't you just tell me what this is really about," Lorri said, not liking the way the interview was making her feel.

"There is no hidden agenda here, Lorri." Her grandfather fielded this one. "You've been through an ordeal, and I'm concerned about you."

"What does it matter how long I was on the boat?"

"I'm trying to figure out how long you went without food," the doctor replied.

"How did you know I went without food?"

Dean could have kicked himself for allowing this conversation to go on here and not in the privacy of their room. His mind scrambled to make light of the fact that she was not the same girl he remembered. At least, not yet.

"Commander Tyler is just guessing that you might not usually be this thin."

Lorri looked into her grandfather's eyes and smiled at the smile she saw there. She had been through an ordeal, an ordeal so fierce that she had stopped trusting even those who loved her.

"I'm sorry," she began, but the doctor put his hand up and flashed a smile of his own.

"The apology should come from me," he said. "I need to let you finish your meal. How can you think clearly on an empty stomach?"

Lorri went back to eating, and Dean was

pleased to see the tension pass. He had not meant to plot against her or go on the attack. He'd seen men come back from battle in great need of care. He was swiftly learning that it was entirely different when it was his own granddaughter. He would stay close but let the doctor finish in his own way, not worrying about the details. Anything Lorri couldn't remember from the last week would surely be covered by Lieutenant Riggs.

Seven

"I've got a meeting this morning," Dean told Lorri early the next day. "Will you be all right?"

"I'll be fine. I'll probably lie here for a while and then take a bath."

"Good. When I get back, we'll eat breakfast and try to find some other clothes for you to wear."

Lorri agreed, thinking that might be a very good idea. She kept to her bed even after he left, and although she thought about getting up — a bath sounded wonderful — it wasn't long before she fell back to sleep.

"What day and time did you get to the island?" Dean asked Rigg as soon as he thanked him for rescuing Lorri.

"Saturday the fourteenth."

"Just five days ago?" he confirmed quietly, not seeming anywhere near as fierce as all the rumors.

"Yes, we got to the island at about eight bells. We needed repairs. We found Miss Archer when we heard her singing."

A heartfelt smile came to the admiral's lips.

"Let me guess, a mixture of hymns and the latest songs hitting the airwaves."

"That about sums it up."

"She has all the words memorized the first time she hears a song. Put something to music and Lorri has it." The admiral paused for just a moment. "Josie was her biggest fan."

Rigg watched the other man, whose attention had strayed to a place in his mind. Both of Rigg's parents were alive, as were both of his brothers. He had no reference point to losing someone as close as a granddaughter. Clearly the man was hurting.

"Did you leave the island that day?"

"No, the next. I put a man in charge of her, and we got some food to her as soon as we could. She had found an excellent water supply and was sleeping in the plane, which was in a small clearing."

"And did she talk to you about what happened?"

"Not until Tuesday."

"What did she tell you?"

"That Clarence Fuller, the pilot, did all he could. She described the rain as being all around them. They couldn't see a thing. She said the trees rushed up to meet them, and all was black with the rain still coming hard. Her sister wouldn't answer her." Rigg made himself tell the painful details. "It took her days to dig the holes. She buried the pilot first because she couldn't put Josie in the dirt at that point. She took Josie's locket and put it on.

"It sounds like she ate what food she could find, which wasn't much, and had plenty of water. She was a little confused and disoriented from time to time, but until she saw you from the office window, she hadn't fainted.

"We stopped again near Cooley, and she had an encounter with another boat crew. It was upsetting to her, but she handled herself well."

"Did you report the men?"

"No, sir. Miss Archer would not elaborate on what happened."

"So she might have been hurt?"

"No, sir. My men saw a sailor touch her hair and try to detain her by grabbing her wrist. My men were on hand a moment later, and Miss Archer was able to walk away."

"Do you know what was said to her?"

"No, sir."

Dean fell silent for a moment. Rigg watched him and waited.

"Where did she sleep on the boat?"

"In my bunk. I took Ensign Westland's bunk. I hung a sheet to give Miss Archer privacy."

Dean's eyes were suddenly intent.

"And your men were gentlemen?"

"Yes, sir. I would swear to it."

Dean didn't need to ask about Rigg's conduct. His gut told him there would be no offense there.

"Did you see the graves?" was the next question, coming on a rather hoarse voice.

"Yes, sir. They were in another clearing."

Dean's eyes closed for a moment. He tried to fight the tears, but it was no use. Rigg came to his feet. He went to the coffee pot, filled two mugs, and returned to the table.

Dean opened his eyes when he heard the mug placed in front of him. He stared down at it for a moment and then reached for his handkerchief. He blew his nose and took a moment to compose himself before reaching for the hot drink.

"I think you should also know, sir," Rigg said without permission, "that we had Zeros almost as soon as we left the island. We traveled in daylight and took down two planes, but one got away."

"And where was Lorri during all of this?"

"On her bunk. We also had a storm the night before we made port. She was very seasick."

Dean was without words. It wasn't enough that Lorri was plane-wrecked and had to bury her sister. She had also been on the boat when it was under enemy attack and experienced a storm only days later. The emotions running through him were so varied and strong that for a long time he said nothing.

Rigg was quiet as well. Again he was having to imagine this for someone he loved and could see why it would be nearly impossible to take in.

"When do you leave here?" Dean finally asked.

"Not for a week at least. Our problems can't be patched up any longer."

Dean nodded and stood. Rigg also came to his feet and saluted.

"Thank you, Lieutenant." Dean released Rigg with a return salute and moved on his way.

Lorri was finally out of bed, running water to take a hot bath, when she realized that her period had stopped and no longer needed her attention. It hadn't run its normal course, but she knew better than to expect that.

For long moments she shivered, not with cold but with some undefinable emotion. The water was hot all around her, but she felt bruised, and her skin ached.

"Josie," Lorri whispered, not wanting to cry but not sure she had a choice. "I can't even visit your grave. I know you're not there, but somehow I want to be near that marker."

Lorri's hand went to the chain and locket around her neck. She squeezed her eyes shut, but hot tears still found a path down her face. She hadn't known that anything could hurt this much. Her father had died when she was ten. She had cried and felt lost for a long time, but that pain was nothing to this.

And as always, the need to see her mother squeezed painfully around her heart. Ruth Archer never quite left her consciousness. She had missed her mother while working in Australia — at times she'd been dreadfully homesick for her and for her sister — but this was different. All at once Lorri felt five years old again. She felt abandoned and alone, and in such need of her mother that she could hardly think straight.

She breathed heavily, trying to control herself, but it was no use. Harsh sobs broke from her throat. Sinking as deeply into the water as she could get, she sobbed in agony, only able to form a few coherent words to God.

"Please help me," she whispered. "Please help me to get home."

"How'd it go with the admiral?" Hugh asked as soon as he saw Rigg.

"I think all right. He might want to see me again."

"Will he be around that long?"

"He didn't say when they were leaving."

"Did you see her?"

Rigg shook his head, his gaze hooded.

"The men have been asking about her."

Rigg nodded. "If I see Admiral Archer again, I'll tell him."

Quinn came looking for Rigg just then. His news about the parts for their repairs was so disheartening that it drove everything else from Rigg's mind.

"Someone had a hot bath," Dean teased Lorri as soon as he let himself back into the room. She was still in the chair, her hair damp, the room a little moist.

"It felt nice."

"I'll bet it did. PTs are not known for their fine bathing facilities."

"I didn't know a bathroom could be that small," Lorri said, and Dean smiled at his first glimpse of the woman he once knew.

"How about some breakfast?"

"With coffee?"

"Yes, ma'am."

"Then I'm all for it."

Lorri set her grandfather's Bible aside and followed him from the room. It was early, so many officers and enlisted men were in the mess hall. Lorri sat in the separate dining room for the officers, her gaze almost immediately going to the windows that separated them. In doing so, she spotted Lionel. Not even thinking to tell her grandfather where she was going, she stood and went to him.

"Hello, Lionel," Lorri said as she approached him where he stood by the coffee urn, greeting him with a smile.

Lionel smiled right back, pulling his hat from his head in the process.

"Hello, Miss Lorri. You're looking well."

"Thank you. I wasn't sure if you would still be here."

"We have repairs to make."

"And then where do you go?"

Lionel grinned as he said, "Back out on patrol."

A quiver of fear raced through her, unexpected and almost confusing.

"Are you all right, Miss Lorri?"

"Yes, I just felt afraid for a moment."

"For us?"

"Yes."

"That's kind of you, Miss Lorri, but we won't go until the *Storm* is fully ready."

Lorri nodded, not able to explain her memory of having been aboard during an attack. She glanced around a bit, and that's when she noticed that Lionel was holding a cup of coffee.

"I should let you get to your breakfast before it gets cold."

Lionel nodded kindly, not anxious to be away, but not certain how long he should detain her.

"You take care of yourself, Miss Lorri," he put in after a few heartbeats of silence.

"You do the same," Lorri urged him as well.

She moved back to the officer's mess, finding her grandfather waiting in the doorway.

Dean knew no end of emotions as he watched her come to him. He hadn't wanted to disturb her conversation, but having his granddaughter talking with ease to an enlisted man was not something he ever expected to see. Clearly she was very comfortable with this sailor.

"Are you ready for breakfast?" he asked when she was close.

"Yes. Did I hold you up?"

"Not at all," he answered, giving her a smile of reassurance and still trying to figure out the odd emotions moving through him.

In the midst of this he realized it didn't matter. She was safe. She was not unscathed, but she was alive, and he was going to get her home. He would deal with his own odd mix of emotions at another time.

Eight

Harmony Hills, California

Ruth Archer stood at the living room window, her eyes going from the driveway to the street and back again every few seconds. She had told herself she was ready. She had prepared as best she could, but in her heart she knew that when she saw Lorri without Josie her heart would break all over again.

For a moment she let her mind go back to the day her father-in-law's telegram arrived. Max had not heard the door. Ruth had stood still for long moments, her mind trying to grasp the words. *Lorri found. Josie lost.* Ruth thought they would be branded on her heart forever.

And now she waited. Not every day since, but certainly today. A second telegram had come. Dean and Lorri were on their way. They would be home this day: August 16, 1945.

A car slowly trailed up the street and drove past. Ruth sighed quietly and turned from the window. It was silly to stand there for what might turn into hours. She would want her strength when Lorri finally arrived. Ruth settled into a chair in the living room, one that still gave her a view of the street, and began to think about the little she knew.

Neither telegram had provided her with details. The ranch had reported what they'd known: Lorri and Josie had left Carson Point in a plane on June 1. The plane was piloted by Clarence Fuller, and the three of them never arrived at their destination. In her mind the miles of ocean had stretched forever. The chances of survival were slim. And yet she hoped. That was the type of person she was. She was not going to decide it was bad news but wait for word. There was no point in crying over imagined events. And when worry came, she confessed it and reminded herself that the Lord Jesus Christ was in control.

Nevertheless, seeing those words — *Josie lost* — had plunged her into a place she'd never visited. She didn't know why it was different from burying a mother and a spouse, but she knew firsthand that it was. In sudden pain, her breath caught in her throat, her heart realized she wasn't even able to bury her daughter. She had been lost at sea.

"Mother?" Max's voice sounded from the stairway just before she entered the room.

"Yes, Max."

"I shut Jo's door. Was that all right?"

Ruth looked at her youngest child — no longer a child but a young woman — and tried not to hold on too tight. At the moment she wanted to tell Max that she was never leaving home.

Ruth gave a small shake of her head.

"It's not all right?" Max questioned.

"It's fine, honey. My mind wandered for a moment."

Max sat down and stared at her mother. Ruth stared back. Max was the first to speak.

"I don't want to cry when I see Raine."

"Why not?"

"I don't want that to be her first memory, me being a big baby."

"So you don't think she'll cry; you don't think I will?"

Max sighed. "I guess we all will — maybe even Grandpa."

"He just might."

"I just wish I knew what happened."

This was not the first time Max had

voiced this, and even though they had spoken of it, Ruth warned her again.

"Don't let your curiosity overrule your good sense, Maxine. Whatever happened, it must have been awful. Lorri will tell us when she's ready. We're not going to pepper her with questions — not today, and not ever."

Max nodded, her face composed, but the questions still pestered her. Was Raine really all right? How could Jo die but not Raine? Where in the world had she been all this time?

For a moment a shudder ran over her. At times when she thought about her oldest sister never coming home, she ached with pain. The news was still so new that Max was quite numb inside, but every so often pain washed over her, pain so acute that it took her breath away.

Watching her, Ruth saw her daughter's anguish but opted not to question her. She believed she knew the answers. And if they spoke of it just now, they might be in tears before Lorri and Dean arrived.

Ruth's eyes went to the window. She hoped it would be soon.

Gasoline rationing was over. Stories on vegetables, canned fruit, and fuel oil — all released from restriction — filled the newspapers. Nearly every article concerned the winding down of the war or life after the fact. Nearly four weeks after being united at the base in Australia, Dean and Lorri now waited at the U.S. Naval Base outside Harmony Hills, California, for their ride home. They shared a newspaper, heads bent as they devoured the words.

Thankfully it was not a long wait. After just a bit of detail work, a sailor appeared and told them the car was ready and waiting.

The newspaper had been a diversion. Lorri was so anxious to be home, she couldn't stop the pounding of her heart. She was on her feet and headed to the waiting car before the man finished speaking.

Ruth had meant to relax, but by the time the car pulled into the driveway, she had been back at the window for some time. Her first reaction had been to run outside, but she knew instinctively it was the worst thing she could do.

Instead she stared at the gaunt figure of her daughter as she climbed from the interior of the vehicle. Tears already streaming down her face, Ruth watched Lorri pause and look up at the house. Without warning,

Lorri's gaze swung to the window. Ruth's and Lorri's eyes locked for just a moment, and then both were on the move. They met just inside the front doorway, tears unchecked, arms reaching to grab and hold on for dear life.

"Mother, Mother," Lorri sobbed, not able to get close enough.

Later it would hit Ruth very hard that her daughter was painfully thin, but right now her arms didn't notice. Right now her baby was home. Her baby was alive.

"Here we go." Dean's quiet voice came to Ruth's ears as he gently propelled them out of the doorway and into the small foyer just outside the living room. Not until Dean did this did Lorri notice her sister standing to the side, waiting her turn.

"Oh, Max!" Lorri cried, an arm going out to drag her in.

Their small cache of luggage inside, Dean shut the door on the world and stood back and watched. Tears filled his eyes as he stood and waited, dreading the story he would later have to tell his daughter-in-law.

"I need to sit down," Lorri said after a time. She'd been feeling good, strong even, but the last few minutes had taxed her.

Dean stepped forward and helped her into the living room and onto one of the chairs. Max sat at her feet, and Lorri looked down at her.

"Your latest picture didn't do you justice, Max. You've become a beautiful young woman."

"Don't say that, Raine. You'll have me bawling again."

Lorri laughed in comfort and delight. She sounded like the same old irrepressible Max she'd always known. Lorri reached to stroke her dark, thick hair, amazed at how shiny and full it was.

"Do I smell turkey?" Lorri suddenly noticed.

"Mother has one in the oven."

Lorri looked across to where Ruth sat on the sofa.

"You're baking a turkey?"

"With all the trimmings," Ruth told her with a smile.

"Thank you, Mother." Lorri smiled across at her and willed herself not to cry again. She glanced around the room, not wanting to feel like a stranger but not sure she had a choice. It was a very long time to have been away.

"You need to sleep, don't you?" Dean spoke up.

Lorri rolled her eyes. "I hate being so transparent."

"Just stretch out on the sofa, Raine," Max suggested. "I'll talk to you until you drop off."

"That sounds wonderful."

Lorri found three people fussing over her in the next few minutes. A blanket was laid over her and a pillow placed comfortably under her head. Lorri laughed a little at the way they hovered.

"Sleep as long as you like," Ruth said, kissing her softly on the cheek.

"Don't let me miss dinner."

"I won't."

Dean stroked her hair and smiled into her eyes before following Ruth from the room. Max, back on the floor, as close as she could get, looked into her sister's eyes.

"I missed you, Raine."

"I missed you too, Max." Lorri reached for her hand.

"But you'll be glad to know," Max launched in immediately, "that I've sworn off boys for good."

Lorri chuckled. Looking into her sister's beautiful face, she knew that resolution would last only a day.

Max told her the reason, explaining that boys her age were just too immature and that she was going to wait for five years at least. Lorri wanted to hear it all. She wanted to take in every word, but Max lost her before she could get to the good part.

Dean found Ruth in the family room that sat off of the kitchen at the back of the house. She stood in front of the patio doors, her eyes on the cement patio and yard beyond.

"I'm sorry, Ruth," Dean said as he joined her at the window. "I'm sorry I couldn't warn you."

"Where has she been, Dean? Is she ill? Am I going to lose her too?"

"No, she's not sick. She's been on an island without enough food."

Ruth turned her head, looking nauseous at the thought, and then frightened at the next thought to enter her mind.

"Did Josie starve to death?"

"No, she and the pilot died on impact."

The word "impact" jolted Ruth again. She took Dean's arm and led him to the sofa.

"Dean, I need you to tell me everything."

Dean Archer owned a dog he named Buddy. He had been bought as a puppy and adored from the moment the family met him. The girls had been asking for a dog, and Dean and Ruth had finally relented. Dean had had only two conditions: The dog must be a golden retriever, and it must be a male.

I live with four women. My dog will be a male!

The girls had teased him over this declaration for weeks.

What no one had foreseen was the way Buddy would take to Maxine Archer, 11 years old at the time.

Buddy started each night at Dean's bedside, but before morning he would move to Max's room and be there when she awoke. He waited for the moment she came home from school, and if he was in the house, rarely left her side. Any word or gesture from her was life and breath to the beautiful, sweet-tempered dog.

And so it wasn't very surprising that when Lorri dropped off to sleep on the living room sofa, Max went to the garage door and let Buddy inside. She went directly back to the floor by the sofa, Buddy's warm fur close at hand, and stared into her older sister's face, trying to remember the face she used to know.

Lorri had been years younger and certainly more filled out the last time Max had seen her. This version — older and thinner — took a little getting used to. Max knew it was still her sister inside, but there was no

132

missing the changes. She hoped she hadn't stared too much before Lorri had fallen asleep.

Tears came without warning. Max didn't want to cry anymore. Her head already ached, but there was no help for it. Turning so she wouldn't wake her sister, she buried her face in Buddy's side and cried like a lost child.

Lorri woke alone. Completely disoriented and fuzzy with sleep, she needed a moment to realize where she was. A smile lit her face as she took in the familiar green drapes and carpet. It was just as she remembered it; not a thing had changed.

"You're awake," Ruth said as she peeked around the corner and then came into the room.

"Only just."

"Hungry?" she asked after she'd bent to kiss her.

"Yes," Lorri answered as she pushed slowly into a sitting position. "But I have another pressing matter first."

Her mother smiled as she came off the sofa and headed for the small powder room under the stairs. Ruth went back to her dinner preparation in the kitchen, knowing Lorri would join her. She was whipping the potatoes when Lorri came in, her eyes searching every detail.

"You got new canisters." Lorri went toward the set of four white containers covered with every color of flower. She peeked in each one and even stuck her finger in the sugar. In the past Ruth would have shooed her away, but not today. Probably not ever again.

Trying not to stare at the changes in her daughter, Ruth began to talk while she worked. Lorri sat on the stool that was tucked under the counter.

"Grandpa Stewart sent me a check for my birthday, and I picked those out at Brennan's Department Store. It was between the canisters and a new rug for the hall. The canisters won out."

"They're perfect in here. How is Grandpa Stewart, by the way?"

"Doing well. He talked about visiting next summer, but I don't know if his legs are up to it."

Ruth was speaking of her father, who still lived in her home-town of Coleman, Minnesota. They hadn't seen each other since the war broke out.

"I need to write to him," Lorri mentioned.

"He would enjoy that."

"What can I do to help?"

"It's all done. I'm just about to call Max and Dean."

"Where are they?"

"Your grandfather had a phone call to make, and Max took Buddy outside."

"I haven't seen Buddy!" Lorri suddenly realized, and was off the stool and headed for the door.

Not caring that she now had three people to bring to the table, Ruth put the meal on and then rang the little dinner bell Josie had given her as a joke one Christmas. Joke or not, it did the trick. The family appeared, the girls crowding into the powder room to wash their hands and Dean taking a seat at the head of the table. Ruth had to reposition the table so the four of them could sit around it, pleased that it would stay that way for some time.

It was a surreal moment for all. Months had passed and turned into years. Lorri was back, but not Josie. The three sat for a moment waiting for Dean to bow his head, but when he did, he said nothing. Tears clogged the admiral's throat, and he couldn't swallow past them. Time passed and people sniffed in an effort to control themselves.

At last Dean managed four words. "Thank you, Father. Amen," he said in a hoarse whisper that freed the occupants of the table to look up and find others with swimming eyes.

"This won't do," Ruth said briskly, forcing herself to sit up a little straighter. "Now, Dean, if you'll carve that bird, we'll have a hot meal."

"Yes, ma'am."

Bowls were passed, and all worked to stem their emotions. When Lorri had her first bite, she laughed softly.

"I think the men aboard the *Every Storm* would envy me now."

"What's the *Every Storm*?" Max asked before she thought, but Lorri didn't seem to mind.

"The PT boat that rescued me."

Max's eyes got huge, but she stopped herself from any more questions. Lorri didn't seem to notice.

"This is delicious, Mother," Lorri said.

"Thank you, dear."

"What, Max," Lorri asked between bites, "no other questions?"

"Well," she answered, her voice quiet with distress, "I didn't want to ask anything I shouldn't."

Lorri put her fork down and looked at her family. They looked back at her, knowing they were all treading on new ground.

"Have you all decided that I can't be

questioned?" Lorri asked quietly.

"We didn't want to be insensitive," Ruth answered, and Lorri nodded.

"I do appreciate that, but you can ask me if you want to know something."

"All right," Ruth said.

The four went back to their meal, and surprisingly, Dean was the one to break the silence.

"Why don't you tell Max about the head on the PT boat?"

Lorri smiled. "You've never seen anything so small, Max. It made the powder room look like a dance hall."

"And was there only one?"

"No, there was also one for the crew."

"Where did you sleep?"

"In the officer's quarters."

"Where did they sleep — the officers?"

"Well, Lieutenant Riggs slept in there too, but Ensign Westland moved in with the crew. At least I think that's how it was. I was a little dazed during that time."

"You slept in with the lieutenant?" Max asked, her voice speaking volumes.

"He hung a blanket," Dean told her, his voice dry.

"Did he tell you about that?" Lorri asked Dean, surprise in her voice.

"Yes." His voice was still dry.

Ruth was quiet during all of this, certain that the details would be emerging over quite some time and trying not to think about having to tell Max the hard part.

Lorri spooned cranberry sauce onto her plate.

"I didn't think you could even buy cranberry sauce at this time of the year," Dean commented.

"You spend so much time in the grocery store," Ruth teased him gently, smiling when he laughed.

No more questions came up at the table. Lorri couldn't eat all she'd put on her plate but didn't worry. As she helped with the dishes, she was already planning on a turkey sandwich before bed. And maybe a little more cranberry sauce.

Ruth heard the soft knock on her door not long after she'd climbed into bed. She was still sitting against the headboard with her diary and told whoever it was to come in.

"Mother," Max whispered as she peeked inside.

"Come in, Max."

Max slipped inside and sat on the edge of the bed. She looked at her mother, not wanting to do anything to make her cry but so desperate for answers that she couldn't sleep.

"Did Grandpa talk to you? Did he tell you what happened while Raine was asleep?"

"Yes."

"Can you tell me?"

"Yes, and it was not my plan to keep it from you, but I didn't know how to go about it when Lorri was still awake."

Max nodded and waited.

"I'm going to keep it brief, Max, for both our sakes," Ruth began, tears already filling her eyes. "There was a storm, and the small plane they were in crashed on an island, not in the ocean like we talked about. Clarence Fuller and Josie were killed immediately. Lorri was on the island alone for six weeks before a PT boat stopped for repairs and found her." A shudder ran over Ruth's frame, but she made herself continue. "They took her to the base at Seaford, and your grandpa was there. From there it took some time to arrange passage home."

Max was silent. She had pictured the ocean and not realized the part about an island, but it made such sense.

"So Josie, I mean, her body, will just stay on the island?"

Ruth nodded, not able to speak.

"What island was it?"

"I'm not sure it even has a name."

Max looked confused, and Ruth waited.

"So did Lorri have to bury Josie and the pilot?"

Ruth could only nod.

The younger woman's face crumpled with grief and tears, and Ruth reached for her daughter. Max sobbed against her mother's nightgown, certain that she had never known such pain.

For long minutes they clung to each other, trying to weather this new blast of grief and live to tell about it. Imagining all that Lorri had been through was dreadful, but the sudden thought of asking details of her was so abhorrent that neither one could even conceive of that.

"Here," Ruth handed Max a tissue, "blow your nose."

Max sat up, eyes red and puffy, and used the tissue. She took some long, shuddering breaths and realized her headache was back.

"I couldn't sleep," Max admitted. "I wanted to know, and I couldn't stop thinking about it."

"I know, honey. It's awful, and that's why I didn't want us to press Lorri to tell us."

"Does she know that we know?"

"I'm not sure she's thought about it one way or the other. As you can tell, she's still not herself."

Max nodded.

"Your grandfather told me that she's more filled out now than when he first saw her."

"She had a sandwich before she went to bed," Max reminded her mother, trying to be hopeful.

Ruth nodded. "She's home now. And we'll take care of her, and she'll be our old Lorri again."

"The only thing missing is Jo."

Ruth internally flinched at those words, but Max had always been open and honest with her feelings, and she never wanted her to be something she wasn't.

"Oh, Mother!" Max suddenly grabbed her hand. "Who's going to tell Ken?"

"Your grandfather."

Not believing it possible to have more tears, Max cried again. She didn't stay long in her mother's room as her headache became worse and she longed for her bed, but every time she thought about her sister's fiancé, fresh tears threatened. Finally heading to her room, she climbed into bed and fell asleep with Ken Showers' face in her mind.

Nine

Dean knew someone was up and about. Buddy's collar jingled as his head came off the floor, and Dean heard footsteps in the hall. He waited for water to run in the bathroom but heard nothing as he slipped from the bed and into his robe and slippers.

Once in the upstairs hallway, a glow from the downstairs told him he'd been right. He headed that way, not bothering to be overly quiet so he wouldn't startle whoever was downstairs.

It was Ruth. She sat in the living room, curled onto a corner of the sofa, her head buried in her arms. The light on the table burned next to her, but the rest of the room was in darkness. Dean took the other end of the sofa and quietly waited. It didn't take long.

"I can't stand it, Dean." Her voice was

thick with emotion. "My baby's last memory of her sister is having to bury her. I can't stand it."

Dean was silent as she cried. He had already been forced to digest this fact, but it wasn't much easier for him to accept.

"Not only is Josie gone, but Lorri had to bury her. The thought of it pains me until I don't think I can breathe."

She had looked up at him, and Dean just let her talk.

"You buried a son and a spouse, Dean. And now I've done both. I grieved for Tom — you know how much I miss him — but losing Josie is different."

"It is different." Dean's voice was low and sad. "Losing my Maxine was unbelievably painful, but losing Tom was like losing a part of myself. I don't know if there's any other way to describe it."

"I think you must be right. A corner of my heart is constantly on Josie, but now that I have details, Lorri's in that painful corner as well. When I picture her digging in the dirt . . ."

She couldn't go on, and Dean wasn't sure that she should. For some time neither one spoke. Ruth would cry and then contain herself. Dean sat in his quiet agony. Eventually he began to pray.

"Dear Father, I thank you for bringing Lorri back to us. Thank You that she's home safe. Help us to endure this pain, Lord. Jo is with You, and that should bring us great joy, but right now we are lodged in our pain. Please don't let us lose sight of You and Your plans for each of us. Please help us. For Your sake and in Your Son's name, amen."

"Thank you, Dean," Ruth whispered.

"It will come, Ruth. I promise you. Your grief will turn a corner, and the intensity will pass. God understands all about losing a child. Just keep going back to Him."

Ruth could only nod because the tears were starting again. Dean came close and gave her a hug before leaving her on her own. He knew there was little he could do. To some extent, all of them would have to walk this path with God alone.

"She sleeps a lot," Max said to her mother at lunchtime the next day.

"Yes, she does."

"Is she really all right?"

"Yes, she was checked by a doctor at the base in Australia. There's also a huge time change to deal with, and it's simply going to take some time to get back to normal."

Max wanted to ask how much time but knew that was being unreasonable. She knew it would never be quite the same again. The thought saddened her, so she tried to think about something else.

"Summer's going by fast," she said.

"Yes, it is."

"I'm not going to want to go back to school."

"It's still more than three weeks away and your senior year." Her mother smiled at her. "You might have fun."

"That's what Arlene says." Max spoke of her closest friend.

"Did you talk to her this morning?"

"Yes, she called."

"Sounds like she was trying to cheer you up."

Max didn't want to tell her mother that she'd been crying again so she said nothing.

Ruth would have questioned her, but they heard Lorri on the stairs.

"Good morning," Lorri greeted.

"Good afternoon," her mother said in return.

Lorri groaned in self-derision. "My bed felt so good, I just kept rolling over and going back to sleep. Hey, Buddy," she added, bending to pet the dog who had come up to greet her.

"I've got lunch ready if you're hungry," Ruth said around a yawn.

"You sound tired."

"I am," Ruth admitted, wanting to be honest.

Lorri looked at her mother. She didn't look tired except a little around the eyes. Lorri knew the fatigue was over her home-coming but didn't know how to offer help.

"Is there anything I can do?" she asked, her voice reflecting uncertainty.

Ruth went to her and spoke once her arms were around her.

"All the news is very new for us, Lorri. I don't believe my thoughts will keep me awake every night, but they did last night."

Lorri looked into her mother's face. She was the most beautiful woman Lorri had ever known. Her eyes reflected her caring and love, and Lorri was still trying to convince herself that she had finally made it home.

"Why don't you come and get me when that happens, and we can talk?" Lorri suggested.

"Right now you need your rest, but maybe sometime I will."

Lorri nodded, knowing it had to be her mother's decision but realizing for the first time that childhood had completely fallen away. She had departed for Australia a woman, certainly, but this was different. If she'd been forced to put it into words, she probably would have failed, but in her heart she knew a great change had taken place.

At the moment she didn't know how she felt about that. There was no need to yearn for freedom — she'd never been held captive by her grandfather or mother — but right now she felt like a contemporary to her mother and not a member of the next generation.

"Are you all right?" Ruth asked, having watched an odd expression chance across Lorri's face.

"Yes, just thinking about some things."

Ruth smiled a little. "I think we'll be doing a lot of that."

Lorri sighed. It was so lovely to be understood. She slipped her arms around her mother again and hugged her tight. They embraced until Max said that lunch was on the table.

"Did you get the butter?" Ruth asked Max on Saturday morning, studying the grocery list in her hand.

"Yes. And the oatmeal and the crackers."

"What kind of crackers did you find?"

Max grabbed the box from the shopping cart and held it up for her mother.

"Oh, those are good. We haven't had those for a while."

"Are you making soup?"

"Yes."

"What kind?"

"Cream of potato."

"Oh, my favorite."

"I thought you might enjoy that."

Once a month Ruth went to the PX on the base and stocked up, but for small amounts of everyday items, they used the local grocery store. Today there was an additional reason: They didn't want to be that far from home.

Lorri found the note about her mother's whereabouts as soon as she arrived in the kitchen. Still getting used to the idea of being at home, she moved slowly, getting herself a cup of coffee and adding a bit of milk.

She had just settled in at the table, the newspaper open in front of her, when her grandfather came in from the garage. He poured his own coffee and joined her.

"How did you sleep?" Dean asked.

"I must have slept well because I can't remember anything after lying down."

"Do you feel rested?"

Lorri made a face.

"Give it some more time."

"Where were you?" Lorri realized she'd heard the car.

"I had to run to the base." Dean paused for a sip of coffee. "I have to leave next week."

Lorri didn't comment. Her heart had done an odd little flip-flop in her chest, and she only looked at her grandfather.

"I'll be gone about a month and then home for good."

"Do Mother and Max know?"

Dean shook his head. "I was just told."

Lorri bit her lip.

"It'll be all right," Dean said.

"Where will you be?"

"Hawaii."

"What if you don't come back?" Lorri asked the only question in her mind.

"I'll come back."

"Would God do that, Grandpa? Would He make us say goodbye to someone else right now?"

"I don't think so, honey. We have to trust that He knows what we can take."

Lorri told herself to calm down. She told herself to trust. God had proved His faithfulness so many times; there was no need for her to doubt now.

"Are you all right?"

"Yes," she was able to answer truthfully.

"I'd rather you weren't leaving, but I'm not going to panic."

"I have to tell your mother and Max when they return."

Lorri only nodded. For some reason she wanted to panic again but pushed the temptation away. Her grandfather was right: God knew what they could handle.

"Max, what are you doing?" her mother asked while she loaded the bags into the car and Max stood — not helping — looking back at the store.

"I think those two girls are giving away kittens."

"That's just what we need," Ruth said with mild sarcasm.

"I was thinking the same thing."

Ruth finally stopped and looked at her very serious daughter. Max looked right back.

"Let's take a kitten to Raine."

Ruth opened her mouth to say no, but the word didn't come out. She looked at Max and then to the front of the store.

"Please, Mother," Max entreated softly, bringing Ruth's eyes back to her.

"We don't know if there's a kitten in the box that's just right for your sister."

"But we could look."

"Yes we could, but it can't be just any kitten."

"That's true. We'll only take it if it's just right."

"Can I trust you to decide, Max, or is your heart going to be lost the moment we get over there?"

Max's smooth brow dropped in thought.

"You'd better decide. If you don't think it's just right, we'll go away, no matter how much I want it."

"You're sure? We could save ourselves a lot of misery by simply not looking."

"But then Raine won't have a kitten, and I just know she would love it."

Ruth had to nod in agreement over that. Lorri had been heart-broken over leaving her cat behind when she'd taken the position in Australia. When they had to write and tell her that Mr. Boots had died, it had been a terrible day for Ruth and Max.

"All right. We'll go look."

Max threw her arms around her mother, making the older woman laugh.

"It's perfect, don't you see? If we take a kitten, we'll just go right back inside and get some food and things."

"You've got this all worked out, haven't you?"

Max's smile was very self-satisfied. She

helped load the rest of the bags into the trunk and nearly skipped as they moved back toward the store.

On the bench out front, the huge store windows behind them, sat two little girls, clearly sisters. In front of them was a box. They smiled when the Archers approached, looking a little shy when they stopped in front of the box.

"Hello, girls," Ruth greeted them, and they chorused their hello in return.

"Oh, Mother," Max breathed after she looked inside the box. Sitting alone was one small kitten, a striped tabby with huge eyes and ears a little too large for the rest of its body. The kitten's face was adorable.

"It's the last one," the older of the two girls spoke. "The other two were taken earlier."

"How old is the kitten?"

"Seven weeks. She was born on June 29."

"It's a female?" Max asked.

"Yes, we call her Muffin."

Max laughed and said, "What a cute name."

At the sound of the little girl's voice, the kitten moved toward that side of the box and put her paws up for some attention. The other girl gently petted the top of her head, her eyes on the pet.

Max made herself stand very quiet and still. She thought it the perfect cat for Raine and their household, but it was her mother's decision. Max prayed that God would work a miracle in her mother's heart and she'd decide to take the kitten home. She knew she was being dramatic and wasn't sure it was a great idea to pray about something so insignificant, but pray she did.

She comforted herself with this one small fact: Raine knew nothing of this. Even if their mother walked away from the box, no kitten in hand, Raine would never know a thing.

"Where's Lorri?" Ruth asked Dean when he came to the driveway to help with the groceries.

"She's baking a cake."

"Was she hungry for cake?"

"I don't know, but I had to tell her that I'm leaving again, and I think she needed to get her mind off of that."

"When?"

"Next week. I'll be gone about a month and then home for good."

Ruth nodded. She'd been living with this military man since very soon after her husband died. It was nothing new, but never what she would term easy.

"Grandpa." Max spoke from behind him, and he turned. His eyes went from Max's eyes down to the kitten in her arms and then back again. Max's smile was infectious, and Dean couldn't help himself: He grinned back at her.

"Let me guess, someone was giving them away in front of the market."

"Won't Raine love her?"

"Her? You brought another female into the house?"

Ruth and Max were still laughing when they heard the door. Max rushed around the house to hide the kitten and wasn't seen.

"I'm glad you're here, Mother," Lorri began the moment she was close. "I can't find the vanilla."

"We're out, dear. I brought some from the market."

"Oh, good. Where's Max?"

Ruth looked around as though she'd just noticed.

"You didn't pass her on your way out?" she misled her daughter shamelessly.

"No."

"Well, she must have run to the neighbor's."

Lorri grabbed a bag of groceries, giving it little thought until she got inside. The moment she did, she glanced out the window and spotted her sister in the backyard.

"What is Max doing?" Lorri asked of the room in general.

"Why don't you go out and see," her grandfather suggested.

Lorri gave him a confused look but still went. She slipped through the patio door and was almost on top of her sister before she saw what sat at her feet.

"Oh, Max, you got a kitten!"

"No, *you* got a kitten."

Lorri stopped, her mouth rounding in surprise.

"You got me a kitten?"

"Yes! Isn't she the cutest thing?"

"She's adorable," Lorri said, giving Max a hug and then hunkering down close to the small creature.

"Her name is Muffin," Max volunteered. "Isn't that cute? Come here, Buddy," Max suddenly called. "Come and see Muffin."

The women laughed hysterically when every hair on Muffin's body stuck straight out. Her back arched, and she was ready to do battle until Lorri stroked her back.

"Be nice, Muffin. This is Buddy."

"He was here first," Max put in, causing Lorri to laugh.

Inside the house, watching them from behind the screen door, Ruth spoke to Dean.

155

"I hope you don't mind another pet. Max was so excited."

"I don't mind at all," he said hoarsely, and Ruth knew that if she looked at him, she would be in tears.

I never imagined her out of the picture, Father, Ruth prayed, her mind full of Josie. *Not at any time did I see this coming. I never dreamed . . .* Ruth couldn't go on. She wasn't angry — just trying to keep her balance in a world that had suddenly tipped. A new pet was delightfully fun, but someone was missing. From now on, there would always be someone missing.

"Mother," Ruth heard in her sleep. She tossed a bit on the pillow, hearing Josie's voice in distress but unable to lift her arms to touch her. It was a helpless feeling, and Ruth begged herself to respond.

"Mother." The voice came again, and this time Ruth felt the bed move. "Mother, please wake up."

"Lorri?" Ruth woke with a start and realized her daughter was standing next to the bed.

"Mother, can I talk to you?"

Ruth didn't hear the tears in her voice until just then.

"Come on." She shifted over and lifted the covers. "Climb in with me."

It was too much for the younger woman. She dissolved into tears and began to sob the moment her head touched her mother's pillow. Ruth, feeling as helpless as she had in the dream, wrapped her arms around her daughter and pulled her close.

"I can't stand it," Lorri cried, feeling as if she were being torn in two. "It's only been a few months, and I miss her so much. I don't think my heart can take it."

Ruth knew that it was too soon for the hurt to be gone, but she didn't say this. She let Lorri talk and cry.

"Why do I keep thinking about all the things I've said and done that I regret?"

"Like what?"

"Like that time when I took the biggest slice of cake even though it was Josie's birthday."

"Honey, you were eight years old at the time. It wasn't like that in the recent past. It hasn't been like that for years. You and Josie were the closest sisters I've ever known. There was no competition. You adored each other."

"Then why can't I think of that? Why is there no comfort?"

"Maybe you're looking for comfort in the wrong places."

"You're probably right," Lorri admitted,

her voice reflecting the humility she felt. "What do you take comfort in, Mother?"

"The promises of God, and knowing that I loved Josie and she knew it. I take my greatest comfort in knowing where she is because of what she believed." Ruth's voice had grown thick with tears.

"I've made you cry."

"It's just going to be that way for a while," Ruth said, having faced this already. "We're going to be sad, and, at times, convinced that we'll never be joyful again. But I know better. I know God is bigger than that."

Tears that had never really receded became fresh again. Lorri desperately needed the reminder of God's goodness. She seemed to forget so easily these days. Everything slipped away easily lately. Suddenly her body felt so bone weary that she couldn't move. She wanted to go back to her bed but couldn't summon the energy.

"I'm so tired," she managed, only to feel her mother's soft kiss.

"Go to sleep," Ruth told her, but Lorri was already gone, sleep bringing relief from the memories that troubled her.

"Did you wake Lorri?" Dean asked Ruth when she arrived in the kitchen the next morning. Ruth looked tired and a bit worn but was dressed and ready for church.

"No. She ended up in my room last night, very upset. Then this morning she slept through my alarm clock and all my getting ready to go, so I know she's still exhausted."

"I'll stay with her," Max volunteered.

Dean and Ruth turned to her.

"Please don't make me go," she asked softly. "I'm just not ready to have everyone looking at us yet."

"But the church family has known about Josie's death for two weeks, Max. Why would people stare today?"

"Because with Grandpa back, they'll be looking for Lorri. And on top of that, I can't stand for her to wake up and find the house empty."

Ruth looked to Dean, who nodded his head.

"Next week, Max," Dean stepped in and told her. "The three of you need to go next week. The first week is the hardest, and putting it off won't change the inevitable."

"Not to mention, the church family only cares, Max. They've cried buckets with us. Never underestimate their power to love and comfort us."

Ruth gave her a hug before having some

breakfast, grabbing her Bible, and hurrying out after Dean.

Max played with Muffin until the kitten fell asleep next to Buddy's tail. When that happened, she went upstairs and planted herself in the chair in her mother's room, her mind picturing all those days Lorri woke on the island to find herself alone. Max hated to have it happen here. If Lorri slept until noon, Max would wait.

Ten

"How are you?" Cora Andrews asked Ruth as soon as the service was over.

"In shock," Ruth answered, knowing how honest she could be with her closest friend. "You wouldn't know Lorri if she was alone and you passed her on the street. She's so thin, and there's very little of the old sparkling Lorri right now. It's going to sound awful, but Josie's death is worse now that Lorri's home. I've never had one without the other, and it just seems all wrong."

"I've done nothing but pray for you for days," Cora said, willing herself not to cry and make her friend's grief more difficult.

"I can't tell you how much I need it. School starts soon, Cora, but I won't be out much. Tell the women at Bible study that I just have to see to our needs at home right

161

now and not put too much on myself. If Lorri decides she would like to attend study," Ruth added, "then we'll come, but I'm not planning on it."

"Let us know if there's anything we can do."

"I'll do that. Dean is leaving this week and will be gone about a month, but then he's home for good."

"Can we have the three of you to dinner after he leaves?"

"Ask me that in a week, Cora, will you? Lorri's just not up to much right now, and we're all going to need to take it slowly."

"Is that why she's not here?"

"Yes, she was awake in the night and completely spent this morning. Max stayed with her."

"I'm glad. Max needs that right now."

"I think you must be right. Tell Arlene to keep calling though. Max appreciates it so much."

"Even though they've sworn off boys for good?"

Ruth laughed and Cora joined her. It felt good to laugh, even if only for a few moments.

"Have you been sitting there long?" Lorri asked of Max when her eyes finally opened and she found her sister close by with Muffin in her lap.

"Off and on. I had to run down and get this little monster from under the fridge. I can't believe you didn't hear Buddy's bark."

"I don't think I heard a thing. Not even my own dreams."

"How do you feel?"

"Pretty good," she said around a yawn. "You're all ready for church. What time is it?"

"It's late. I stayed home with you."

"I'm sorry, Max."

"It's all right. I wanted to stay. Grandpa said the three of us will go next week and get it over with then."

Lorri nodded, having had some of the same thoughts, and then reached for the kitten. "This is the cutest cat I've ever seen."

"She's a little character too," Max told her. "She likes to drag things around. I think she was in the process of dragging Buddy's play sock across the kitchen when he barked at her. She shot under the refrigerator to hide. It took some work to get her out."

"What did you have to do?"

Max looked as guilty as she felt.

"I coaxed her with a tiny piece of leftover turkey. Mother would have a fit if she knew."

"Mother's never had a fit in her life, but I'm sorry I missed this spectacle."

"Why don't you get up, and I'll make you some breakfast."

"Do I smell beef roast?"

"There's one in the oven."

"How close are we to lunch?"

"About an hour maybe."

"I'll just take a long shower and wait for lunch."

Max didn't look overly happy about this, so Lorri didn't move from the bed. Muffin had settled in to sleep, and Lorri absently wondered what her mother would think of that.

"What's the matter?" Lorri asked her sister.

"You don't eat enough. I worry about you."

"I'm not sick, Max, I just can't hold much these days."

"But what if lunch is longer than an hour away? You must be getting hungry."

"I'll have a snack," Lorri said to please her.

"Okay!" Max was on her feet before the word was fully out of her mouth.

"I'll grab a quick shower and be right down."

Max scooped the kitten off of her

mother's sheets and inspected the area for hair. Their mother was not fond of pets in her bedroom.

"I think it's all right," Lorri said after looking around as well.

Max laughed a little and Lorri smiled. Two things they knew: Their grandfather liked male pets, and their mother was patient with the pets until they passed the threshold of her room.

"It's good to have you back, Admiral," Pastor Higgins said. "We've missed you."

"Thank you, Pastor. I have to leave again this week, but I won't be gone long."

"Is there something we can do for Ruth and the girls?"

"I can't think of anything just now, but before I forget, I need to mention something to you. Not until I saw the bereavement announcement in the bulletin for the Murphy family did I realize we haven't even talked about a service for Josie. I need to mention that to Ruth before I leave, so she might be calling you about that."

"Certainly. Anything we can do. I assume you would want to have it once you return?"

"Yes, that's what I was thinking."

The conversation between the men closed soon after that, and it wasn't long before

Ruth and Dean were back in the car. Not wanting to bring it up at home just yet, Dean broached the subject of Josie's service the moment they pulled onto the street.

"I was just thinking of that," Ruth admitted.

"And what were you thinking?"

"That we need to do something. I just don't know what."

"I haven't come up with any ideas either, but I will tell you that I want all four of us to agree. And I want it to wait until I get back so Lorri has more time to get on her feet."

"Oh, yes, thank you, Dean. You're certainly right. The girls and I can discuss it while you're gone, and then we'll all put our heads together as soon as you arrive back."

The car stopped at a red light, and Dean turned to look at his daughter-in-law.

"Are you going to be all right?"

"You mean while you're gone?"

"Yes."

"I don't plan to be overly busy, and I think that's best. Max goes to school in just a few weeks, and we'll just enjoy each other for the time being."

"That's a good plan. I wish I didn't have to go this soon, but it couldn't be helped."

"We understand, Dean. You know that."

Dean nodded. They did understand. It was a way of life for all of them. He had not been required to move all over the countryside, but being away from home was too often the norm. He was up for retirement next year, and although there were aspects of military life he would miss, he was more than looking forward to it.

Wednesday arrived before anyone was ready. Dean had to be at the base at eight o'clock, and the family was up to see him off. Ruth didn't cry, but Lorri and Max grew very emotional when Dean bent to pet Buddy and stroke his ears.

"It'll go by fast," he told them, hugging each for a last time. "I'll be home and under foot before you know it."

He didn't linger, but mercifully, with one last wave, slipped into the car that had been sent and was whisked down the street.

The women stood on the front lawn for a while, no one speaking. They didn't dare look at Buddy, whose soft brown eyes had followed his master and still looked down the street. Ruth was the first to go inside, and eventually her daughters followed.

Lorri had been home for little more than a week when she decided to visit Josie's room.

Down the hall from her own, Josie's room was shut off from view by the door Max had closed.

The room was stuffy and still when she opened the door, and for long moments she stood on the threshold and told herself to breathe.

Every inch of the room shouted Josie. Her favorite color, light peach, was everywhere. There were touches of green and tan, but peach was the predominant shade. Lorri walked in tentatively, her heart beating painfully against her ribs, and stood looking around.

The bulletin board over Josie's small desk still had things from high school. The only change in the room was her mother's sewing machine. It was set up under the window, and no dust marked it. Surprised at the thought of her mother sewing in here recently, Lorri wondered if maybe she'd just come in to dust.

"I'm glad I found you in here," Ruth said from the doorway, her voice betraying no particular emotion. "Why don't you go to your closet and pick out a dress for church on Sunday. I'll alter it for you."

Lorri couldn't help but look down at her figure. She was still underweight, her clothes baggy and hanging on her.

168

"I think it will be embarrassing on Sunday."

"Why is that?"

"I don't know. I just feel like I'll be something of a spectacle."

"I guess in a way you might be, but it won't last long. And I don't think anyone will press you about details, so don't worry on that."

"Mother?" Lorri had a sudden thought.

"Yes?"

"Why haven't you pressed me for details? Don't you want to know everything?"

"Of course I do, but I see no point in making you do something you don't want to do. When you're ready to talk, you will."

Lorri only nodded. There wasn't much she could say to that. She wasn't as ready to talk about Josie's death as she'd originally thought, and it was a relief to know that her mother was not waiting impatiently.

"Go get your dress," Ruth ordered gently, thinking they both needed a change of subject.

Lorri did what she was told, grabbing the first dress she saw, her mind still very much on the conversation with her mother. She went back to the room and slipped into it, standing still while her mother tucked and pinned.

"Have you been doing much sewing?"

"Mostly repairs," she answered around the pin in her mouth. "Max wants some new skirts for school, but you know I won't start those until the night before she goes back."

Lorri laughed a little. When it came to sewing, her mother had always procrastinated. The things she repaired and made from scratch were beautiful, but she didn't enjoy it much and put it off for ages.

"There," Ruth stepped back. "Look in the mirror and see what you think."

Lorri stepped to close the door and examine herself in the dress. A genuine smile came to her lips, and she turned back to her parent.

"I think you're a magician."

Ruth only smiled and helped Lorri ease the dress off without dislodging the pins or poking herself. Just minutes later she was seated, the machine flying at top speed.

"Have you been in here much?" Lorri asked from the bed.

"Define 'much.' "

"I don't know. It feels empty, but it also feels like you've been sewing in here."

"Not sewing," Ruth answered, her eyes on the machine. "But after I got your grandfather's telegram, I slept in here a few nights."

The color drained from Lorri's face. For

some reason this never occurred to her, and the thought was surprisingly painful.

"Don't think about it," Ruth said, having thrown a swift glance at her. "In fact, you'd probably better check on Muffin."

"All right. Did you want me to come back and try on the dress again?"

"I'll hang it in your room. Let me know if it needs anything else."

Lorri put her arms around her mother, suddenly desperate to touch her.

"I love you," Ruth whispered into her daughter's hair.

Lorri whispered it right back and slipped from the room.

Early the next morning, the house still quiet, Lorri sat in the living room and dangled a piece of yarn in front of Muffin, waiting for her to notice. It didn't take long. Instantly on the attack, Muffin jumped after the yarn, tiny claws splayed, ready to take on the world. She rolled herself around the offending piece of string, clearly in charge, and wrestled it to the carpet. Lorri sat contentedly and watched her subdue it and then drag it around a bit.

When the kitten settled back against Lorri once again, she went back to thinking about the verses she'd just read in Deuteronomy, the ones where Moses asked the children of Israel to think about their God. She reread the verses she'd marked in her Bible one more time.

O Lord God, thou hast begun to show thy servant thy greatness, and thy mighty hand. For what God is there in heaven or in earth, who can do according to thy works, and according to thy might? . . . For what nation is there so great, who hath God as near to them, as the Lord our God is in all things that we call upon him for?

Lorri's heart became quiet within her. She was not of the nation of Israel, but she knew God had chosen to be near her as well. Not for a moment did she doubt this, but the days ahead were sure to be a test. For this reason, Lorri tried to memorize the last verse, knowing she would need to be reminded in the very near future.

"A picnic?" Ruth questioned her youngest daughter during breakfast on Saturday, no excitement in her face. "Today?"

"Yes, at the beach! It's so hot, and you know we'll have fun."

"Along with the 10,000 other people who will be there." Ruth's voice was dry.

"We can go to Sand Hill Beach. It's never as crowded."

Ruth was more than a little skeptical, but

Max's face never lost hope. Ruth looked at her older daughter, who only smiled, her brows raised in amusement.

"Did you put her up to this?"

"No."

"You're sure?"

Lorri only laughed. She loved the coast, and everyone knew it. What they didn't know is how swiftly her mind went back to a couple of small scraps of beach in the middle of the Pacific. First the one where the plane crashed, and then the island where she was confronted by rude sailors. The memory of that time was all at once surreal and frightening.

"Are you all right, Raine?" Max was the one to notice.

"Yes," Lorri tried to smile. "Just thinking of something."

The room grew quiet, uncomfortably so. Max wanted so much to be sensitive, but she also wanted to know if she'd done something to upset her sister.

"Did I do something?"

"You didn't do anything, Max," Lorri felt relieved to say, and also admitted, "I was thinking about the islands."

"What was it like, Raine? Did you swim?"

"I went to the beach very little. I was afraid of being spotted by an enemy ship, so

I stayed in the trees. A few times I was so cold I went and sat in the sun and sand, but mostly I kept to the trees."

"You said two islands," Ruth mentioned.

"The PT boat needed repairs, and we stopped before getting to the base in Australia."

"Did something happen?" Ruth asked without thinking, her daughter's face was so vulnerable just then.

"A little run-in with sailors from another boat. It just scared me."

Ruth couldn't stop the tears that flooded her eyes. Lorri had been through so much, and then to be frightened by men from their own military. Her daughter looked distressed over the tears, and Ruth knew it was time to lay it out on the table.

"You see how it is, Lorri. I do want to know what happened, but it's going to be upsetting, and then you're not going to want to tell me." Ruth gestured helplessly with her hands. "I don't feel like I can win."

Lorri didn't know what to say, but Max was not at a loss for words.

"You just have to do it, Raine," she told her. "When you're ready, you have to tell us. We might cry and be in pain, but it can't be as bad as not knowing."

Lorri nodded, all of them crying now.

"I think a picnic to the coast is just what we need," Ruth said at last. "I'll start on some lunch. You girls gather everything else."

They were not the happiest crew, but everyone went into motion. Muffin was made comfortable in the garage, but Buddy was to join them. Picnic basket packed and ready, they left at midmorning, the beach less than a 30-minute drive away.

They were certain to all come home tired and sunburned, but Ruth had been right: Right now an outing was the best medicine.

Lorri sat quietly in the pew next to her mother for the evening service and thought about how painless it had been that morning. Many people had hugged her and welcomed her back, but she caught very few pitying glances and no one questioned her about her appearance or Josie. And she had needed to hear the sermon about God's faithfulness and patience.

Being back this evening at the more casual service felt wonderful and normal, as if she were reclaiming her life. Josie was missing, but Lorri didn't let her mind dwell on that. Amidst these thoughts she spotted her younger sister.

"Well, Max might have sworn off boys,

Mother, but they haven't sworn off her."

Ruth looked up from that morning's sermon notes and glanced around the church pews. She spotted her youngest daughter sitting with Arlene Andrews. Not far from the two young women were three boys. They were talking among themselves, but their eyes strayed continually to the two girls, who seemed oblivious to them.

Ruth smiled and even laughed a little.

"And it certainly doesn't help that she got a little more color yesterday," Lorri went on. "She's more beautiful than ever."

"She is beautiful, isn't she?"

"Have you just realized that?"

"No, but I don't dwell on it. It's her sweetness and sense of humor that you really notice."

The women looked over just then to see Max expressing herself with a funny face. They both laughed, and this was the way Cora Andrews found them. She had a hug for Lorri and then for Ruth.

"How are you?" she asked them both sincerely.

"We went to the beach yesterday," Ruth told her, realizing they hadn't spoken that morning.

"I can see the burned noses."

"We were just commenting that Max

looks better than ever with pink on her cheeks and nose."

"As if Max needed any help," Cora said with a comical roll of her eyes.

Pastor Higgins was moving toward the pulpit just then, and all over the church, folks got settled in their seats. Max came over in a hurry and sat close to her sister.

"It's great to have so many of you joining us tonight for communion," Pastor Higgins began. "I want to open things up for testimonies, but before I do that, I have some thoughts I want to share, some reminders from our last communion.

"Communion is not a period at the end of the sentence. It might seem that way since Jesus is nearing the end of His ministry on earth, but in truth, this was a starting point for the disciples. We can't come to the table lightly. Our hearts have to be right before God, and in that, many think that this latest time period in their life has come to a close, but that's not the case.

"Communion is the start of a new time. Until we meet again around the bread and cup, we need to remember our actions this night. We need to keep this event in our minds when temptations crowd in. Tonight is the beginning, not the end. Reflect, certainly. Make sure your heart is clean and confessed before God, but don't stop there. Determine to partake tonight and to stay holy until we partake again."

Lorri needed these words so much. It had been a long time since she'd partaken in the Lord's Supper, and never had she looked at it in light of a new time.

Help me, Father, she prayed. *I want to go from here to be mindful of You and more obedient than I ever have been before.*

Lorri looked up to see that her sister and mother were praying too. She bowed her head again and asked God for the same thing for them.

Lorri's and Josie's trunks arrived from Australia on Wednesday. Lorri was not prepared for this. She had missed some of her things but was in no way wanting. A truck pulled up, and a delivery man came to the door. Ruth signed for the trunks and stood back while they were placed in the living room.

Emotions surged through her as she remembered packing those trunks with the girls so many years before. A letter from Ian Colins, addressed to Lorri, accompanied the keys, and she sat down to read it. She read out loud.

"Dear Lorraine, I don't know where to start. Our sorrow for you and for ourselves is difficult to describe. The children miss you both so dreadfully. I hope you can write to them when you feel up to it.

"We comfort ourselves with the fact that if you are reading this, you are home with your family as you need to be. I hope time will heal all wounds and that you will find great happiness in the near future. If ever you should wish to return to us, you would be most welcome.

"Our hearts are with you, both today and in the future. Sincerely, Ian Colins.

"P.S. Clarence Fuller's family requested your address. I hope it was all right to give it to them."

Lorri looked up into her mother's eyes and found that Max had joined them.

"Clarence Fuller was the pilot?" Max confirmed.

"Yes. I've been thinking about how I would get a letter to them, so I hope they write."

The three women looked at the boxes. No one looked overly eager to dig in.

"What shall we do?" Ruth finally asked.

"I'm in no hurry to open Josie's, but I don't have to be around if you want to."

"I don't," Ruth said. "What about you, Max?"

"No, I'll wait."

"Let's try to get it up to her room then.

What about yours, Lorri?"

"Can we just put it in the corner in here for now?"

"Of course. Here," Ruth said, getting right to work, "we'll put it here behind the chair."

With a good deal of pulling and panting, the trunks were moved. Lorri's fit well behind the chair — not invisible, but certainly out of the way. It was no easy task to get Josie's up the stairs, but once there, the three of them breathed a little sigh of relief. They shut the door. For the moment, Josie's trunk did not have to be dealt with.

Eleven

Thursday evening found the three Archer women dining with the Andrews family. Ruth and Cora had been close for years, and Max and Arlene's friendship went back to first grade.

Cora and her husband, Leonard, also had three sons, all grown and gone from home. Like Max, Arlene was the baby and a senior in high school. Her father was the principal at school. He was unfailingly kind and fair, and the student body loved him. He had a way with young people, and Lorri, without even realizing it, was more open with him than she'd been with her own family.

It didn't happen until after dinner when they were settled on the back porch with tall glasses of iced tea. Leonard began to ask questions of Lorri, and she found herself sharing, barely aware of the other four people who sat and listened in silence.

"What's the hardest part about being back?" Leonard asked first.

"Being here without Josie. I don't think I realized just how much we'd done together. I can probably count on two hands the times we slept away from home and weren't together."

"Did you ever think about the changes that would come with her marriage?"

"Yes, but thinking about something and living it are two different things, don't you think?"

"Yes, they are different. I was just curious if the two of you ever discussed it."

"Not really. I often told her I envied her, and she usually told me it was just a matter of time and I'd be caught as well."

Leonard smiled.

"Is that what she called it, being caught?"

Lorri smiled back.

"Ken always said that he chased Josie until she caught him." Lorri sighed. "They were so perfect for each other."

"How is that?"

"Both so kind and caring."

"Who's perfect for you?"

Lorri's smile slanted a little.

"I don't know. I guess that's the other

hard part. I think Josie should be the one to still be here."

"Because she had a fiancé?"

"Yes. Even more hearts are involved where Josie is concerned. Ken and his whole family will grieve for her."

"And they wouldn't have grieved for you?"

Lorri looked surprised by this.

"You didn't think of that, did you?"

Lorri could only shake her head, her face full of amazement.

"If Josie were here, she'd be in the same pain that you are right now," Leonard explained gently. "As would Ken. As would his whole family."

Lorri was speechless. Such a thing had never occurred to her.

"You still count, Lorraine. You still matter. You're here because God has a plan. It won't erase all the pain you feel over losing your sister, but you mustn't forget that you're vital to Max and your mother right now. They wouldn't trade you for anything."

"But I wish they could," Lorri admitted, her voice catching a little. "I wouldn't want them to have to choose, but I wish God had. I wish the plan had included Josie and not me."

"All the wishing in the world won't change the way things are. I think God understands how you feel; in fact, I'm sure of it, but don't spend too much time telling God He made a mistake. It's a waste of time and energy, especially energy. Trying to do God's job is exhausting. We're just not equipped for it."

Lorri looked him in the eye.

"Every student at Harmony Hills High School, past and present, loves you. Do you know that?"

"I love them," he said simply and then smiled widely, his eyes holding hers. "Some I love more than others."

Lorri smiled, feeling tears pricking at the back of her eyes but determined not to give in to them. She glanced around and realized how she'd monopolized the conversation.

"This wasn't very polite of me," she began but stopped when she read the faces around the patio. They needed this too. Her mother looked ready to cry, but then she'd been warned about that.

"Do you feel bad, Mother," Lorri had to know, "that I haven't shared more of this with you?"

"No, dear. I really am ready to wait for you."

"Well, I want to know everything, for

heaven's sake!" Max suddenly burst out, sounding so aggrieved and angry at herself that the company had to laugh.

"What's so funny about that?" Max asked, still frowning. "I should be scolded or something, and you're all laughing."

"It's your honesty, Max," Leonard told her. "It's so refreshing."

When the laughter died down, the sisters looked at each other, Max very contrite.

"I'm sorry, Raine."

"Don't be, Max. I'll get there. I'll tell you. I just might need a little more time."

"Don't listen to my complaining anymore, Raine." Max was frowning again. "I need to be spanked."

Lorri could only smile at her, and Max couldn't help but smile back. Cora felt as though she could move for the first time.

"More iced tea, anyone?" she asked.

They all wanted refills, and the timing was just right. While Cora did the honors, Arlene hummed a song that got Lorri singing. One song led to another and Lorri sang — usually alone — for nearly 30 minutes.

Max and Ruth were utterly silent. It was the first time they'd heard her in more than four years. If asked, they would have said they could have gone on listening all night.

Buddy was oblivious. Asleep on the kitchen floor, dead to the world, he had no idea that his tail had been spotted as the enemy. Muffin was approaching, turned to the side, back arched and hair on end, ready to pounce. She didn't expect to be caught.

"Muffin!" Lorri scolded her, bringing the kitten to a halt but no more relaxed. Her eyes a little wild and still on the hunt, Muffin went swiftly back to the tail.

Just coming on the scene, Max laughed so hard that she woke Buddy, who moved his tail and foiled the whole episode.

The women kept on laughing when Muffin attempted to look innocent. Buddy sniffed her, and she actually began to purr.

"What a fake," Max complained. "She was about to get you, Buddy."

The dog, loving any attention from Max, went to her, tail wagging. Not to be left out, Muffin curled around one of Buddy's legs, her motor still running.

"Have you been crying?" Max asked, suddenly spotting what her sister was doing at the kitchen table. Around her lay discarded tissues, and in front of her was a small stack of envelopes.

"I'm writing to the children. It's harder than I thought."

"A separate letter to each one?"

"Yes. I want them to know how proud I am of them." Tears filled her eyes, but she kept on. "I want to remind them of all their progress and how much Josie and I loved being their teachers."

"Mr. Colins said you could go back." Max had taken a seat across from her sister, Muffin on her lap. "Will you go?"

"No," Lorri said with a definitive shake of her head. "I don't think I could do it without Josie, and I really don't want to try."

"I'm glad, Raine. I don't want you to be gone again."

Lorri smiled across at her.

"You're going to be the first to go. School starts in a little over a week."

"You have to remind me." Max's sigh was dramatic, her head going back. Lorri could only laugh at her. "It's not funny, Raine. Mother hasn't started on my clothes, and I know the year is going to last forever."

"Do you know what I just realized?" Lorri said, sitting up very straight. "Josie has some clothes that would look perfect on you."

Max looked a little shocked, so Lorri rushed on.

"You don't have to go through the whole trunk, Max, but let me get her dresses and

187

skirts out. Over the years, we found some very cute clothes in Australia."

"What about you? Don't you want to wear them?"

"I'm shaped a little differently than you and Josie. And I'm not as tall. We never traded clothes much. It just didn't work."

"I don't know, Raine," Max began, but Lorri was already on her feet.

"If they make you sad, or if it feels odd to you, I'll just put them back. Okay?"

"Okay," Max agreed, wondering if she might regret it, but she was about to be surprised. Max had never seen the clothing that Lorri hauled into her room. There was no sentimental attachment at all. And her sister was right; they fit and looked sensational.

Ruth came in from the neighbor's to find her daughters in a fashion parade. Max was using the hall as a runway, and Lorri was commentating.

"Maxine Archer is wearing a stunning navy skirt with a pointed waistband. She's matched it with a snow-white blouse, sporting just a hint of lace, perfect for school or that special afternoon date." Lorri paused for just a moment. "Unless of course, you've sworn off boys for good."

"What are you two doing?" Ruth said, smiling at their antics.

"I'm giving Max a new wardrobe for school. Josie and I found all kinds of cute things in Australia."

"This skirt is beautiful." Ruth studied tiny buttons and detailing at the waist.

"Which reminds me . . ." Lorri was on the move again, this time to her own trunk in the living room. Her mother and sister followed, and Lorri handed Ruth a skirt, similar to the one Max was wearing, and a blouse in pale pink.

"Try these, Mother."

Ruth didn't even think about protesting. New clothing, homemade, store-bought, borrowed, or handed down, was always fun.

"Oh, Mother," Max exclaimed. "That blouse is beautiful with your dark hair. You should wear pink more often."

"I don't think I realized how close in size we are, Lorri, but I don't want to take this from you."

"I can't wear it right now anyway. When I'm back to my normal size, I'll borrow it back from you."

"You're getting there," Ruth suddenly said. "I was noticing yesterday that you're filling out."

Lorri glanced down at herself before saying, "It's nice not to be as tired."

"But she was crying." Max felt their

mother had to know. "She's writing to all of the children."

"That would be hard, but it's very sweet of you."

"I miss them," Lorri admitted. "When my mind started to go on the island, I couldn't remember their names, and that was scary."

"Why did your mind start to go?" Max asked.

"The hunger, I think. As soon as I got some real food, things became clearer, so I have to assume that my brain needed nutrition."

"And that didn't happen until you were on the PT boat?"

"Right. They fed me even while I was still on the island."

"They didn't take you right away to the boat?"

"No, they had repairs to make, and I stayed put until it was time to leave." As soon as Lorri said this, she started to laugh.

"What's the matter?" Ruth had to know.

"It's not funny at all, but I can't help laughing. I disappeared when they were ready to leave. The lieutenant was so angry. He was always such a gentleman, but at that moment, I think he could have strangled me."

"Where did you go?"

"To see Josie's grave one more time."

"Did you tell him that?"

"No." Lorri shook her head, wishing she had explained. "I wasn't thinking too clearly. I should try to write him, but I don't know where I would send the letter."

"He didn't stay angry at you, did he?" This was important to Max.

"No, not at all. He was very kind."

"Shall I tell you what I'm thinking right now?" Ruth said. The girls looked at her. "You've lived another life, Lorri. It's odd as a mother to be so disconnected from my daughter, but it's true. You've stepped into a world that Max and I can't share with you. Dean could. He would understand, but all I can do is try to imagine what this must have all been like."

"I'm glad you don't know." Lorri's voice was sober now. "I don't want you to know what the war looked like. I had just a glimpse, but I wish I hadn't even had that."

This time no one questioned her. Lorri was thinking about the way the guns had exploded and the enemy aircraft all around them. She had held on for dear life, sure she was going to end up in the water and drown, all the while wondering which would be easier, drowning or starving to death.

191

"Are you all right?" Ruth had been watching her face.

"Yes," Lorri said and decided to tell them. "The *Every Storm* came under attack on our way to base. I hid in the lieutenant's bunk, but I could hear everything. I didn't think about it until just now, but they were amazing men, having to fight like that. I can't help but wonder if the crew made it through the war."

"Maybe Dean can find out for you."

Lorri nodded. "I'll ask him when he gets home."

Silence began to descend, but Ruth would have none of it.

"Thank you for the skirt and blouse," she said.

"You're welcome. I have some other things you should try."

"I'll do that when you can wear them again."

"Why not now?"

Ruth shrugged a little. "Because in a very short time you're going to be your normal size again, and you might feel differently when that time comes."

Lorri opened her mouth to argue, but Ruth forestalled her with a raised hand.

"Thank you for wanting to be so generous, but I have plenty of clothes to wear."

"And you can always raid Raine's closet if you change your mind," Max suggested helpfully.

Her voice was so matter-of-fact, as if she could picture her mother doing that very thing, that her family laughed. Loving to make her family laugh, Max grinned with pleasure before going to change her clothes. Once in her room, she looked at all the outfits Lorri had brought from Josie's trunk and realized her mother probably wouldn't have to sew at all before school began.

"That was quite a sigh," Leonard commented to Arlene on the way home from church. "Anything wrong?"

"I just miss the old Max. I know it sounds selfish, but sometimes she's so sad and quiet."

"Give her time, sweetheart. I think there's more to all of this than any of us quite realize, and that's bound to be very hard."

"What do you mean?"

Leonard and Cora exchanged a glance. Did they tell their daughter some of the things Ruth had shared with her friend? It would certainly help Arlene understand, but was it fair to the Archer family?

"Let's just say that Lorri has been through quite a bit, and that's bound to affect Max."

"Do you know what it is, Mom?"

"Yes."

"Did someone hurt Lorri?"

"No, it has to do with Josie's death."

Arlene knew there had been a plane crash. She had wondered but never asked how Lorri had survived. The facts had never been explained to her. Arlene now asked God to take care of her friend and to help her think less of herself. Beyond that, she didn't let herself dwell on what the details might be. She realized she didn't want to know.

"There's something we need to talk about," Ruth told the girls on the way home from church on Sunday. "I told your grandfather that we would discuss it, and I keep putting it off."

"Why is that?"

"Because I'm tired of crying."

The girls didn't know what to say to this, so they made the remainder of the ride in silence. However, they were not going to let their mother off the hook. Both Lorri and Max followed her up to her room, their actions very clear.

"I thought it could wait until after lunch," Ruth said when Lorri and Max sat on the bed and stared at her.

"Now is a good time," Lorri said pointedly.

Ruth saw no escape. She sat in the chair near the bed and made herself begin.

"Your grandpa and I want to have some type of service for Josie, including a headstone at the cemetery next to your father."

Lorri felt sick to her stomach and called herself every type of fool. *Why did you push this? Why did you have to know right now?*

"I like the idea," Max stunned her family by saying, unaware of Lorri's turmoil. "I wish I could see where Josie is buried or even a picture of it. I'm glad we'll have something here." Not until Max was done did she realize that Ruth and Lorri were staring at her. She looked uncomfortable and apologized.

"No, don't be sorry, Max," her mother put in. "I'm glad I know how you feel."

"But I think I upset Lorri."

"Are you upset, Lorri?" Ruth asked.

"Yes, but not with Max. The whole idea just takes some getting used to." Lorri tried to say this without crying, but it didn't work. They didn't know the details. They didn't understand the way she had dug in the dirt for days, using a thin rock and her bare hands, in an effort to give her sister a proper grave and one for Clarence Fuller as well. It all came flooding back to Lorri, and she buried her face in her hands and sobbed.

"I'm sorry, Raine. I'm sorry," Max said, arms around her and unable to stop her own tears. "I didn't mean to hurt you."

Lorri couldn't speak. She hugged Max, who looked so much like Josie, and tried not to remember. Dry of tears just now, Ruth had pulled her chair a little closer, waiting for the storm to pass. Handing tissues to the girls so they could wipe their faces, she spoke when they looked at her.

"Your grandfather had two conditions: that we wait for him and that we all agree. It doesn't matter how long it takes, but until we all agree on the best way to handle this, we won't do anything. Do you understand?"

Lorri and Max nodded.

"It won't be a fun time, but it doesn't have to be all painful. We can have a funeral service, casket and all, or just a memorial service with no casket, or something in between. It can be private or include the whole church family."

"The church family has been wonderful," Lorri said, thinking about the hugs and warm smiles she'd been getting the last two weeks.

"Yes, they have, and they loved Josie too."

"Would we really want to have a casket that had nothing in it?" Max asked.

"It could have some things in it, special things that remind us of Josie," Ruth answered.

"You can do that?"

"We can do anything we want."

"What does Grandpa want?" Lorri asked.

"He wasn't very specific, except about wanting a proper headstone."

Max looked at her sister. "Do you know what day Jo died?"

"June 1."

"That was three months ago yesterday," Max said. "It doesn't seem that long."

"It's not for us," Ruth reminded her. "We didn't get the telegram about the plane being missing until the fifth. And even then we didn't have any details."

"What did the telegram say, Mother?"

"Just that your plane never arrived and there was a search going on."

"Did you assume we were lost?"

Ruth sighed. "I pictured all those miles of ocean and tried not to imagine your small plane in the water, but it wasn't easy."

"Clarence said the weather report was for clear skies, and when a little rain started, he joked about not being able to trust anyone anymore." Lorri shook her head, still amazed. She was back in that little plane. "There was no warning. We were suddenly in a downpour, lightning flashing all around us and the wind tossing us all over the sky.

"It felt like forever. Clarence had joked a little more, but then he was quiet. Josie felt sick with the motion, and I had a headache from my head being thrown against the window. I don't know how long the storm actually lasted, but at least an hour, maybe more. Clarence shouted at us to duck just as we crashed into the trees.

"The impact knocked me out. When I woke up, all was dark. There was a huge gash in the plane on Josie's side, and the rain was pouring in. Josie and Clarence wouldn't answer me, and I couldn't get my seatbelt undone." Lorri closed her eyes with the memory.

Ruth took her hand. "Don't think about it anymore, okay? We don't have to know right now."

Lorri looked into her mother's eyes.

"Do you ever think about yourself, Mother? Do you ever take care of yourself first?"

Ruth's smile was crooked.

"You know me, Lorri. I just don't want you to have to live it over again and again."

"I'll probably not have it all clear in my

mind for months. I keep remembering things that happened. They were so vivid at the time, but then they completely slipped away."

Ruth reached up and cupped her cheek. "I'm so glad you're home. I missed you so much."

"Josie and I talked about that. Neither one of us would have left if we'd known we would be gone for so long."

"Sometimes I feel cheated," Max admitted. "You and Jo were away for so many years, and I didn't get to see her again."

"We talked about you every day, Max. Our hearts were never gone."

Max felt tears again, and she already had a headache. It was on the tip of her tongue to say she didn't want to cry anymore, but Muffin took care of it for her. All three women caught movement in the hallway and looked over to see Muffin dragging an underslip from Lorri's room. It was heavy enough to outweigh her, but she wasn't giving up. They laughed so loudly and suddenly that they startled Muffin. Deserting the undergarment, she rocketed down the stairs.

Twelve

Max looked beautiful for her first day back to school. She wore the navy skirt and white blouse that were Josie's, and her hair was pulled back with a red ribbon. It wasn't hard to imagine that every male head in the school was going to turn in her direction.

Lorri and Ruth were a little at loose ends when she left, and it didn't help that Buddy stood at the picture window in the living room and watched forlornly as she walked away.

"It'll be Christmas break before we know it," Ruth said, going for another cup of coffee. "Never do the days pass so swiftly as when we're on the school calendar."

"Why is that, do you think?"

"I guess because it's all blocked out in the sections of time. September will quickly give way to October, and then Thanksgiving will be here in the blink of an eye. Christmas and the new year always rush in, and just like that," Ruth snapped her fingers, "the school year is half over. Second term goes just as fast."

"And what do you do with yourself all day?"

"The same routine I've always had. Wash on Tuesday, clean on Wednesday, Bible study with the women on Thursday, and marketing on Friday or Saturday."

"Plus a thousand little jobs that seem to get done by themselves," Lorri added, and Ruth smiled, pleased at her observance.

"Never forget that I love it, Lorri. I love taking care of my family, and I'm always thankful that your grandfather offered us a home. I'm not sure what I would have done."

"Mother, why haven't you married again?"

Ruth's head tipped in thought.

"If the truth be told, Lorri, I wish I had, but I never met anyone who I thought might be a good father to you girls. Certainly not the way Dean has been. I don't mean to make it sound like men were lining up; the few men in the church family who were my age didn't want a ready-made family."

"They don't know what they were missing," Lorri said, looking at her lovely, sweet mother and thinking that she would be worth any amount of adjustment a stepfather might have to make.

"Well, I don't know about that," Ruth said as the doorbell rang. "I don't dwell on it. Never have and never plan to."

Lorri stayed at the table while her mother went to the door. She came back with a tearful Cora Andrews, coffee cake in hand.

"I'm just the biggest faucet in the world," Cora was saying. "I can't believe Arlene is a senior. She'll be gone before you know it. And you know how spoiled I get in the summer with Leonard around. And now he's gone too." Cora used a hankie and then looked up to find compassion on their faces.

"Would you like some coffee?" Lorri offered.

"Yes, please," Cora said, accompanied by a sniff. "I was supposed to babysit for Martha Jones today, but the baby has a cold so she canceled her outing."

"That would have helped keep your mind off your loneliness," Ruth said kindly. "But instead, we'll have to eat this cake and cry with you."

Cora couldn't help but chuckle at Ruth's playful tone.

"Tell me something, Lorri," Ruth said conversationally. "Have you ever tasted one of Cora's coffee cakes?"

"Not for a very long time."

"Well," Ruth continued, cutting and serving as she talked, "I think it might take a good five days of crying for you to get over this, Cora, so we'll expect you each morning this week."

This was the start of laughter and light-hearted conversation. The morning didn't pass without a few more tears, but the women were very glad that Cora had dropped by, coffee cake and all.

"Hey, Max."

It was just after lunch, and Max had been studying the class list in her hand, unaware of anyone else in the hall. She stopped and looked up to see Johnny King addressing her.

"Oh, hi, Johnny."

"Are you headed to Algebra?"

"Yes."

"I'll walk you."

"All right."

Max didn't read too much into this. She had known Johnny for years. He was remarkably handsome, and it seemed that he had dated more girls in school than any other boy. Max had not been one of them.

"The summer was certainly good to you," he said about halfway down the hall.

"What makes you say that?"

"The way you look."

Max smiled at the compliment but didn't let it go to her head.

"How was your summer?" she asked.

"Good. I worked but still spent plenty of time at the beach."

Max didn't comment because she didn't know what to say.

"Rumor has it that you and Arlene have sworn off boys."

Max couldn't stop her smile. She hadn't expected that to get around but didn't mind that it had.

"We find it's easier that way."

They were at Max's class, but Johnny wasn't done.

"I'll just have to see if I can find a way to change your mind," he said.

Max only smiled and said she had to get to class.

"Max," Johnny called her name one last time and waited for her to turn. "I heard about your sister. I'm sorry."

"Thanks, Johnny," Max said quietly as she slipped into the classroom. She was unaware that Johnny stood and stared at the door, almost making him late to his own math class.

Some 48 hours later, the laughter and fun time with Cora was but a memory. A letter from Clarence Fuller's family had arrived. Lorri read it, her heart squeezing with pain. But not willing to waste any time, she went to the kitchen table with pen and paper, planning to write back to them directly.

Her intentions were better than her efforts. She addressed the letter but got no further. Where did one start? What did one say? Each time Lorri thought about the emptiness for them, she felt as though she were dying inside. She didn't know what Clarence's beliefs had been. She didn't know if his family had comfort about his eternal whereabouts or not. And if they did comfort themselves that Clarence was in heaven, was the comfort based on belief in Jesus Christ, or were they under the false impression that because he was a good person, that must count for something?

Ruth came through the kitchen about 20 minutes later to find Lorri pacing around the table, anxiousness written all over her.

"What's going on?"

Lorri handed her the letter.

Ruth read it and then looked to the table.

"You don't know what to say, do you?"

"No, I don't. You have me. You have me here to tell you about this and answer your questions. They don't have anyone. How much do they want to know? And where do they believe he is?"

Ruth sighed. These were all very good questions, but she had no answers.

"I wish Grandpa were here to ask."

"Why don't you hold the letter until he returns?" Ruth suggested.

Lorri looked to be considering this when the phone rang. Ruth answered it and was on the line for a time. When she got back to the kitchen table, Lorri was nowhere in sight, so she went back upstairs to work.

"Mother," Lorri called to her, and Ruth went to the top of the stairs to see her. "I'm going for a walk. I'm taking Buddy. Muffin is in the backyard."

"Did you want me to come along?"

"No, I'll be all right."

Ruth waited only until she heard the front door close. She moved down the stairs and to the kitchen table. Lorri had not added a word to the paper.

You know all about this family. You know their hearts and needs. I can only tell them what I know and that I'm praying for them. Please help me to word the letter gently. Help me to be clear and kind. Clarence was very brave. I just want them to know that.

Lorri had walked all the way to the park and now sat on a bench to pray. Silent tears rolled down her face as she asked God to help her. Buddy sat quietly at her feet, but Lorri wished he were on the bench so she could hide her face in his coat.

A couple walked by with a baby stroller, and Lorri felt vulnerable and exposed. She started the long walk home, unaware of the way her mother paced in the living room, guilty of worry. Ruth met her at the door, looking relieved and upset all at the same time.

"You were gone so long," Ruth said, her arms still around her.

"I'm sorry. I didn't keep track of the time."

Ruth looked into her face.

"Did the walk help?"

"I think so. I'll let you read the letter when I'm done."

Ruth nodded, ashamed of how fearful she felt but thinking she knew why. Lorri had just come back. The thought of losing her was almost unbearable. There was no excuse for worry, but if she was going to offer one, that would be it.

★ ★ ★

Max came in the door from school to find
the kitchen empty. She was ready to run upstairs to find her mother when she spotted
her in the backyard.

Stretched out on two loungers were her
mother and sister. Her mother was reading a
book, but Lorri was sound asleep, Muffin
curled in the crook of her arm. Max let herself quietly out the door and sat at the foot
of her mother's lounger.

"I didn't hear you come in," Ruth said.

"I just got here." She glanced at Lorri. "Is
she feeling all right?"

Ruth reached for the letter. "She wrote
this today. I wrote my own copy of it, so if
you're not up to reading it, I can show you
mine later."

Max started on the letter. The details she
had already imagined, but when Lorri spoke
about Clarence Fuller's bravery and kindness, Max's heart felt broken. Her words
were kind but frank about his death and
burial. She talked about all the flights they'd
shared together over the years, always land-
ing safely until this time when the elements
rose up against them. Max felt drained after
reading it and understood why Lorri was
sleeping.

"What did you think?"

"I think they'll appreciate all she said, but it won't be easy to read."

"Easier than not knowing," Ruth said.

Max had to nod. "Yes, that's true."

"How was school?" Ruth had forgotten to ask.

"All right."

"Tell me something that happened today that you loved."

Max thought a moment.

"We had a pop quiz in science and I got 100 percent."

"On only the third day of school? I'm impressed. Now tell me something that wasn't so fun."

Max made a face.

"I think there's this boy who's getting serious about me."

"Do I know him?"

"Johnny King."

Ruth frowned. "I thought he had a girl."

"He's had many, but word is out that Arlene and I have sworn off boys. I think he sees it as some sort of challenge."

Ruth had to smile. When Arlene and Max had first come up with their plan, everyone gave it a week, but they'd been true to their word. There was very little talk of who was cute and who was dating whom. And Max had been correct: Life was much easier without all of that.

"So what will you do?"

"Just keep being kind and saying no."

"Good."

Mother and daughter exchanged a smile before Max proclaimed she was starving. When she returned to the patio, she had a snack, a pitcher of lemonade, and three tall glasses of ice. Ruth joined her daughter in the refreshments, but Lorri slept through the whole thing.

Ruth stared down at her pillow that night, seeing the note and a little box. She saw that it was Lorri's handwriting and wondered when she'd had time to do this. Ruth sat on the edge of the bed and read the note.

Mother, Josie bought this for you about six months ago. I found it in my trunk. I don't know why she never sent it. Maybe she was saving it for your birthday.

Ruth opened the box and found a brooch inside. It was shaped like a gold bow with a gold locket hanging beneath. It so perfectly fit her taste that for a moment she didn't think she was going to survive.

How will I do this? she asked of God. *How will I possibly keep on without my Josie? She knew me so well and loved me so sweetly. I want to hold her once more, Father. I want to kiss her soft brow and tell her how much she's loved and missed.*

Ruth couldn't think any longer. Holding the brooch close and rocking a little with the pain, she sat on the bedside and begged God to help her through the agony. Her words were incoherent and rambling, but she knew God understood.

She prayed until she was too tired to sit up and then laid her head down on the pillow. Placing the brooch on the nightstand where she could see it, she fell asleep with the light on, her mind full of her oldest child.

"Another week has passed," Ruth announced, addressing Max and Lorri on Saturday morning, "and we still haven't talked about Josie's service. I want to know what you want."

"What do you want, Mother?" Max asked, realizing Ruth had never said.

"I don't think I want a memorial service with many people talking. Pastor Higgins knew Josie for about two years before she left, and I just want him to speak."

"I'm okay with that too, but the thought of an empty casket bothers me," Lorri admitted. "If everyone wants that, I can get used to it, but it still seems strange to me."

"I was getting used to the idea," Max said.

"I mean it wouldn't be open, but it could still have Josie's picture on top, that pretty one in her blue dress."

"What do you think, Lorri?" Ruth asked.

Lorri rolled her eyes.

"I was thinking the casket would be open. I don't know why, but that's what was bothering me."

"So that's not going to bother you so much?"

"No, it's fine."

"What day does Grandpa come back?" Max wondered.

"Thursday or Friday. He said he'd send word."

"Do we know what day we're having the service?"

"No, I was going to wait for Dean to decide. He just wanted us to talk about some of the details ahead of time."

So she would remember everything for the next week, Ruth wrote down all that they talked about. A feeling of unreality crept in from time to time, but she made herself concentrate. When the list was complete, she had the girls read it over and note any additional ideas.

That done, it was time to get to the grocery store. Lorri offered to go with her. Max stayed home. Arlene was coming over, and the two of them were scheduled to work on a big project for English class.

"Are you in the mood for grapes or cherries?" Ruth asked Lorri.

"Cherries."

"Bing or Royal Ann?"

"Bing."

"Wow, you're easier than Max. She has to think about things until I tell her I'm moving to the next aisle."

"Maybe she's had too many choices."

"The war took care of that. She's just indecisive," Ruth said. Then she asked, "How was the food in Australia?"

"It was good but different. I'm sure they would say the same about ours."

"I haven't told you this, but you have an accent."

"Do I really?"

"Yes, it's very slight, but certain words take on a life of their own."

"Such as?"

"Well, anything that ends with an *a* now has a slight *r* sound to it."

Lorri's look over this was comical. "Like what?" she demanded.

"Like Australia. It comes out Australie*r*."

Lorri started to giggle. She hadn't thought about it, but it was true. She did say things differently, but they sounded fine to her own ears. She said as much.

"I'm sure they do," Ruth agreed. "But if you don't mind, when we get home, you can show me where *Australier* is on the map."

Lorri began to giggle again, and Ruth only shook her head. Lorri was pushing the cart and in no hurry about it. Ruth stepped up the pace, thinking that at this rate they were going to be gone all day.

"Permission to break our agreement?" Arlene asked, interrupting the studying long enough to speak.

"Permission granted." Max went along.

"Word in the hallways is that Johnny King is completely smitten with you."

"I'm getting that impression."

"You didn't tell me this."

"We've sworn off boys."

"But at this moment we're off the record, so tell me now."

"He waits every day and walks me to Algebra."

"Do you like him?"

"No."

"Not even a little?"

"He's all wrong for me, Arlene. He *used* to come to church, and he's dated every girl in school. I don't want a man whose eyes roam that much and who does Christianity part-time. I've been happier not thinking about boys, and I intend to keep it that way."

Arlene nodded, and Max's head went back over her book.

"One more question."

"All right."

"Do you think he's cute?"

Max looked up. "Still off the record?"

"Yes."

"He's an absolute dream."

Arlene went into gales of laughter, which ignited Max's own giggles. Nevertheless, they did not allow the distraction. When the laughter died down, they went right back to work.

"It felt longer than a month," Lorri confessed to her grandfather, hugging him once again.

"For me too. You look great."

"Do I?"

They had settled in the living room, Buddy all but climbing into his master's lap.

"Yes, you do. How's Max?"

"She's wonderful."

"Still off boys?" Dean asked of Ruth.

"Yes. There's a boy who likes her, but she's handling it very well."

"Only one?" Dean asked, a twinkle in his eye.

Ruth scoldingly shook her head in his direction.

"Do you know what I'd like to do tonight?" Dean suddenly asked.

"What?"

"Go to the football game. Harmony Hills plays at home tonight, don't they?"

"I think they do. Max would know."

"Shall we go?"

Ruth and Lorri smiled at his enthusiasm, completely ready to agree. They were still talking about it when Max came in the door.

"Grandpa!"

She was overjoyed to see him, questions pouring out of her as she sat close to him on the sofa.

"So when do you leave again?"

"Barring the unforeseen, I don't."

"What were you the most hungry for?"

"Your mother's beef roast, mashed potatoes, and gravy."

"Did you see any of the men who rescued Raine?"

"No."

"The radio news talked about the signing of the official surrender papers. Were you there for any of that?"

"No, but I did see some of the U.S. prisoners after they were released. They were overjoyed to be free."

For the moment Max ran out of questions. She sighed a little and sat contentedly next to her grandfather. Dean looked over at her, his eyes filled with love.

"Max, is there a home football game tonight?" Lorri asked.

"Yes, we play Valley."

"Grandpa wants us to go."

"Truly?" she asked of Dean.

"Sure. How does that sound?"

"I have to call Arlene!" Max bolted from the room, an action that had its usual effect: Everyone laughed.

Thirteen

"I needed that," Lorri told her mother as they mounted the stairs much later that night.

"Why was that?"

"It felt normal. I didn't think anything would ever feel normal again. It was sad that we lost, but I still enjoyed it."

"Your father played football," Ruth said. They were almost to their rooms.

"I remember seeing the pictures."

The women parted for their own beds. Lorri was ready for sleep, but Ruth had made the most amazing discovery. She had gotten ready for bed but then curled up in the middle of the mattress with her photo albums. It took only seconds to find Tom Archer in his football uniform. Ruth touched the picture lovingly, missing him still.

"I've been in such shock," she whispered to the image of his face. "Josie's not just with our Lord Jesus Christ, she's with you too. Our girl is in heaven with you, Tom, and I didn't even think of it."

Ruth hugged the album close to her chest, lifting her face toward the ceiling.

"Thank You, Lord, for reminding me. Thank You for letting Tom have one of our girls."

"You wrote to Ken?"

"Yes, I sent word, but it's impossible for him to get away."

Ruth nodded, trying to imagine Josie's fiancé being able to join them for the service.

"I also called Ken's family this morning," Dean went on, "to tell them the time and date of the service."

"Do you think they'll come?"

"I think Mr. Showers will, but he said Mrs. Showers is pretty shook up."

Again Ruth could only nod. It was all coming together so swiftly. The funeral was one week away — a Monday morning — with a private graveside service to follow. Pastor Higgins would officiate, handling the music and such. The Oceanside Funeral Home would handle the other details.

Ruth didn't know the last time Tom had been so much on her mind. She realized she needed her husband here. She was burying a child. It was only logical that he be here beside her.

"What's the matter?"

Ruth looked startled. She hadn't realized Dean was still sitting there.

"I was thinking about Tom, wishing he was here beside me," she said.

"I've thought about him a lot lately. Maxine too," Dean said, naming his late wife.

"We've said goodbye to many, haven't we?"

"I guess we have. I don't think about it all the time, but we have certainly known grief before. And if I have my way, you'll know grief again," Dean said, shocking Ruth's eyes a little wide. "I don't want to bury any more of my family, Ruth." His voice deepened with suppressed emotion. "I'm sure you understand."

Ruth reached for his hand. "I certainly do, Dean."

Dean gave her hand a squeeze and rose from the table. There would be tears enough in a week's time. He didn't want to start now.

"Something wonderful happened four months ago today," Pastor Higgins told the mourners who gathered in his church on

Monday, October 1, 1945. "It wasn't wonderful in every way for everyone concerned, but it was wonderful for Josephine Archer.

"You see, Josie knew where she was going. She hadn't planned on dying that day, but it was all right that she did. I don't mean that no one would hurt, miss her, or be sad, but when a heart has things settled for all of eternity, it changes the way we look at her passing.

"Josie's grandfather and mother met with me. They told me that they wanted everyone to know what Josie believed and why she believed it. It's no secret. It's all spelled out in God's Word. Josie Archer knew she was a sinner and needed a Savior. She also knew from Scripture that the only salvation is from God through His Son. So when Josie was still quite young, she humbled herself before God and believed on Him for that salvation.

"And because God always keeps His promise, we know that her belief in Him was settled for all time. I stand before you today with a heart that is both heavy and light — heavy for the loss of our dear friend and sister but light in knowing that her rightly placed faith has secured her a place in heaven forever."

The family listened to these words in the

same state that Pastor Higgins delivered them. Their hearts were both heavy with hurt and joyful with the fact that Josie had believed on Jesus Christ to save her.

Pastor Higgins went on to speak about Josie, her age, her family, and her accomplishments, but before the service ended, he reminded them once again that believers do not need to mourn without hope. Hope was found in the death, burial, and resurrection of Jesus Christ.

"Hello, Mr. Showers," Ruth greeted as they climbed from the cars at the cemetery.

"Hello, Mrs. Archer. I'm sorry to see you under these circumstances."

"I'm glad you could come. How is Mrs. Showers?"

Mr. Showers' eyes grew suspiciously moist.

"She's in a bad way right now. She can't stop crying, and she didn't want to come here and upset everyone even more."

"Please tell her I'll write to her soon and that we understand."

In the face of this kindness, Mr. Showers could not speak. He pinched his lips tightly together, nodded, and turned toward the grave site. It didn't help that the first person he saw was Max. She was so like Josie in face and frame that it was startling.

He forced his eyes to Lorri, who stood next to her. She looked very different from the last time he'd seen her. She was still lovely, but thinner and missing the sparkle he had previously witnessed. Ken's father thought about what she'd gone through with her sister and understood anew why his wife could not stop crying.

"You can come in closer," Pastor Higgins invited, directing the small group. Mr. Showers and the Andrews family were the only ones the Archers had invited. There were many dear folks in the church family, but they had limited the invitations to keep things simple.

"I think you've handled this all very well," Pastor complimented the family. "You've been wise in keeping the numbers down and keeping this private, but I can't help but wonder if there might be some things you wish to say. I didn't plan a long sermon for this time at the grave — you don't need that — but I did want to give you a chance to share."

The group was quiet for a moment, but then Leonard Andrews had something on his heart.

"I remember the first time Josie babysat for Arlene. I don't remember if any of the boys were home, but Arlene didn't want us to go out that night. She was dreading staying with a new sitter, and then Josie came. We weren't gone that many hours, but by the time we got home, they were fast friends. Josie had even been willing to help Arlene build a fort on her bed, and the two had climbed in together to read a book."

Arlene had buried her face against her mother to hide her tears, but the adults were all smiling amid theirs. Josie had been special and fun, and no one was surprised by this story. Dean was the next to share his heart.

"If it's true that a man never plans on burying his child, it's ten times as true concerning a grandchild. We are certainly not the first to stand in grief around a graveside, and we won't be the last, but that fact doesn't always soften the hurt." Dean paused, wanting to finish but finding it hard. "I'll keep on because the Savior has a plan, but I'll miss you, Jo. More than I can say."

Ruth couldn't manage his words. Her face crumbled, and she sobbed with the ache inside of her. Dean moved close to put an arm around her, and Max turned helplessly to Lorri.

"Say something, Raine," she cried. "Tell Jo how I feel, because I can't right now."

Lorri's head hurt with the pressure she felt inside, but she made herself speak the first thing that came to mind.

"Thank you, Josie, for your sweet heart and godly spirit. We'll always love you. We'll never forget you. And heaven will be a more precious place in our hearts because you're there waiting for us."

No one else could speak. Pastor Higgins read a few verses from the Psalms and closed in prayer. Mr. Showers and the Andrews moved toward the cars, and the Archers took a few more minutes by the casket.

In a way it was helpful that Josie wasn't in that box. Only Lorri could actually picture where her body was, and the others naturally tried. They stood and talked for a few moments, and then Dean said it was time to leave. There was rescue in those words. Josie had been gone four months, but things had not been complete until today. Painful as the days ahead might be, the process of moving on needed to begin.

"Hey, Max," Johnny King called to her, stopping her on the front steps of the school at the end of the day on Tuesday. Max had stopped in only long enough to get her assignments and now was ready to walk home.

"Hi, Johnny."

"Where have you been the last few days? Were you sick?"

"No," Max shook her head but didn't elaborate. Johnny, much brighter than his grades showed, didn't press her.

"I saw you at the last home game," he offered.

"Oh, yeah, that night we lost to Valley."

"There's a home game this Friday night. Do you want to go?"

"I'll probably just go with my family, but thanks for asking."

Johnny's deep blue eyes studied her. She was unique, he knew that. His only regret was not pursuing her — and only her — years before.

"I guess I didn't take it seriously when you said you were swearing off boys."

"It's easier that way right now," Max said.

Johnny smiled that smile that had turned many hearts.

"Easier for who?"

Max couldn't stop her answering smile.

"I've got to get home."

"I can give you a ride." The offer was made in his most charming voice.

"No, thanks. I'll see you tomorrow."

"Bye, Max."

Johnny didn't care who witnessed it. He stood still and watched Max until she was out of sight. The rumors all around school were that Johnny King had finally lost his heart, and to a girl who didn't want him. Johnny wouldn't have admitted it under threat of torture, but the rumors were very true.

"Lorri, you've got to see this," Ruth called very quietly from the edge of the living room.

Lorri came around the corner and had to cover her mouth to keep from laughing. Buddy had taken up his usual place in front of the picture window to watch Max walking away to school, but today Muffin had joined him. Perched on top of Buddy's head, the half-grown kitten sat comfortably, taking a view of the out-of-doors as though she'd never seen it before.

Ruth grabbed the camera and tried to get a photo, but Muffin spotted Lorri and came to her.

"Oh, she moved."

"She might do it again," Lorri said, cuddling the cat in her arms.

"She's a little character, I'll say that much for her."

Ruth put the camera away, and Lorri, a little at loose ends, followed her. Ruth gathered her gloves and gardening tools and went into the backyard.

"Do you think Max was ready to go back today?" Lorri asked from across the garden.

"Probably not, but putting it off was not going to accomplish much."

"There must be kids all over the school who are in the same boat."

"I'm sure you're right. The war has ended and the mourning and rebuilding will begin."

Lorri began to hum "I'm Looking Over a Four-Leaf Clover," and Ruth smiled as she worked on the flower bed at the back of the house. Sure enough, it wasn't long before Lorri began to sing. The doxology was next, then "White Christmas."

"Mother," Lorri suddenly said, cutting off midsong. "I've been meaning to ask you something, but I don't know how to word it."

"Do you have it figured out now?"

"No, not really."

Ruth turned her head and smiled at her.

"Just ask, Lorraine. We'll figure it out together."

"I guess I want to know why you never ask, *Why us?*"

"Why us?" Ruth questioned her, trying to understand.

"Yes. Do you remember that woman from so many years ago who had lost her twin sons in a fire? She was sharing how she was dealing with it, but all the time she talked, she said she didn't know why God would do that to her.

"We never spoke of it, but I got the impression that you and Grandpa didn't agree. I remember your face registered concern or some other emotion. Do you recall it now?"

"Yes, I do recall. I wasn't at all happy with the things she said."

Lorri waited, but her mother didn't go on. She waited a bit longer and pressed her when there was more silence.

"So why, Mother? Why don't you ask God, '*Why us?*'"

Ruth turned fully to face her daughter and spoke frankly.

"Why not us, Lorri? Why not our family? We've never been promised a hedge that keeps away all pain and loss and suffering. God will do as He pleases, and it pleased Him to take your father and Josie home. I can't ask God why until I'm willing to ask why not."

"Oh, Mother," Lorri breathed, "I think you're wonderful."

"Do you?"

"Yes. You don't try to help God."

"Is that what you do?"

"Sometimes."

"What did you try to help with lately?" Ruth was using the trowel again.

"I didn't want Max to go back to school. I think there should have been some type of holiday all this week so she could be home."

"That's sweet of you to want to take care of her."

"It's me wanting my way and sure that I know what's best. I'm not sure how sweet that is."

Ruth turned back to her.

"Are you being too hard on yourself? You miss Josie, so you naturally want to have Max around to love and protect."

Lorri shrugged, thinking her mother might be right. She did miss Josie, more than she could have imagined, and Max was so much fun.

Lorri realized she'd sat around long enough. Going back to her song, she began to help her mother in the garden.

Early October brought the World Series — the Detroit Tigers defeated the Chicago Cubs four games to three. Ava Gardner married band leader Artie Shaw. General Electric announced the construction of the world's most powerful electron accelerator, which could direct steam at the speed of light and cut through nearly 12 inches of armored plate. And advertised as the "first pen to write underwater," a ballpoint pen offered by Gimbel's of New York had 10,000 eager buyers on its first day of sales.

Lorri kept up on all these events through the newspapers and the radio as October faded into November. The days were cooler now, the nights especially so. Warmer skirts, slacks, and sweaters came out of wardrobes.

Lorri was almost back to her normal size, her appetite still improving and with it a desire to cook and bake. Rare was the evening when she did not put dinner on the table, and because meat was becoming more available, the selections were varied and interesting.

"Pork chops," Dean said one evening, sitting down with pleasure. "It's been a while."

"Lorri smiles at the butcher, and he gives her the best selection under the counter."

"Mother!" Lorri said, sounding faintly shocked, but both Dean and Max were laughing.

"I think you should swear off men, Lorri," her sister advised. "It's the only way to live."

"How is that working for you?" Lorri asked.

"Just fine," she told her with a cheeky smile. "I've been asked out more this year than all my other years combined, but I just say no."

"But does that get us thick, center-cut pork chops from the butcher?"

No one around the table expected this outrageous remark from Lorri, and they nearly choked on the food they were chewing.

"Lorraine Susan Archer!" It was her mother's turn to be shocked.

Lorri tried not to look too pleased, but it felt good to give back a little.

"On a more serious note," Dean cut in, thinking it might be more than time. "I've heard from Ken."

This had the effect he expected. All eyes and ears were attentive.

"He'd like to visit later this month, probably after Thanksgiving, but only if it won't be too upsetting."

"Well, of course he should come."

"It might be upsetting, but he needs to come."

"What day?"

All three women had spoken at once, and Dean tried to wade through it all. He waited until the table grew quiet.

"He's not sure what day. He'll send word."

"How is he doing?" Ruth asked.

"His letter didn't say." Dean's eyes swung

to Lorri. "I can imagine that he will want some details. Are you sure you're up to this?"

"Yes. Tell him to come anytime."

The table was a bit quiet after this, but only until Max made her announcement: "I almost blew up the science room today."

What followed was a hysterical account of mishaps and mislabeled containers. No one was hurt, but Max was in her element, entertaining her family with the tale. She managed to singe the tiny hairs from the backs of her fingers but otherwise was unscathed.

"And I still got an A," she said simply, wrapping up the tale and making her family laugh once again.

First Lieutenant Kenneth Showers looked wonderful. He had flowers for Ruth, a warm handshake for the admiral, and hugs for Lorri and Max.

"Sit down," Ruth urged. "It's so good to have you back."

"It's good to see you too. I've been concerned about all of you."

"We're doing well. We've wondered about you."

Ken smiled a little. "I'm not sure I believe it yet." He looked to Max. "You look so much like Josie these days, Max. It's hard not to stare."

"Does it make it harder?" she asked compassionately.

"Not hard to be around you, but hard to believe that Josie's not coming back."

Max didn't know what to say to this, but it didn't matter. Ken's eyes swung to Lorri.

"I heard a pretty horrendous story about you."

Lorri shrugged a little, not sure what to say.

"Do you feel like telling me about it?"

Lorri didn't let herself ponder on whether she felt like it; she just started in. She was vague about the crash and even the burial, hoping he wouldn't notice. She glossed over as much as she could — for his sake — and ended by telling how the crew of the *Every Storm* had found her.

Lorri finished and looked him in the eye, knowing in an instant that he wasn't going to go for it. He looked at her, as kind as he'd always been, but the questions were in his eyes. They weren't long in coming.

"There was no one on this island but you?"

"That's right."

"Did you find a shovel of some type in the plane?"

"No."

"So you dug in the dirt with your hands?"

"Well, I found a flat rock, and that helped."

Ken never took his eyes from her. He'd seen awful things on the shores of Europe, things he never wanted to think about again, but he hadn't been forced to bury someone he loved.

"Don't spare me, Lorraine."

No one missed his use of her full name, especially Lorri.

"Josie was dead," Ken went on, "but you were not. Right now I want to find out about you."

"It was awful," she heard herself admit. "My sister and Clarence Fuller were dead, and I've never felt so alone. At first I wanted to die with them, but then I realized there would be no one to tell my mother what happened to Josie, so I did what I had to do."

"You had water?"

"Yes, there was a spring, so I had all the water I wanted. Food was not so easy."

"What did you eat?"

"I tried the different plants and berries. I was working hard and felt I had to have food, but it wasn't that easy."

"Working at digging?"

"Yes. The first berries I tried burned my mouth so badly that I had blisters. Another kind made me vomit, and another was so bitter I couldn't swallow it. The only ones that didn't make me sick were hard to find, so I ate leaves that weren't as bitter."

It never once occurred to Ken that her family hadn't heard all of this. He never even looked their way. It was the same for Lorri. It was as if she and Ken were alone in the room together.

"And all the while you dug?"

"Yes. It took me about five days to finish the holes."

"You did separate holes?"

"I couldn't bring myself to bury them together. It was hard, but I don't regret it."

"And then what? What did you do all day after that job was done?"

"I spent a lot of time next to the graves. I felt a little better, even though Josie couldn't hear me. In the mornings I would search all over for our things, but I only found a few pieces of our luggage and some scraps of clothing. I found a shoe that probably belonged to Clarence."

"How long, Lorri?"

"Was I on the island? About six weeks. I don't know if I would have made it much longer. I was pretty weak by the time the boat arrived."

Ken just looked at her. His father had

warned him about the changes in her, but he thought she looked good. Maybe a little thin, but healthy.

"I'm sorry, Lorri," Ken said at last. "Josie wouldn't have wanted that for you. She would have wanted to protect and take care of you. I don't know if there was ever a letter from her that didn't mention you. I know you did everything together. In fact, I worried about it, because I feared we wouldn't live close after the wedding."

If he kept it up she was going to cry, and she didn't want that. She wanted her own question answered.

"I have something to ask you."

"All right."

"You don't seem upset." Her voice didn't betray the turmoil she felt inside. "Were you still in love with my sister?"

"I was going to tell you about that, and yes, I'm still in love with your sister. I always will be, but my family noticed it as well. I don't show my emotions easily, but it's bigger than that, Lorri. You see, I hadn't seen Josie in over five years. Her letters meant everything to me, but sometimes they would take six months to find me. Our love and our plans had to be placed in a far corner of my mind so I wouldn't get my head blown off."

Lorri's hand came to her mouth. "I'm sorry, Ken. I'm sorry I said that."

"No, Lorri, honey." Ken's voice was filled with understanding so that he sounded like the big brother he'd been planning to be. "I wasn't scolding you. I'm glad you asked. I was going to tell you anyway so you would never doubt my feelings for Josie. I was so honored I was to become a part of this family."

For the first time they became aware of the others. Max had buried her face in a sofa pillow, and Ruth sat with her eyes closed. Dean's face gave nothing away, but he watched his older granddaughter very closely.

"I'm sorry if I shouldn't have pressed her in that way," Ken said quietly to the admiral.

"I think it's all right, Ken. I'm glad Lorri felt she could tell you." He looked to Lorri. "Are you all right?"

"I am, yes. I think it helped to talk about it. And Ken," she said, adding a few more words, "you need to know that Josie adored you. If she didn't have a new letter, she read your old ones. You never left her heart for a single moment."

The man who had said he didn't show his emotions cracked a little. His eyes closed in pain and longing, and he sat very still for several seconds. When he looked up, the admiral was ready with a rescue. He asked Ken about his life now, his immediate plans for the future, and where he would be stationed. Ken stayed and visited with the family for another hour.

"I have Christmas presents for you," Ken ended his visit by saying, stepping back to the front door to retrieve a large bag.

"But Christmas is almost a month away," Ruth protested with a laugh.

"But I probably won't get back this way for a while. And I wanted you to have them."

She had done well to that point, but his words caused tears to come to her eyes. Ken had a tender hug for her and for the rest of them before going on his way.

"I want him to love again," Ruth said when the door had been shut. "I won't tell him that, but I'm praying that he'll love again."

Her family was too emotional to comment, but everyone nodded their agreement.

Fourteen

"Dean Archer," Ruth said in a whispered, scolding tone on Christmas Eve. "What are you doing?"

"What are you doing up?" he shot back, having been caught in the act.

"I heard all this bumping around and thought we had burglars."

"And what exactly were you going to do when you found burglars?"

"I don't know, but I wasn't going to lie there and wait to be murdered in my bed!"

Dean had to laugh. She sounded so exasperated but had been speaking in a whisper the whole time.

"Are you going to tell me what's going on?" Ruth asked, just as she realized that Dean was standing in front of a dark piece of furniture that came to his waist.

Having watched her gaze and seeing no

240

help for it, Dean stepped to the side so Ruth could see what he was attempting to hide. Ruth took in the wooden console and wide dials of a very large radio, and her eyes widened.

"You bought a new radio?"

"Shh," Dean hushed her, which caused them both to giggle, neither aware that it was already too late.

"What's going on?" Max said as she joined Lorri on the top step.

"I think they're sneaking in a big Christmas gift."

"They're not being very quiet about it," Max said around a yawn. "What do you think it is?"

"I don't know."

The word *radio* drifted from below just then, and the girls looked at each other in surprise. Trying desperately to contain their own laughter, they sprang up and ran to Max's room, the closest.

"A radio!" Max whispered, her eyes huge with excitement.

"We'll have to be surprised in the morning," Lorri ordered. "Don't forget."

"I won't. It sounds like it's going in the family room, so we'll just stay in the living room like we always do."

"All right."

The chimes in the hallway struck 12 times just then. Lorri smiled at her sister.

"Merry Christmas, Max."

"Merry Christmas, Raine."

They hugged and went back to their beds, but sleep was miles away.

"Merry Christmas!" the Archers shouted when Leonard Andrews opened the door.

"Merry Christmas! Come in, come in. Cora, they're here."

Hugs were exchanged and bowls and platters of food were passed off to be refrigerated or enjoyed on the spot. Two of the Andrews' sons were home, Scott, the oldest, and Ray, the youngest of the three boys. Bob, the middle of the boys, was married and having Christmas with his wife's family.

"It smells wonderful in here," Ruth said.

"It's the cider. Let me get you a mug."

"Thank you."

"Would you like cider, Lorri?"

"Oh, hi, Scott. Thank you, I would."

In the kitchen, Cora waited for her son to look at her, but he would not. She blocked his way to the kettle of cider on the stove top, and that wrung a smile from him and also brought his eyes up.

"Yes," he said very quietly, "you were right."

Cora couldn't stop her huge grin. She had told her son when he arrived the day before that Lorri Archer had done some growing up since he'd last seen her, and was in fact beautiful. Scott had not seemed overly convinced. Cora knew no end of pleasure to have him tell her she was right.

"Behave yourself," he told her softly before slipping out of the kitchen to give Lorri the cider.

"Thank you," Lorri said, smiling up at him, not remembering his hair as being so light. "How have you been, Scott?"

"I'm doing well."

"You must be done with school?"

"Yes, I'm at Falcon these days. Mostly in development."

"Sounds interesting. Is this a busy time for you?"

"Yes, we had only half of yesterday off and today. It's too hectic to close down."

"Well, that's a good problem, isn't it?"

"Yes," Scott laughed. "Put like that, it is. What are you doing to keep busy right now? Are you headed back to Australia?"

"No, I'm sticking pretty close to home."

"You have an accent."

Lorri shook her head. "Mother and Max

say the same thing."

"It's very charming," he complimented her, and Lorri was surprised to find herself blushing.

Scott noticed it and observed accurately, "I think you need to get out more."

Lorri laughed a little before agreeing, "You're probably right about that."

A feast was in the making, and Lorri excused herself to help in the kitchen. Scott joined his sister and Max in the living room, where he noticed that Ray was rather taken with their guest. He mentally shook his head until he heard Max telling them about the new radio Dean had bought for Christmas. Suddenly Max had his attention as well.

"Did my eyes deceive me, or did Scott Andrews show some interest in you, Raine?"

"Did my eyes deceive me, or did Ray never take his eyes off of you?"

Max, who had flopped down on the end of her sister's bed, smiled.

"It was a fun day, wasn't it?"

"Yes, it was. Are you still sworn off boys?"

"For the most part."

"What's the other part?"

"Oh, I don't know. When someone like Ray shows interest, it has an effect."

"What kind of effect?"

"Pleasure, I guess. It probably doesn't help that Arlene wants us to marry her brothers and all be one big, happy family."

Lorri's brows rose on this announcement. She had enjoyed seeing Scott, but marriage had never entered her mind.

"Do you never think about marrying, Raine?"

"I did before Josie died, probably because she had Ken, but I haven't given guys much thought since."

"I keep seeing guys who would be perfect for you."

"Like who?"

"Clint Corbett."

"Do I know him?"

"He plays the organ at church. His wife died about two years ago, and he has the cutest little girl."

"I don't think we've ever met."

"You don't sound like you want to meet him."

Lorri wasn't sure if Max would understand, but she had to try.

"I still feel a little lost, Max. I'm so thankful to be here and not in Australia, but even here I feel slightly displaced. The thought of meeting someone new right now only adds to that feeling. Does that make sense?"

"It does. I won't push you."

Lorri caught the compassion in her voice and felt her own compassion, compassion for the younger sister who just wanted her to be happy.

"Well, if you spot a man and you're sure he's the one, you'd probably better at least nudge me."

Max smiled. "I love you, Raine."

"I rather like you too."

These days they didn't pass up opportunities to hug. With a final Merry Christmas and a hug to go with it, Max went to her room so they could both go to sleep.

"I'm thinking about returning to women's Bible study after the new year, Lorri," Ruth mentioned a few days after Christmas. "Would you like to go?"

"I would, yes. Is there a reason you haven't gone until now?"

"I just felt I needed some time."

"What are you studying?"

"Hospitality, among other topics."

"Who teaches it?"

"Betty Higgins."

"Sounds interesting. What day is it?"

"Thursdays."

"I'd like to go. What Thursday do you start back?"

"I'll have to ask someone about that. It might be right after the first, or it may be the next week."

"Where do they hold it?"

"Pastor and Betty's house."

In the midst of this conversation, it struck Ruth that she was very blessed. She had known loss and heartbreak, but her family was all around her. Dean's retirement was coming up in August, and that was a blessing too. Gone would be the days when he was away for weeks and months on end. Max was having her best year in school, and God had blessed her decision not to be so taken with boys. She was the happiest Ruth had ever seen her, even amid the grief.

And Lorri was an added bonus. Like most mothers, she wanted to see her middle daughter loved and married, but for the moment she was here, and the simplest of conversations was warm and comforting to Ruth's heart.

"That's a faraway look," Lorri commented.

"Just counting my blessings."

"Did you number me?"

Ruth didn't answer. She simply put her arms around her daughter and held her close.

"1946," Arlene said, leaning against Max in the backseat of the car. "Can you believe it?"

"I'll be 18 this year," Max said. "I think that's old."

Leonard and Cora didn't comment from the front seat, but they smiled. Max had that effect on them.

The Archers had given a last-minute slam-bang New Year's Eve party, but that wasn't enough for the girls. Arlene had asked to have Max overnight, and Ruth had given her permission.

"I'm going to give boys another chance this year," Arlene proclaimed.

"Not me," Max argued. "If Prince Charming doesn't fall into my lap, I'm staying where I am."

"What about Lorri? You're still looking for her, aren't you?"

"Yes, but I don't tell her who I find. She doesn't want that right now."

"He'll have to fall into her lap too."

"Now I think we've had enough of that, girls," Leonard said from behind the wheel. "Dean would not approve of you letting boys sit on your lap."

Arlene and Max, a little sleepy and very content, found this highly amusing. They

laughed the rest of the way to the Andrews',
and Cora wondered if they would sleep at all
this night.

February

"Where's Lorri?" Dean asked of Ruth
long after the service ended. Ruth had
thought she was already in the car, so she
began to look around. She looked back in
the sanctuary and around the foyer until she
saw Max headed their way from the parking
lot.

"Mr. Andrews is talking to Lorri," she informed them. "She said she would be along
shortly."

It was on the tip of Ruth's tongue to ask if
Lorri looked upset, but she told herself to be
patient. It also looked as though it was going
to rain, but Ruth kept her mouth shut on
that issue as well.

"Is she going to come back in here?" Dean
asked. "Or should we wait for her in the
car?"

"Well, Mrs. Andrews and Arlene are already sitting in their car, so I guess we could
do that."

Ruth decided that it was an odd conversation. She didn't mind Lorri talking with
Leonard. In fact, she was pleased. He had
such a way of coaxing words from anyone he

met, but the suddenness and privacy alarmed her a little.

"Here she comes," Max said before they could even reach their vehicle.

They looked up to see Lorri walking swiftly toward them. She was just the way they remembered her now. Home for almost six months, she looked and acted like the Lorri of old.

"Is everything all right?" Dean asked, having been curious as well.

"Everything is great, but I have something I need to discuss with you."

"With Leonard too?"

"No, I can call him when it's all settled."

On this cryptic note, they climbed into the car, and Lorri waited only that long to begin.

"Mr. Andrews says that Madrone Elementary School needs an aide to finish the year. The first- and second-grade teachers are both expecting, and the school board approved one helper for both rooms. Mr. Andrews has spoken to the principal there and told him he might have someone for the job. Then he asked me."

Max screamed and threw her arms around her sister.

"Oh, Lorri!" Ruth said, turning in the front seat to see her. "This is just what you asked the women at Bible study to pray about. I'm so excited for you."

"It's only until June," Lorri continued, her voice beginning to fill with excitement. "But maybe that will lead to a permanent position of some kind. What do you think, Grandpa?"

"It sounds perfect. When would you start?"

"Well, if I let him know today, Mr. Andrews would call Madrone's principal in the morning and tell him I'd like an interview. If he likes me, I'll have the job."

"He'll like you," her grandfather said with a confidence that made the rest of the family smile.

"Nervous?" Max questioned her sister over the breakfast table.

"Terribly. I can't even eat."

"You're going to do fine," Max reassured her. "The children will love you."

"But will the teachers?" Lorri fretted. "I wish I could have met them."

"If they're expecting and someone is there to help, they'll love you," Ruth said from the kitchen, her voice dry.

Max laughed, but Lorri didn't even smile. She played with the handle of her coffee cup, her oatmeal getting cold in front of her.

"Look at it this way, Raine; it's Wednesday. Even if you're miserable, you'll only have three days this week."

Lorri's shoulders began to shake. "Your logic is amazing. What about the remainder of the year?"

"You don't worry about that right now. Just worry about this week."

"Don't worry *at all*," their mother put in pointedly, placing lunches on the table next to her daughters.

Within 15 minutes they were both out the door. Ruth stood at the window with Buddy and Muffin, reminding herself that the order not to worry applied to herself as well.

"Okay, Edith, is this a capital *I* or *T?*" Lorri asked the little girl next to her.

"It's a *T.*"

"In that case, why don't you make his hat a little longer?" Lorri crossed the *T* with her fingernail. "Right now he looks like an *I.*"

The little girl smiled up at her as if her dream had come true, and Lorri gently rubbed her back. Lorri glanced up to the front and found Mrs. Beach smiling at her. Still knowing nothing but relief, she smiled right back.

Mrs. Beach taught first grade. She was five months pregnant, her ankles swollen and uncomfortable. Mrs. Carter was the second-grade teacher. She was six months along in her pregnancy, and had a little more energy than Mrs. Beach. Both women were kind-hearted, competent teachers, and very appreciative of Lorri's quiet presence and efforts.

Lorri was there to offer relief. She did the physical jobs. She took recess and lunchroom duties, found missing hats and umbrellas, stood with the children while waiting for parents to arrive, and at the end of the day, picked up the rooms and did the final checks on windows and locks.

Most days Lorri spent mornings in the second-grade room and afternoons with Mrs. Beach and her class. She had small breaks throughout the day, especially when the teachers read to the class.

For the most part the children were well behaved, but on occasion, Lorri would escort someone to a special chair at the front of the second-grade room. It was a chair of shame because everyone could see who was in trouble, and most children didn't want to sit that close to the teacher when the reason was not positive.

For three weeks, from 8:00 A.M. to 3:15 P.M., Lorri had basically been run off her feet. But she was enjoying it. The children were delightful, and it felt good to have a schedule. She missed the long talks with her mother, long walks with Buddy, and finding new recipes to try, but she made up for those on the weekends as best as she could.

"Miss Archer?" questioned the little girl who was finally done with her lesson.

"Yes, Edith?"

"This is ready to check."

Lorri thanked her and took the paper, adding it to the pile she would check during story time. A swift look at the clock told her that was just 15 minutes away.

Edith went back to her seat, and Lorri felt a moment of relief. She signaled to Mrs. Beach, who acknowledged her with a nod. Lorri slipped from the room and tried not to run. She suddenly realized she'd needed to use the bathroom for the last two hours.

Max and Arlene saw Johnny coming toward them, but never in a lifetime did they believe he would bypass the table full of his male friends and join them at their table in the lunchroom. They were wrong. He sat down at the table next to Max and looked across at Arlene.

"Do you realize that commencement is in three months?" he said.

"I think so," Arlene said, trying to catch up. "Is there a problem?"

"Yes, there's a problem. All this time and I still haven't convinced a certain someone to go out with me."

Max's hand came up to cover her smile, but Johnny didn't look at her.

"Well," Arlene did her best to sound compassionate, "she hasn't given you much encouragement."

"Do you think she might feel a little sorry for me?"

"Not a chance," Arlene stated flatly, and Johnny finally turned to Max. She was eating the cookies from her lunch, her eyes brimming with amusement.

"Those cookies look good."

"Here, have one," Max offered.

"Thanks."

Johnny watched her while he ate, wishing with all his heart that she wasn't so sweet and pretty. Watching him right back, Max knew what was coming.

"Come on, Maxine," Johnny said, using his most cajoling tone. "One date."

"And what will one date accomplish?"

"You'll see how charming I am and fall for me."

"There's no end to your modesty, is there?"

Johnny put his arms out wide and asked, "What's there to be modest about?"

The girls had had enough. Both told him he was pitiful as they rose from the table to leave. They were laughing when they said this, so Johnny knew he was forgiven, but it still didn't work: no date with Maxine Archer.

"Ruth," Betty Higgins called, "why don't you start our prayer time with an update on Lorri. How is she liking the job?"

"Oh, thank you for asking. She's enjoying it so much. She is a little tired, but she comes home with a new story each night, and it sounds like the children and other staff members love her."

"How is it for you, Ruth?" Betty asked. "Are things pretty lonely at home?"

"A little, yes, but it's such an amazing blessing to have Lorri back in California after all these years; I just enjoy her every chance I get."

The time for sharing prayer requests and then praying usually lasted for 30 minutes. Routine called for the women to then start on their current study book or topic. If many women had prayer requests, they simply spent the whole time talking about those things and then praying together.

Today was just such a day. The lives of many women had been affected by the war. They still grieved and ached with the loss of loved ones. Ruth didn't share from her own heart, but she certainly understood the helplessness and feeling of loss. Indeed, Josie was often on her mind.

No small amount of tears were shed this day, and Ruth, when it was finally time to go home, found that she had a headache. She debated how to handle it: take Buddy for a long, leisurely walk, or lie down and sleep for a time.

Sleep won out. Buddy didn't look ready to leave the yard, and Ruth found she had no energy to spare. She lay down just before lunch and didn't wake for two solid hours.

Fifteen

Lieutenant Donovan Riggs continued his walk down the school corridor, certain he was seeing things. He had been in something of a hurry, but now his pace slowed almost to a crawl. His eyes were centered on one person, and he needed time to think.

It was she, Miss Lorraine Archer, looking as he'd never seen her. She was some 20 yards in front of him, directing children to stand still as they waited for their parents. It took some time for her to turn in his direction, but when she did, Rigg couldn't help thinking what 20 well-placed pounds could do to a woman's figure.

It had been an especially long day. While Lorri was not frustrated, she was more than a little tired. The children were moving off swiftly, but two little girls remained at her

258

feet: Helen Peterson and a first-grader named Violet.

Lorri didn't know what made her look in the other direction, but her heart nearly stopped in her chest when she did. Coming very slowly toward the group, and in uniform, was the lieutenant. The girls didn't notice him, but Lorri made some swift deductions.

"Violet," she asked softly, "what's your last name?"

"Riggs," the little girl answered absently, intent on a spot on the pavement.

Lorri asked the question just in time. A moment later, Violet spotted the lieutenant and ran to him. Lorri watched as Rigg swung her up into his arms and kissed her cheek.

"Goodbye, Miss Archer," Helen said just then, and Lorri regained her composure long enough to turn and send her off with a wave. She turned back, only to find the lieutenant had come a little closer, Violet still in his arms.

"Your daughter?" Lorri asked.

"My niece."

An "oh" shaped Lorri's mouth, but no sound followed.

"How are you, Miss Archer?" Rigg asked, his eyes watchful.

"I'm very well, Lieutenant. How are you?"

"Fine."

"Did you all come home safely?" Lorri asked, suddenly remembering the men. "Is everyone all right?"

"Yes, we did arrive home safely. It's kind of you to ask."

Even as Rigg answered, he wondered whether he should tell her that Ellis had been diagnosed with cancer and Lionel's wife wanted a divorce, but he kept the thoughts to himself.

"I'm glad. I've thought about all of you many times."

"We thought about you too," Rigg admitted, barely able to take his eyes from her. She was beautiful. Nothing about her before gave a hint concerning her normal appearance. His men would have fallen apart had she come aboard looking like this.

"Uncle Donovan?" Violet interrupted his thoughts. "Are we going home?"

"Yes," he told her, having almost forgotten his brother's oldest child. "We'll go right now."

Lorri had caught the stare and understood what he was thinking. Her smile was a little knowing when she bid the lieutenant goodbye, and his amused grin told her he knew he'd been found out.

"Goodbye, Violet," Lorri said. "I'll see you Monday."

"Goodbye, Miss Archer."

"Goodbye," Rigg said to Lorri, his gaze catching and holding hers for a moment.

Lorri could only move her hand in a small wave. She hadn't remembered much about him, not the color of those green eyes, certainly, and after looking into them, she'd had nothing to say.

Long after Lorri should have collected her things and gone home for the weekend, she was still moving slowly through the motions, checking the classroom and making sure all was in order.

She made the walk home in the same way: not the least bit rushed, as if she had all the time in the world. She didn't hurry until she was in sight of the house. Then it was suddenly very important to tell her mother who she'd seen.

"Did you know he was stationed here, Grandpa?"

"No, honey, but it's an awfully big base."

"What did he say?" Max wanted to know.

"Not too much. The *Every Storm* and her men came back safely, and he was at school to pick up his niece."

"Did he think you looked different?" Dean asked, hiding a smile.

Lorri, on the other hand, could not hide hers. An almost dreamy, satisfied smile stretched her lovely mouth until the whole family witnessed it.

Ruth and Max looked at each other and then to Dean, but he was smiling at Lorri.

"I think," Ruth began, sounding calmer than she felt, "that I want you to tell me every detail."

"All right," Lorri agreed without hesitation, explaining that he was there to pick up his niece, and that they spoke for a few moments.

Ruth didn't press her, but the moment she got her father-in-law alone, she didn't spare him.

"Dean Archer, I wish to know exactly who this young man is who makes my levelheaded daughter smile like a smitten teenager."

Dean couldn't help laughing a little. "I noticed that too."

"But you're not concerned?"

"Lieutenant Riggs is a fine young officer. I did a little checking on him after the fact and learned that our Lorri couldn't do much better."

Ruth's mouth opened, but Dean put his hand up.

"I wasn't matchmaking, Ruth, I just wanted to know who this man was. I was very impressed when I debriefed him at Seaford and wanted to know more."

"And what did you learn?"

"He finished OCS at the top of his class. He has a college education. He left a full-time job after Pearl Harbor to enlist. He's close to his family, some of whom live here and others who live in northern California. And his faith in Jesus Christ is very real."

Ruth took a big breath. "I've never seen Lorri look like that."

"You're too used to it from the old Max."

"I guess so. So what do we do now?"

"Not a thing," Dean told her, a bit sternly. "If Lieutenant Riggs wants to get to know our Lorri, he knows what he has to do."

"So what did he look like?" Max asked her sister when they were alone that night.

Lorri bit her lip.

"Tell me, Raine."

"He's dreamy, Max," Lorri admitted, her voice almost at a whisper. "Dark hair, green eyes, and tan. I couldn't believe it."

"He didn't look like that before?"

"He might have, but I was pretty weak."

"It was his looks," Max said outrageously. "They turned your knees to water."

The two of them giggled, way too pleased with themselves.

"Seriously, Raine, do you think you'll see him again?"

Lorri shrugged. "He didn't say why he was picking up his niece. So I don't know."

"Do you hope you see him again?" Max asked, watching her sister's every facial feature.

Chewing pensively on her lip, Lorri met Max's inquiring gaze.

"Yes." She nodded a little. "I do."

"A rather amazing thing happened today," Rigg told his brother and sister-in-law that evening. It was after dinner, and the kids were in bed.

"What was it?" Jim Riggs questioned him.

"When I picked Vi up, I saw the woman we rescued off that island."

Dorothy, Jim's wife, had been bent over some mending, but her head came up in a hurry.

"She was at the school?" Dorothy asked.

"Yes. I asked Vi about it on the way home, and she said she's the helper in the first- and second-grade rooms."

"Miss Archer?"

"You know her?" Rigg asked.

"I've met her several times, usually when

she's helping the children with rides at the end of the day. She's extremely sweet."

"I think you might be right."

Something in his brother's voice, or rather the lack of expression, caused Jim to look at him and then his wife. Jim didn't say anything, but Dorothy wasn't above a little teasing.

"Am I all wet, Donovan, or did she look a little different when you found her?"

It was said without laughter, but Rigg knew she was having him on. He settled a little more comfortably in his chair and smiled at her.

"She looked very different," he told her, his green eyes dancing.

"Do tell," Dorothy coaxed, leaning forward a little.

"Let's just put it this way: If she'd looked then like she looked today, I'd have had a riot on my hands."

Dorothy loved this. She started to laugh out loud until her husband warned her that she was going to wake William, their baby.

Rigg didn't stay much longer, telling them he needed to get back to the base, but in truth he wasn't in much of a hurry to leave. His brother and wife had bought a small house and turned it into a home. Rigg never tired of visiting them and the children. As he drove away, he wondered if Dorothy would need him to pick up Violet again in the very near future.

Ruth returned from the grocery store to be greeted with the sounds of Glenn Miller. Loud band music came from the family room, and as soon as the first bags were on the kitchen table, she went that way.

Her daughters were dancing. Side by side, they slid sideways and hopped into place. They clapped, snapped their fingers, and laughed breathlessly as they went through different motions and turns.

Ruth could only stare. Her daughters had never been to dances. Where had they learned some of those intricate moves?

"Come on, Mother!" Lorri called when she spotted her, not even breaking stride.

"Where did you learn to dance?" Ruth demanded.

"Josie and I would play the radio in our room and make up our own moves. I'm teaching Max."

Max, who was keeping up just fine, grinned at her mother and added her own invitation.

"You'll like it," Max sweet-talked, but Ruth only shook her head and slipped back into the kitchen.

When the girls realized she was unloading the groceries, they cut the music off and went to help. Both were still panting.

"As if the two of you don't get enough exercise," Ruth commented, handing bags to Dean, who had just returned from the Saturday morning men's Bible study.

"Who's been exercising?"

"We were dancing," Lorri explained.

"Was I invited?" Dean asked, making the girls laugh.

"You're going to give them ideas, Dean," Ruth chided.

"Like what?"

The four had carried all the bags inside to the table, and now Ruth and Dean faced off.

"Like such things are all right. You should see some of these moves."

"But it was just the two of them, right?"

"Yes," Ruth grudgingly admitted.

Dean looked as though he was going to laugh, and Ruth's eyes narrowed a bit.

"When they dress up and head out to the dance halls, I'll step in," he told her, still a hint of laughter in his voice.

Ruth looked at the girls, her eyes speaking volumes. The girls did not want to disappoint her and were about to say so, but she spoke first.

"We've never talked about such things. I

always assumed you knew, but now I'm going to ask. You do realize that such motions in front of men are completely improper?"

"Yes," Max said, and Lorri nodded in agreement.

"We won't dance anymore if you don't want us to, Mother," Lorri put in.

"So you don't have a problem with it, Lorri?" Ruth asked.

Lorri smiled a little. "I lived for four-and-a-half years on a cattle ranch in the middle of nowhere, Mother. Friday nights can be very long and lonely. Josie and I were just having fun. I wanted to have the same fun with Max."

Ruth had to admit that she hadn't looked at it in that light. Nevertheless, everyone could see she was in a quandary.

"I think your mother needs to work this out, girls," Dean put in. "And until she does . . ."

Both girls nodded, not needing their grandfather to finish. The groceries were put away and lunch was readied without another word on dancing. Lorri, however, had plenty on her mind. The whole episode with her mother had made her feel like a five-year-old, and she wasn't sure how she felt about that.

★ ★ ★

Rigg didn't make a move in their direction, but from the pew he'd chosen, his eyes followed the Archer family as they entered into church on Sunday. Rigg had visited this church in the past but had never seen the admiral. Right now he felt surprised speechless. The way they greeted others and made their way to a certain pew told him they were at home here.

Rigg liked this church, but he hadn't been stationed in the area long enough to get settled anywhere. His eyes studied the back of Lorraine Archer's head, and with a sideways quirk of his mouth, he wondered if this might be a church he should visit more often.

"I need to break our agreement," Max said to Arlene at lunchtime on Tuesday, not about to keep it to herself any longer.

"Okay," Arlene agreed. "What's up?"

"My sister saw the man who rescued her off the island."

"Where? Did he come to the house?"

"No, it was all by coincidence. His niece goes to the school where Raine works."

Arlene's mouth opened. "And they saw each other? Did they talk?"

Max nodded.

"Max," Arlene frowned. "That's not breaking the agreement."

"The next part is," Max leaned close and whispered. "She hopes she can see him again."

"Isn't he married?"

"No, what made you think that?"

"I don't know. I just assumed. Did she say what he was like?"

"She says he's dreamy. Raine never talks like that."

Arlene's hands came to her cheeks. She was so excited for Max's sister that she wanted to squeal, but they were in the lunchroom, and that wouldn't have worked at all.

"Well, this looks exciting," a familiar voice said. "You must be talking about me."

"Every moment, Johnny," Max said with mild sarcasm, watching him hide a smile.

He ate lunch with them often and was always amusing and a gentleman, but Max knew he wasn't the man for her. He knew how she spent every Sunday, but he never so much as asked about her faith in Christ. Max believed that if Johnny really wanted to get to know her, he knew how to go about it.

It was never her intent to play games with his heart. She did nothing to lead him on, even though he flirted outrageously with her most days. Max wasn't completely immune to it, but she worked hard. She had determined a long time ago not to let him work his way into her heart.

Today he was especially fun, and he looked great, but Max Archer was keeping her guard up at all times.

Lorri was doing it again. On Monday she'd done it; Tuesday too. Now Wednesday rolled around, the school day coming to an end, and Lorri wondered if the lieutenant would pick up his niece. And she didn't just wonder but once outside with the children took swift peeks behind her every few seconds.

And she wasn't sure why. Did she just want to look at him again? Did she hope that they could talk for a while? Did she hope to see interest in his eyes? It was all so confusing that it gave Lorri a headache, but still she thought about the lieutenant. And because of that, she wondered whether he thought about her.

"Miss Archer, I can't find my paper."

Lorri bent down to help the little boy at her side, and in the next instant, Violet Riggs' mother came for her.

Well, that answers one of my questions, Lorri thought, trying not to think about the rest.

271

★ ★ ★

"We're going to be grandparents," Cora told Ruth the moment Bible study was over.

"That's wonderful, Cora," Ruth said softly, matching her friend's tone. "Or is it?"

"I don't know." Cora sounded as confused as she felt. "At the risk of sounding selfish, I feel too young."

"You don't sound selfish, but this is new territory for you. Had it not been for the war, I could have been a grandmother a long time ago and feeling just like you."

"I never thought of that, Ruth. Josie and Ken would have been married years ago."

"I haven't dwelt on it, but it's come to mind more since Josie's death. I'm glad she didn't leave a child behind, Cora. Ken would do fine as a father — he'd be wonderful — but I hate it when children don't have their mothers."

"I'm sure that stems from your own childhood, Ruth. You know firsthand how hard it is."

Ruth nodded.

"What do you hear from your dad these days?"

"His legs aren't doing well. I'm hoping after Dean retires this summer that the two of us can drive back to Minnesota to see him. I don't think he'll ever make the trip out here again."

"Does Dean like the idea?"

"Yes, we've got it tentatively planned for the fall. It should be beautiful in Minnesota in the autumn."

The women were silent for just a moment. Ruth sat up a little straighter and looked at her friend.

"How did we get off on me? Now tell me everything! How is Janice feeling and when is this little person coming?"

Cora smiled at Ruth's enthusiasm and felt her own excitement rising. She gave her all the details, and when she was done, felt a little better. Getting out the catalog when she arrived home, Cora took a long time paging through baby clothes and furniture.

Lorri told herself to breathe, but she was finding it a bit hard. A week later — the next Friday — the lieutenant was coming toward her again. Lorri thought she should explain that he didn't have to park and walk over, he could just pull up to the curb, but then he'd be gone much faster, and Lorri discovered that she didn't want that at all.

"Uncle Donovan!"

He'd been spotted, and Lorri smiled as

his niece ran to assault him. Clearly they were fast friends. Lorri had two other children to get off, but when she turned back, Rigg was still standing there. It gave her no end of pleasure.

"How are you?" he asked.

"I'm doing well. How about yourself?"

"I'm glad it's the weekend."

"It's always nice, isn't it?"

"Very."

His gaze was so watchful that Lorri wondered if they were still talking about the weekend. She didn't want to read things that weren't there, but her heart was definitely acting up.

"My mother wrote you a letter," she suddenly confessed.

"Why did she do that?"

"Well, I think she wanted to thank you."

Rigg nodded, his eyes filled with understanding.

"We weren't sure where to mail it, and we forgot to ask my grandfather, so it's still sitting at home on the desk."

Rigg nodded, and Lorri told herself to hush.

"Did you want me to give you my address?"

"If you don't mind."

"I don't mind at all."

"I'll just get some paper from the room," Lorri said, starting that way.

"Miss Archer?"

"Yes, Violet."

"Do you still have to go to school?"

"Well, I stay a little longer and close things up, and then I go home."

The little girl walked beside her, as if she were headed back to class, and Lorri was aware that Rigg was somewhere behind them. She slipped into the room and grabbed the first piece of paper she could find. She handed it to Rigg, who had produced a pen and wrote out his address, his penmanship neat.

"This should take care of it. Please tell your mother that whenever she gets a chance to mail the letter, I'll look forward to reading it."

"I'll do that."

"Can we walk you to your car?"

"Well, I still have to close up."

"We can wait," Rigg offered, not at all in a hurry to leave.

"Well, actually," Lorri said, looking as flustered as she felt, "I walk."

"In that case, we'll give you a lift home."

"You don't have to do that. It's probably out of your way."

"If it's close enough for you to walk, it can't be much out of our way."

275

Lorri looked flustered again and found the lieutenant smiling. She assumed she looked like a blushing teenager, so she turned away to finish her work in the room. She didn't expect Violet to follow.

"You lock the windows?"

"Um hm. I check each one."

"I can't reach the windows."

"I think you'll be able to reach them before you know it. How old are you right now?"

"Six."

"When will you be seven?"

"In April."

"You see what I mean? You're almost seven, and that means you're a very big girl."

Violet smiled shyly but with great pleasure, and Rigg, watching from near the door, winked at the little girl when she looked his way.

"I have to check the other room, but I'll hurry."

"You don't need to hurry," Rigg said calmly, and Lorri stopped rushing to look up at him. She hadn't realized how closely she'd come to stand in front of him or that he was so much taller than she was. Rigg's face gave nothing away, but Lorri felt herself blushing. She stepped back and slipped out the door, Violet on her heels.

"Do you help the second-grade room get closed too?"

"Yes," Lorri said, glad for the distraction. Hoping she hadn't forgotten any details, Lorri closed up that room, checked all locks, and gathered her sweater and handbag. Trying not to appear as rushed as she felt, she presented herself ready to go, Violet still at her side.

"All set?"

"Yes, thank you for waiting."

"It's our pleasure, isn't it, Vi?"

The little girl only smiled at him as she wasn't sure what he meant. Lorri hung back a little, following the two of them to a 1935 Ford.

"Oh," Lorri said without thought. "It's your car."

"Whose car did you think it would be?"

"I thought it might be one from the base."

Rigg's smile started slowly but grew very wide.

"Spoken like a woman who lives with an admiral."

Lorri laughed, hoping she wouldn't blush again.

"In you go," he said to Violet but waited with seemingly all the patience in the world for Lorri to sit down in the front seat.

The ride was made in near silence. Lorri

gave directions, but there was no small talk. Lorri turned in her seat to say goodbye to the little girl in the back. She slipped out before Rigg could come around and help her.

"Thank you for the ride," Lorri said through the open window on her side.

"You're welcome." Rigg had bent to see her face.

Lorri waited until they pulled away and waved once more. She walked to the house, not sure her feet were touching the ground.

Sixteen

"Oh, it's you, Lorri. Did I hear a car?"

"Yes," Lorri answered her mother, still in a bit of shock. "Lieutenant Riggs gave me a ride home."

Ruth stopped the mixing bowl and looked at her daughter.

"I told him about your letter, and he gave me his address." Lorri held out the paper.

Ruth took the paper and studied it for just a moment. Her eyes were soon back on her daughter.

"How did this come about?"

"Well, he came to get Violet again and then stayed to talk. He then offered to walk me to my car, and I had to tell him I walked."

"That was certainly kind of him."

"It was, wasn't it?"

Ruth watched her face.

279

"You look a little disoriented."

Lorri shrugged a little. "I think I spent the whole time blushing like I was guilty of something. I don't know what he must have thought."

"And do you care what he thinks?"

"I do, Mother!" she burst out, her arms coming up and every bit of frustration showing on her face. "There's something about him that draws me. I can't hardly think when he's looking at me!"

"Does he spend a lot of time looking at you?"

"My eyes, yes." She was calming a little. "I can hardly look away."

"And so you blush?"

"Yes."

Ruth could see the obvious. She found herself begging God to lead and direct in this situation. She wanted Lorri to find someone, but the mystery of who that would be and what it would all look like was a little scary.

"What are you thinking?" Lorri wanted to know.

"Just praying that we'll all be wise, especially you."

"Do you not trust me about this, like with the dancing thing?"

Ruth looked confused and then surprised.

"It wasn't a trust issue, Lorri. Is that the way I made you feel?"

"A little bit. I felt like a child, sort of ashamed of myself and the good time I had with Josie."

"That was not my intent, and I'm sorry it seemed that way. I do have an issue with today's dances, and it was a huge shock to see you and Max bouncing around. If I'd stopped and thought, I'd have realized it was in the privacy of our home. But it was never about trust. I trust you completely."

"Even in this?"

"This is the hardest time to keep your head," Ruth went on, thinking very clearly now. "When our emotions get involved, they can run away with us. If I see that happening, I'll be coming to you about it, but it won't be because I don't trust you. It will be out of concern, to make sure you are seeing everything clearly. Does that make sense?"

"Yes. I'm glad I talked to you. But I just realized something."

"What's that?"

"I have no idea if I'll even see him again."

Ruth stood for a moment in indecision, not sure if she should say what was on her mind.

"What does that look mean?"

"Do you really want to know?"

"Yes."

"You'll see him again, Lorri. I think you'll see him quite a bit."

Lorri felt a frisson of fear race through her, but it was followed by another emotion: pure, undisguised delight.

"There's a letter for you, Max," Ruth said just before dinner. "It's from Sears."

Max didn't rush. If a letter came and not a package, it probably wasn't good news. She opened it slowly and read swiftly.

"Everything I ordered is sold out!"

"Everything?" Ruth clarified.

"Yes!" Max sounded more than a little disgusted. "What am I going to do?"

"We'll have to try the shops here in town," Ruth suggested.

"We'll pay a lot more." Max was still out of sorts.

Lorri didn't say anything, but she wasn't happy with her sister. They had just come away from the war. Men had died, children were left fatherless, families had split, and Max was unhappy because she couldn't have the clothing she wanted. It was all Lorri could do to keep her mouth shut. She set the table in silence, and when her grandfather came from the kitchen carrying a big pot of stew, he noticed her face. He'd also heard the complaints of his youngest grandchild.

The four gathered around the table and bowed their heads. Dean took a moment, weighing his words, and began to pray.

"Father in heaven, we thank You for the food that Ruth prepared tonight. We thank You for all of her hard work. Thank You for the roof over our heads and the clothes on our backs. Help us not to fall into discontent. Help us not to forget all of Your goodness and to see our blessings. In the name of Your Son Jesus, we pray. Amen."

Bowls were passed and filled with stew. Biscuits and butter made the rounds. The silence went unbroken. Ruth was opening her mouth to ask Lorri to tell everyone about her afternoon when Max spoke.

"I'm sorry I was so selfish about the clothes." She glanced at her grandfather. "I fell into discontent."

Dean smiled at her, thanking God for her tender, sensitive heart.

"Why do you suppose we do that?" he asked her.

"I think it's just what you said, Grandpa. We forget all of God's goodness."

"I think you're right, Max."

Get a hold of yourself, Ruth Archer! was the

silent conversation at the other end of the table. *You're still thinking about Lorri and the lieutenant, and you didn't even notice your other daughter's attitude.*

"How was your day, Raine?" Max suddenly asked.

"Interesting," Lorri said with a smile.

"Tell us!"

"Well, a certain lieutenant came to get his niece again. They gave me a ride home."

Max's open mouth and huge eyes were hysterical.

"I don't think he proposed, Max," Dean said mildly, laughter in his voice.

"It doesn't matter. Raine wanted to see him again, and she did."

Both Ruth and Dean looked to the oldest.

"Is that true, Lorri?" Dean questioned. "Did you hope to see Lieutenant Riggs again?"

"Yes, I did," she stated simply, not angry at Max for sharing. "I'm not sure why, but I did."

"I think I know why," her grandfather surprised them by saying.

Lorri looked at him and waited.

"Well, for starters, he very recently played a pretty important role in your life, plus he's a believer. He's also a gentleman, and I don't think anyone would call him ugly."

Lorri was quiet as she tried to process these words. Yes, she knew he was a believer, and that was the most important fact, but her grandfather had really put his finger on it. The lieutenant was on the island with her. He was the only person in her life right now who could remotely understand what it had been like.

For some reason Lorri desperately wanted to talk to him about that time, but she pictured herself asking and knew it would never work. Not to mention the fact that even if he was willing to speak with her about it, she was sure to cry. She didn't want that at all.

"I think we lost her," Lorri heard Max say. She snapped back to attention.

"Sorry," she said, going back to her stew.

"Did I upset you?" Dean asked.

"No, but you're right. He did play a big part in my life, and I realized that I would love to talk to him about that."

"Maybe you can."

"No," Lorri shook her head with complete certainty. "Asking him would be nothing short of humiliating, and I'm sure to lose my composure."

Dean let it drop. Ruth looked at him and saw that the wheels were turning, but she knew Lorri missed this.

The four finished dinner and then worked together on the dishes. Dean settled himself next to the radio, and the women all joined him. They stayed up way too late but were also up early on Saturday morning. Dean thought a drive to the coast would be fun. The women were all game.

Rigg almost hadn't come. He felt guilty for liking a church for the wrong reasons and then realized that if the admiral went to this church, it must have something going for it. All of that, however, slipped from his mind as he watched Lorraine Archer walk to the front and stand behind the pulpit. The pianist played the opening chords for the song, and Lorri began to sing.

In an instant Rigg was swept back to the island and then aboard the *Every Storm*, where his men would stop in their tracks upon hearing her voice. The words of the song were somewhat lost on him as he remembered those times.

A rather tall gentleman occupied the pew in front of him, so Rigg didn't think Lorri saw him, and for some reason this was a relief. He remembered Friday when she seemed at a loss in his presence, and he certainly didn't want to do anything to interrupt her song.

She finished — Rigg having barely caught the words — and returned to her seat. Pastor Higgins thanked her for sharing and then asked the congregation to open their Bibles to the book of Matthew. Rigg forced his mind to the verses at hand.

Rigg looked around the canteen and spotted Hugh Westland. He headed toward his table and took a seat, knowing he'd be welcome.

The men spoke of Hugh's recent assignment and Rigg's plans to be done with the Navy at the end of June. The men from the boat came up, and Hugh had some new information on Ellis and his cancer surgery.

"I saw Lorraine Archer recently," Rigg stated calmly after some minutes of concentrating on their lunches, effectively bringing Hugh's head up from his soup.

"Where was this?"

"She works at my niece's school," he answered, not in a hurry to mention the way she sang in church.

"How was she?"

"She seemed to be doing fine."

Hugh watched him. The lieutenant was one of the most respectable men he'd met in all of the navy. Hugh had never seen him looking at pin-up magazines, nor had he allowed such pictures in their cabin of the *Every Storm.* Nevertheless, there had been something in the lieutenant's voice that caught his attention.

"How did she look?" Hugh asked.

Rigg couldn't quite contain his smile. "She looks good."

Hugh had a smile of his own. He didn't know why he knew this, but *she looks good* was a vast understatement. The lieutenant had this woman on his mind. He'd be willing to put money on that.

"What are you smiling at?" Rigg asked him.

"You."

"Why?"

"You've got Miss Archer, granddaughter of Admiral Dean Archer, on your mind. Don't bother to tell me you don't."

Rigg opened his mouth and closed it again.

Hugh's smile only grew wider.

"How are you, Lieutenant?" Dean asked after the man had saluted him and Dean had answered.

"I'm well, sir."

"Lorri tells me you gave her a ride home last week."

"I did, sir. I hope you didn't have any objections."

"No, it's fine."

Dean stood quietly for a moment. Thinking about this and doing it was proving harder than he expected. Nevertheless, he plunged in.

"Do you ever think much about the island and Lorri's rescue?"

"I do sometimes. It wasn't a very good time for her."

"No, it wasn't. She's told us quite a bit, but her mother and sister and I can't really picture it all."

Rigg nodded, not certain what to say to this.

"If the chance presented itself, would you ever be willing to talk to Lorri about the island and such?"

"Certainly, sir," Rigg agreed without hesitation. "Anytime you wish."

"Well, that's just it. I can't think that Lorri would appreciate my setting it up, but there might come a time when it would work itself out."

Rigg didn't pretend to know what he was talking about. He nodded slowly, but his face was confused.

"I have the strong impression that if my daughter-in-law saw you at church, she would invite you to dinner."

Understanding dawned.

"I would enjoy that, sir," Rigg said simply,

thinking about the short but kind note he had received from Mrs. Ruth Archer.

"Well, then," the admiral said, clearly done. "Maybe we'll see you Sunday."

"Yes, sir."

Rigg saluted and was dismissed to go on his way. He didn't have anything pressing, but he found himself walking rather fast. His brain, however, was moving faster, still trying to make complete sense of the conversation he'd just had.

"How about this, Max?" Ruth held up a short-sleeved blouse in a check pattern, but her daughter didn't look too thrilled.

The Archer women were in Brennan's Department Store. Max needed some lightweight clothing for spring and summer, but her tastes had changed of late, and nothing much appealed to her. Lorri had the only solution.

"Try this," she said, not asking, but telling.

"I don't know, Raine."

Lorri pushed it at her, and Max went reluctantly into the changing room. Lorri stood right outside the door and waited for her to emerge.

"Is it on?"

By way of an answer, Max emerged in a

spring dress that was beautiful on her. It was made in pastel gingham, and the ruffles and rickrack had not been spared.

Lorri smiled in satisfaction, and Max made a face at her.

"Oh, Max," her mother said. "That's so cute on you."

"I found another one," Lorri offered. This one was a darker gingham with a pinafore styling that Max liked on sight.

And so it went. Lorri and Ruth each found a new blouse, but it was Max's wardrobe that was helped the most. Lorri spotted some shoes just as they were leaving, and she bought them because they were a perfect size and fit.

Somewhat laden down with boxes and bags, the women headed for home. Ruth looked at her girls' satisfied faces and had only one comment.

"Wait until your grandfather sees what we spent."

"I don't know if you should have worn that dress," Arlene said the moment she saw Max at school Friday morning.

"What's wrong? Do I have a tear?" Max bent her head to examine herself.

"No, there's nothing wrong, if you get my meaning."

But Max didn't get her meaning. She stared at Arlene until she heard the voice she heard every day at school.

"Well, now, Maxine. A new dress, and looking better than ever."

Max and Arlene exchanged looks before Max turned to Johnny King.

"I hope you were thinking of me when you bought it," Johnny said, smiling down at Max, mustering all the charm he could manage.

"I don't think I was, Johnny."

"Well, no matter. You don't have to do anything to get my attention. You already have it."

"I have to get to class," Max said, starting that way.

"I'll walk you," Johnny offered.

Max didn't try to persuade him one way or the other, but she thought back to the first month of school when Johnny had done this very thing. Never in her wildest dreams did she think he would still be pursuing her.

For the third Friday in a row, Lorri watched Rigg come toward her. It was much like the week before when Violet spotted him. Rigg lifted her for a hug and a kiss, but neither one seemed in any hurry to leave. The children were all seen off, and Lorri turned to find the twosome waiting for her.

"How are you?" she was the first to ask, telling herself she was not going to talk too much or get flustered.

"I'm fine. And yourself?"

"I'm doing fine."

"I got your mother's letter. It was very nice of her."

"Somehow I think she would say that of you."

It was happening again. They were running out of words and ended up staring at each other.

"Do you have to close up today?" Rigg asked at last.

"Yes."

"Well, we'll go with you, won't we, Vi?"

Lorri smiled down at the little girl so she wouldn't have to look at Rigg and once again found the child by her side.

"I got this wrong on my paper." Violet showed Lorri the lesson when she was back in the first room closing windows and cupboard doors.

"Let me see," Lorri said, hunkering down to look.

"It got marked in red," Violet explained.

"I see that. What letter is this, Violet?"

Lorri asked, having guessed the problem in an instant.

"It's an E."

"What letter does it look like?"

Violet studied it. "An F."

"I think so too. I think that might be the reason it's marked."

"I needed to give him bigger shoes."

"That's right. And next time you'll know."

Rigg, standing again near the door, felt his heart swell in his chest. Something was happening to him. He did not fall in and out of love with the dawning of each new day. Being attracted to a woman enough to want to see her again was new to him. Watching Lorri Archer, seeing her kind ways and sweet temperament, made him wish he could see her each and every day.

Waiting in silence for Lorri and Violet to finish, Rigg remembered the words of the admiral. He knew that now was not the time to ask her about the island, but he wished he could. She had suffered a terrible loss. Was she doing all right? Or was this job just to help take her mind from the matter?

Rigg's mind stopped. He had questions certainly, but no guarantees that she would welcome such inquiries from him. In fact, she tended to blush a bit in his presence.

"We're all done." Lorri was suddenly at

his side. "Thank you, Violet, for helping me."

"You're welcome."

"It was good to see you, Lieutenant," Lorri began, already moving away from them.

"Do you have a car today?" he asked.

Lorri stopped, not wanting to admit that she didn't.

"It's a nice day for walking, don't you think?" Lorri asked.

"It is a nice day, but it's a nice day for a ride too."

Lorri hesitated, not wanting to take advantage or have expectations.

She didn't know it, but he'd already heard from her grandfather that the ride had not been a problem. For that reason, he pressed her, not worrying about the consequences.

"I certainly don't know firsthand, but I would imagine that you get plenty of exercise on the job."

Lorri didn't comment.

"It is Friday, and your feet might be ready for a bit of a rest."

"If you're sure it's no trouble."

"It's trouble free."

Lorri still didn't look overly convinced, but Violet suddenly took her hand.

"You can come with us," she said simply.

Rigg had to hide the pleasure he felt inside. In the face of the little girl's simple statement, Lorri said nothing more.

Again the ride was very quiet. Violet had a question, but Lorri said next to nothing. Rigg, however, was faster once they reached the Archers' driveway. He was at Lorri's door before she could even move, opening it, and standing aside to let her pass.

"Thank you, Lieutenant." She was on the pavement. "I really do appreciate it."

"You're very welcome."

Something in his tone made Lorri look at him. Their eyes held just long enough to make Lorri blush.

"I hope you have a good weekend," Rigg said gently, trying to rescue her.

"Thank you."

Lorri went to the door. She forgot to say goodbye to Violet or even to wave.

Her mother met her inside. She took one look at her daughter's face and knew exactly whose car she had heard in the driveway.

Seventeen

Saturday found Lorri and Ruth working in the garden. Muffin thought it was all for her benefit and was continually in Lorri's way, but Lorri was patient and moved her gently aside, drawing rapturous purrs from her each and every time.

"You didn't say much about your ride home last night," Ruth commented at one point, having wanted to ask for hours.

"There wasn't much to say. It was like last week."

"He asked and you accepted?"

"Well, I guess he had to sort of talk me into it this time."

"Why was that?"

"I don't know. I don't have a thought in my head when he's around, and I just think he must feel a little sorry for me. I don't want him to offer because he finds me rather pathetic."

Lorri weeded around a group of snapdragons, and Ruth worked on the border of the lawn. The conversation, however, was far from over.

"Lorri?" Ruth called her daughter's name, having taken a moment to think it out. "Is that really how it seems to you? I mean, I haven't met this man, but I've never gotten the impression that he would be kind to you out of pity."

Lorri had to think about that. Where all this insecurity had come from she didn't know, but it plagued her. "I guess that doesn't really fit who he is, but I will say this much: Talking to Violet is ten times easier than talking to the lieutenant."

"I would imagine so."

"Why is that, Mother?" Lorri's voice held a hint of frustration.

"Children are so easy, Lorri. They're humble and guileless. We can learn so much from children."

"Like just being who you really are?"

"Yes, that among many other things."

Lorri thought about her mother's words for a long time. She didn't know when she would see the lieutenant again, but she was going to stop worrying about what he thought and just be the person she was.

"I feel like it's all my fault," a tearful Cora told Ruth. "I wasn't all that excited about becoming a grandmother, and now Janice has had a miscarriage. They wanted this baby so much."

"That was just in the beginning, Cora. You haven't felt that way for a while now."

"But I was still so selfish."

Cora broke down then, and Ruth stayed close. She was in her friend's living room, hoping to find some way to offer comfort and support. But in the middle of Cora's words, Ruth thought about the different faces of grief. An unmet child, still taking form in its mother's body, was just as loved as the full-grown daughter she had lost.

Leonard came in from the garage just then. He had not heard the news. Ruth slipped away to the kitchen and started a pot of coffee. She stood next to the stove, watching it brew up into the lid, and began to pray, tears unheeded on her cheeks.

If I didn't believe that You were in control of all, I don't know what I would do. I love You, Father. I love that You love us so completely and that You always know what's best. Cora needed to be more thankful — she knows that — but please comfort her, Lord. Help her in this grief. Help her to trust You for another day and another child.

Ruth cut off when she heard movement behind her. Leonard had come to the kitchen. He got mugs down from the cupboard and brought the cream from the refrigerator.

"This was kind of you, Ruth," he said simply, preparing a cup of coffee for his wife.

Ruth didn't comment, but Leonard still looked at her.

"You know all about grief, don't you?" he said.

Feeling helpless, Ruth shrugged a little.

"It doesn't matter, does it?" Leonard went on. "A tiny unborn person or a grown daughter — it's still so painful."

"I was just thinking that same thing."

Leonard smiled at her. "Join us with your cup, Ruth."

"Thank you, Leonard," she said, watching him head back to the living room. She did fix her own cup and returned to her friends, thankful to be there. When all three were settled in the living room, Leonard began to pray.

"What's the matter?" Max asked when Lorri suddenly grabbed her arm.

"He's here!" Lorri said, her voice low, even though the service was over.

"Who's here?" Max said and then realized. "Where? Where is he?"

"Coming this way," Lorri got out just before Rigg slipped into the empty pew ahead of them, stayed standing, and greeted them.

"Hello, Miss Archer."

"Hello, Lieutenant. How are you?"

"I'm fine," Rigg answered, smiling and wondering how many times their conversations would start this way. His eyes darted to the younger woman beside Lorri, and Lorri caught it.

"This is my sister, Maxine. Max, this is Lieutenant Riggs."

Both women stood, and Max put her hand out to shake the lieutenant's.

"It's nice to meet you, Lieutenant."

"Do you prefer Max or Maxine?" Rigg asked, deciding to cut all formality.

"Max," that young woman told him, smiling at his relaxed manner.

"Max it is," Rigg said, thinking that she was as beautiful as her sister. "Are you by any chance still in high school?"

"I'm a senior."

"I have a brother who's a junior."

"Does he go to Harmony Hills?"

"No, most of my family lives up north in Santa Rosa."

Lorri hadn't known that and found herself listening closely. Max was relaxed with the lieutenant, and Lorri wished her heart was not pounding so hard, a pounding that only grew worse when she spotted her mother across the way. She knew what she must do and waited only for a lull in the conversation to do it.

"Lieutenant?" Lorri began.

Rigg turned to her immediately, almost as if he'd been waiting for her to address him.

"Yes."

"Would you mind terribly if I introduced my mother to you? I know she would wish to meet you."

"I would be happy to meet your mother," he said with all the kindness he could muster. She was looking very strained over the question — far worse than Friday afternoon — and he felt almost desperate to put her at ease.

"She's talking to someone right now, but maybe if you —" Lorri floundered to a halt.

"I'm in no hurry." Rigg understood the unspoken words. "I can wait as long as you like."

Lorri glanced over to find Max watching her. The younger girl gave her a sympathetic smile, and Lorri knew she looked as lost and flustered as she felt. She knew nothing but relief when Rigg began a conversation with Max again.

It took some minutes, but Ruth finally came their way. Many folks had cleared out, and Lorri was glad for that. Lorri watched as her mother approached and saw the very moment when she spotted the man in uniform. Her eyes darted to her daughter, who spoke right up.

"Mother, I want you to meet someone," Lorri began, letting her mother get a little closer. "Mother, this is Lieutenant Riggs, the gentleman who rescued me from the island. Lieutenant, this is my mother, Ruth Archer."

"It's a pleasure to meet you, Mrs. Archer. Thank you for the note."

Ruth had shaken his hand, but she didn't let go. Tears she could not control filled her eyes. Rigg stood patiently, his eyes respectful and not darting away.

"I'm sorry," Ruth whispered.

"It's all right," Rigg assured her, wishing there was some way for her to know it truly was.

"Are you all right, Ruth?" Dean had come up, and his voice was just what Ruth needed. She nodded, let the lieutenant reclaim his hand, and took a moment to compose herself. Still, she was not going to let this opportunity pass.

"Lieutenant Riggs," Ruth jumped in without letting herself think too much. "Are you by any chance free for dinner this Friday evening? We're going to barbecue chicken on the grill if that sounds good to you."

"It sounds delicious. What time would you like me to come?"

"Any time after 5:30. We'll probably eat at 6:00."

"I'll plan on that."

The family said their goodbyes then, Rigg speaking to everyone but Lorri. For her he waited until last, stopping and catching her eye.

"I'll see you Friday."

"Okay." Lorri nodded and managed a small smile. She moved off with her family, asking herself if he meant Friday afternoon or evening. And then she realized it didn't matter. Friday was just five days away.

"She's going to marry him, isn't she?"

Ruth was changing her clothes before starting on lunch but turned from her closet to look at her youngest daughter, who had taken up residence on the bed.

"I don't know, Max."

Max looked at her mother, desperate for answers, and Ruth sat down on the bed, telling herself that lunch could wait.

"What is it you're thinking, Max?"

"He's wonderful," Max said simply. "And he looks at her, Mother, you know, in that special way. He's unbelievably kind; I've never met anyone so kind. I guess Ken is kind too," Max said as an afterthought. "I think that's why Jo loved him, and that's probably why Raine will love the lieutenant."

Ruth just listened. She didn't know what to think, but she certainly understood what Max was talking about. She had stood holding his hand — a total stranger — and then she had cried. His eyes had never left her face. As if he'd been ordered to do so, he stood still and waited for her to make the next move.

"What did you think of him?" Max asked.

"He seems to be very special, but your sister isn't quite at ease, Max, and that's why I'm not going to start looking for wedding dress patterns."

"You should have seen her before you came over. I've never known her to be like that. She was so nervous, but when he looked at her . . ." Max searched for the words. "He was just so sweet and patient and kind! I don't know how else to say it."

But Ruth didn't need to hear it any other way. She knew just what Max had seen. The lieutenant's face flashed through her mind, swiftly followed by her daughter's. Ruth knew the least she could do was pray; in fact, that was the most she could do as well.

"Was I seeing things, or did you seem a little flustered around the lieutenant?"

"You weren't seeing things, Grandpa," Lorri had to admit, starting lunch when her mother didn't come from upstairs. "I'm nervous around him, and I'm not sure why."

"Would it help if the two of you could talk about your rescue?"

"I don't know, but at any rate, that's not likely to happen."

"I wouldn't bank on that," Dean said boldly, not ready to tell her what he'd done. "I'm asking God to give you that opportunity. I think it's just what you need."

Lorri turned to look at him, the salad fixings momentarily forgotten.

"Why do you feel it's so important?"

"It could have been any boat to stop at that island, but it wasn't. It was the *Every Storm*. The skipper could have been married with three kids, but he wasn't. He was a single man who shares our faith in Christ and who now seems interested in my granddaughter.

"None of those things are a coincidence, Lorri. I'm not saying we should book the church, but you and Rigg have some type of future together. Maybe it's only to talk about the island and what that was like for you, but this man is not out of our lives just yet."

Lorri hadn't thought about it that way. It was true that she would like to discuss the island. It came to mind often, and she was tired of pushing it away for fear of mentioning it and upsetting her family, not to mention she would like to hear the lieutenant's side of the story. She was not herself during that time. What could he tell her that she might have missed? What had he thought of the whole ordeal?

Previously the thought of speaking to him about the island caused her to blush in her tracks, but not now. Now she wanted to talk to the lieutenant about it. She wanted to know what he thought.

"Well, Donovan." Dorothy Riggs greeted her brother-in-law with pleasant surprise and a hug just as they sat down to Sunday dinner. "Come in. Have you eaten?"

"No, but don't feel like you have to feed me."

"We have plenty."

"Hey, Donovan," Jim greeted him. "Have a seat."

Donovan did so as soon as he hugged Violet and pressed a kiss to William's small brow.

"How was church?" Jim asked.

"Good. We're still in Matthew. How about you?"

"One of our missionaries is in town, so he spoke this morning."

"Violet mentioned that you gave someone a ride home again on Friday," Dorothy wasted no time in saying.

"That's true," Rigg said, smiling a little. "She's a bang-up little reporter."

"I give her cookies," Dorothy replied cheekily, causing her husband and brother-in-law to laugh.

"Well, as a matter of fact," Rigg continued, "that's part of the reason I'm here. I'm going to the Archers' for dinner on Friday night."

"She invited you?"

"Her mother did. I'm sure it's her way of thanking me."

"What do you think Lorri thought of that?"

"I don't know. She's so nervous around me that I can't quite read her."

Dorothy, who had been ready to make all kinds of suggestions about the future, was struck with compassion. This woman, Lorraine Archer, had been through an awful lot.

"Are you willing to give her time?" Jim suddenly asked, causing both Dorothy and Rigg to look at him.

"If you recall, Ralph met Elsie under uncomfortable circumstances," he continued, speaking of their cousin. "And Ralph had to move pretty slowly during courtship."

"I'd forgotten about that," Rigg said, thinking that Ralph would say it had been worth every moment. He and Elsie were very much in love, their first child due in the summer.

"I have time," Violet said quietly, and the adults realized that she'd been hearing every word.

"I'm glad to hear that," Rigg told her, "because right after lunch we can play a game or go outside. What do you think of that?"

The adoration that always showed in the first grader's eyes for her Uncle Donovan only deepened. The adults knew the conversation was over. And that was probably for the best.

"Do you think we could be any lazier?" Ruth asked of the girls, covering a yawn at the same time. All three of them lounged around the family room and shared the newspaper. Dean was sound asleep in his chair, oblivious to them all.

"Listen to this," Max said, reading from an article. "It says here that an honest army vet paid $20,000 in taxes after winning in a crap game. He'd won $53,000."

"That was honest," Ruth commented.

"Why do you suppose we're so surprised by that?" Lorri asked. "Why don't we expect people to be honest?"

Her mother and sister didn't have an answer. Lorri went back to the Sunday funnies, but her thoughts remained on honesty. If she had been forced to be honest about wanting to see more of the lieutenant, could she have been? She wasn't sure. Considering she rarely put two intelligent words together in his presence, he was being exceptionally patient.

"The funnies are supposed to make you laugh, not frown."

Lorri looked over to find Max smiling at her. Lorri shook her head, much like her mother was wont to do.

"I was thinking about what a bumbling

idiot I am around the lieutenant. Friday night is sure to be delightful." Lorri didn't bother to veil her sarcasm.

"It won't be like that."

"I wish I could believe you, Max. You saw me this morning."

"But the more time you spend with him, the better it will be."

"I don't know if there will be *more time* after Friday night."

"I do."

Lorri looked at her tolerantly.

"Raine." Her sister's voice was the most patient she'd ever heard. "You're going to fall in love with him."

"That may very well be, but it helps when both people are in love."

"He's going to fall too. He won't be able to help himself."

"I wish I shared your confidence."

"You don't have to. Just ask me, and I'll keep telling you what to do."

Ruth loved this. She laughed so hard that Dean shifted in his sleep. The girls started to laugh at their mother but didn't want to wake their grandfather. By silent agreement, everyone went back to the newspaper.

The phone rang that night in Rigg's room not many minutes after he returned from church. The admiral, Lorri, and Max had attended the service, but there had been no sign of Mrs. Archer.

Rigg got to the phone on the fifth ring, assuming that Dorothy was calling to ask him to watch the kids sometime that week. He was wrong. It was his mother.

"Dorothy wrote to me," she wasted no time in saying. "Is there something you want to tell me?"

Rigg had to laugh. "Hello, Mom."

"Well?" Her voice was full of teasing. "Who is this girl?"

"Dorothy didn't fill you in?" he teased right back.

"No, she just asked if I had talked to my son lately. She hinted that there might be a female in his life."

"A female, yes. In my life, not quite."

"Can you tell me about it?" Virginia Riggs asked, this time very serious.

"It's rather unbelievable, but the woman I rescued off that island lives here in Harmony Hills. She works at Violet's school."

"What are the odds of that?"

"I don't know, but I never dreamt I would see her again."

"What is her name — I can't recall if you told me."

"Lorraine Archer."

"How is she doing?"

"I think well. We haven't talked past generalities, but when I met her mother in church on Sunday, I was invited to dinner Friday."

"Are you going?"

"Yes. I'm looking forward to it."

"You wrote that you were trying another church closer to the base. Is that the church?"

"Yes. I just got home."

"Did you see Lorraine and her family tonight?"

"Not to speak to, and I didn't see her mother."

"How is it going at the new church?"

"I like it. The preaching from the Word is very sound. Pastor Higgins addresses the men a lot. It's convicting, but it reminds me of the church there at home."

"I'm glad to hear it."

Rigg heard a small commotion on the other end, and then his mother came back on.

"Your father wants to talk to you. I'll write this week."

"Okay."

"I love you."

"I love you too."

Rigg spent a few minutes with his father,

keeping it brief but glad to have talked to them both. He thought about their conversation for a while. A few words from Dorothy in a letter, and his mother makes a phone call. It must have shook her up a bit.

Rigg smiled at the thought. He would write this week as well, but there wasn't a whole lot to report. He could see the words in his head.

I've met a woman I want to get to know. At times she seems terrified of me. Her grandfather is an admiral. At times I'm terrified of him. If we ever get over our fears, I'll write more.

"Max?" Arlene said for the third time, finally reaching out and touching her friend's hand.

"What?"

"I've been calling your name."

"Oh, sorry."

"You've been distracted all day."

"I'm sorry," Max said again but didn't elaborate.

"What's up?"

Max looked as indecisive as she felt. After a moment she sighed.

"For two girls who have sworn off boys, we sure manage to talk about them enough."

"Is that what this is about?" Arlene made a face. She'd been ready to have boys back in her life for weeks, but Max had not gone along.

"Not about me. It's about Raine."

"Tell me."

Max did, sharing the way their mother had invited the lieutenant to dinner.

"Tonight?" Arlene clarified. "He's coming tonight? No wonder you're distracted."

"I keep thinking about Raine. I don't want her to be embarrassed or anything."

Arlene had been on the verge of asking all about this man, but she held off. Max's sad, distracted face was about her sister, and for these two friends, that was no joking matter.

"We'll pray, Max," Arlene encouraged her.

"What will we pray?"

Arlene remembered something from the sermon the week before.

"That all hearts will be humble."

Max felt as though a weight had suddenly been lifted. Her grandfather had told her at one time that worry was a prideful thing. *We want to be in charge, and when we can't be, we worry. We need to humble ourselves before God and let Him have His way.*

"Thanks, Arlene," Max said with heartfelt honesty. She spent the rest of the day asking God to give them humble hearts during dinner. Each time she started to worry, she confessed it and thought of something else. She was able to report to Arlene at the end of the day that it had gone very well.

Eighteen

"You're here," Lorri said quietly.

"Where am I supposed to be?" Rigg asked, having already hugged and kissed his niece, who was now playing with a small ball she'd pulled from the pocket of her dress.

"I just didn't think I would see you until tonight."

Rigg nodded thoughtfully, trying to gauge if she was pleased or disappointed.

"You don't have to keep doing this," Lorri said, her voice not uncertain anymore. "I truly do not expect you to give me a ride home each Friday."

Rigg smiled, wondering what that had cost her.

"You're laughing at me, aren't you?"

"I'm not." Rigg swiftly schooled his features. "I just don't think I've heard you be so firm before."

"I didn't mean to sound bossy, but I think you feel some sort of obligation. And I don't want you to."

"So if I don't feel obligated, will you be all right with my giving you a ride?"

Lorri had to weigh that one and finally asked, "You think I still need to be rescued, don't you?"

"No, I don't. I can see how capable and strong you are, but I can't see any reason to let you walk home if I'm free to drive you. If I don't pick Vi up or I don't have time to go your way, I won't be able to give you a lift. So far that hasn't been the case."

"You don't feel sorry for me?" she asked the first thing that came to mind.

Rigg laughed. "Why would I feel sorry for you?"

Lorri frowned at him, trying to cover her own smile.

"I don't know," she stated, "but I'm done with this conversation now, and I'm going to close up the rooms."

"All right," Rigg said with a huge sigh, falling in behind her. "I guess I'll come along and feel sorry for you that you still have work to do."

Lorri's hand came to her mouth, but not before Rigg saw the smile. She was covering laughter, and they both knew it.

"Miss Archer?" Violet called, running to catch up.

Lorri turned to her in relief. She had to escape the lieutenant's probing eyes.

"Yes, Violet."

"Are you going to ride with us today?"

"Yes, I am. Are you going to help me with the classrooms?"

"Yes."

"We're such a good team!" Lorri took the little girl's hand and led her away.

Rigg couldn't help but think of his mother. He knew if she could see Lorri Archer's way with her granddaughter, she would fall in love with this woman. Rigg knew something else: He was headed there himself.

"More potato salad, Lieutenant?"

"Yes, please. Thank you, Mrs. Archer."

The five of them were on the patio. It had been swept and cleaned, and the meal they enjoyed at the picnic table was delicious.

A low, mournful howl sounded from the garage door that led to the backyard, and Max looked that way.

"He'll survive," her grandfather reassured her dryly, not even taking his eyes from his plate.

Max glanced at the lieutenant and smiled shyly when he smiled at her.

"What's your dog's name?" he asked.

"Buddy, and he's really Grandpa's dog."

"But he knows you're a soft touch," Rigg guessed.

"Oh, my," Ruth put in. "He certainly figured that out in a hurry."

Max bent over her food, not wanting to admit to anything.

"Did you grow up in California, Lieutenant?" Ruth asked.

"In Santa Rosa, yes. My folks and my brother who still lives at home are there."

"What brought you to southern California?"

"The war. I enlisted after Pearl Harbor."

Conversation moved around the table after that. Rigg had questions for the admiral, and Ruth and Max had questions for Rigg, but Lorri did not contribute. She was attentive but couldn't make any words come out of her mouth.

Rigg was about to give up hope that she would ever be comfortable around him, but then the meal was finished and he found himself alone with Lorri. They had taken comfortable seats on the patio, and for a moment it was quiet. Her family was inside getting coffee and dessert ready. For a moment she wished she'd gone with them, but then she began to think about his family and wondered about Violet's father.

"How many brothers did you say you have?"

"Two. One married — that's Vi's father — and the youngest is still in high school."

"Are you the oldest?"

"No, I'm the middle." Rigg had been looking at her, but her eyes had been on the yard. "How about you? Was Josephine older or younger?"

"She was older. I'm the middle one too."

This time Lorri glanced his way, but her eyes soon went back to the grass her grandfather would probably be cutting in the morning.

Rigg watched her for a few minutes but didn't want to be caught staring. She was a little more relaxed with him today, and he didn't want to spoil that. He looked across the yard, and almost as if she'd been waiting for that very act, Lorri had another question.

"Do you ever think about the island, Lieutenant?" she asked him.

"Yes, I do. How about you?"

"I do think about it, and I ask myself if there's something I need to apologize to you about."

Rigg shook his head. "I can't think of anything."

"Not even when you wanted to leave and I was nowhere to be found?"

"I didn't know about your sister at the time. I realize now where you were."

"I couldn't tell you," Lorri turned to him. "I just couldn't talk about it right then. I'm sorry."

"There's no reason to be sorry. I was too harsh on you."

Lorri looked away, not certain she could cope with his compassion. She suddenly saw herself leaving the island in that small boat and looking back to gain a final glimpse.

"I wasn't going to jump out of the boat," she said.

"What's that now?"

"When we were leaving the island, I think you were afraid I was going to try to return."

Rigg nodded with understanding.

"Just a last look, right?"

Lorri turned to him, her eyes swimming.

"I didn't want to leave her there. I didn't want to leave Clarence Fuller either, but I had to. There was nothing else I could do."

"I saw the graves," Rigg told her. "You did a very honorable thing. A fine job."

"You saw the graves?"

"Yes."

"But you didn't ask me about them. You didn't mention it at all."

"I realize that," Rigg agreed. "Maybe I should have, but you weren't very strong right then, and I just wanted to get you safely away."

"Why didn't you think I would be safe?"

"If the enemy had spotted us, Miss Archer, we would have been in a lot of trouble. It was a very vulnerable predicament to be in."

"And made worse by my presence." Lorri's voice was flat.

"I don't regret a single moment," Rigg told her. "We were proud to rescue you and would do it again."

"You weren't always very happy with me."

To her surprise, Rigg laughed. Lorri turned to look at him.

"I'm sorry to laugh," Rigg apologized, "but you were a bit unpredictable."

"Would you please tell me about it?" Lorri entreated sincerely, leaning a little from her chair. "Some of it is so blurry in my mind."

"What would you like to know?"

Lorri shrugged a little. Her reserve had melted away but now came back like a wall.

Rigg saw it and jumped in. "I'll tell you

what I'll do. I'll just start at the beginning, and if you have a question, you stop me."

"All right."

Her face had taken on that hopeful gleam again, and Rigg, anxious to please her, worked to recall the events.

"I think you knew that *Every Storm* was having mechanical trouble."

Lorri nodded.

"We stopped at the island and ten of us went ashore. I was with Lionel and Quinn. They were a few steps ahead of me and the first to hear you singing."

"I was singing?" Lorri asked, amazed that she didn't remember this.

"Yes," Rigg had to answer with a smile.

"What was I singing?"

" 'The Yellow Rose of Texas.' "

A sudden laugh escaped Lorri, and Rigg thought she looked more beautiful than ever. He forced his mind back to the rescue and continued.

"We didn't try to bring you aboard right away but fed you on the island. Do you remember that?"

"Lionel helped me."

"That's right. I knew I could trust him to take care of you."

"I was hungry," Lorri said, thinking about the food he gave her. She thought it might have been crackers. "When did you find the graves?" she suddenly asked.

"The next morning. Hugh discovered them."

A shiver ran over Lorri, but she still asked, "What did you think? What was that like?"

Rigg debated how to answer and decided on the simple truth.

"I was stunned when I realized what you'd been forced to do, and I just hoped that the other people on the plane had been strangers to you."

Lorri's hand came to her mouth. The memory was tormenting. She could still see herself digging and then having to push her sister's body into that hole because she'd been too weary and weak to lift her.

"I wish I'd left a marker or something," Lorri said, tears in her voice. "I wish I could have done more."

"You did very well. Hugh and I were very impressed."

"We had a service here," Lorri told him, wanting him to know.

"I'm glad."

"We even had a casket."

"What did you put in it?"

"Just little things that reminded us of Josie."

The sound of her sister's name, even coming from her own lips, was too much for her. She broke down and cried. The lieutenant sat still, helpless in the midst of her pain.

"I'm sorry," she managed at one point, working to find her breath.

"Here —" Rigg offered his handkerchief, and Lorri realized she had one of her own.

She took his anyway.

"Thank you," Lorri said, her voice still coming in gasps. "You're going to think that all we do is cry."

"I don't think that, and I would wonder more if you didn't cry."

"She had a fiancé," Lorri suddenly said. "So often I wish it had been me so Josie could have gone on to marry Ken."

I don't wish it had been you, Rigg thought but kept silent, not sure what to say next.

"I think my family forgot that they were supposed to bring coffee and cake," Lorri said as she suddenly glanced behind her, wondering where everyone had gone.

"Before they come with the cake, Miss Archer," Rigg spoke up. "I would like to suggest something to you."

"All right."

"If you have any more questions about the island, please ask me. You can write me at the base if that's easier, or catch me at church or even when I come to get Violet. Okay?"

"Okay. Thank you."

The silence rained down on them again. It was a little uncomfortable, but Lorri didn't try to find her family. She had one more thing to say.

"Thank you for letting me talk to you."

"You're welcome."

"You saw worse things, didn't you?"

Rigg looked at her but didn't answer.

"Oh, I know, you don't want to tell me about it, but I know it was awful for you too."

"At times it was. That's very true."

"I'm glad it's over."

Rigg sighed, his heart relaxing. "So am I, Miss Archer — so am I."

"Where were you?" Lorri asked of Ruth the moment the lieutenant left. "I thought you were coming right out with cake and coffee. What took so long?"

"Well, your grandfather hoped you would have a chance to talk so we stayed away." She smiled at her daughter. "I don't think the lieutenant minded."

"No," Lorri had to agree. "He certainly liked the cake."

Ruth laughed. "I think he wanted to say

yes to the third piece I offered but forced himself not to."

Lorri smiled. "We did talk. I learned a few things."

"Maybe you can talk again."

"That's what the lieutenant said."

"What exactly?"

"That he would answer any questions I have."

And with that statement Lorri realized she was exhausted. It was only 9:00, but her whole body felt weighted with fatigue.

"I'm going to bed, Mother."

"All right, dear."

They hugged and Lorri started up the stairs, thinking someone had added a few steps when she wasn't looking. She went through the motions of washing her face and brushing her teeth, but she was already half asleep. Once in bed, she turned out the light and remembered no more.

"I didn't get a chance to talk to you last night," Max said at breakfast. "How did it go with the lieutenant?"

"It went well. We talked about the island, and that was good."

"Did you cry?"

"I tried not to," Lorri said as she made a face, "but it didn't work."

"And what did he do?"

"He just gave me his handkerchief."

Max sighed. "I tell you, Raine, you don't find his type very often."

"And what exactly is his type?"

"Oh, you know, tall, dark, handsome, kind, thoughtful, and attentive. Not to mention, he shares your faith." Max looked at her sister. "I don't think you'd better let this one get away."

"He's not a fish."

Max found this highly amusing, and when Dean came in, he found the girls laughing.

"Someone must have slept well," he said, getting a bowl for his own cereal.

"Hi, Grandpa. How was Bible study?"

"It was fine. Did you get that lawn mowed, Max?"

"I thought you said it was your week."

Dean smiled. "I had hoped you wouldn't remember that."

Max smiled cheekily at him. "And besides, Arlene and I have plans."

Dean sighed dramatically. "Having to mow that lawn at my age. There's no respect anymore."

The girls had no compassion. They laughed hysterically over this, and Dean gave up with a laugh of his own. He changed into work clothes to tackle the lawn.

★ ★ ★

"Hello, Rigg," said the admiral, wasting no time in greeting him Sunday morning.

"Hello, sir."

"How did things go on Friday night?"

"I think fine, sir. We didn't cover a lot of ground, but we did speak of the rescue, and I encouraged her to check with me if she had any more questions."

"Is that what she did, question you?"

"Some. Sometimes she just talked."

Dean nodded, his mind wandering a bit. Josie's birthday was coming up, and Dean knew it was going to hit all of them.

"I'll hope you'll join us again," Dean invited, realizing he'd fallen silent.

"Thank you, sir."

"Why don't you come and sit with us?"

"All right."

With no further ado, Dean moved to join his family and Rigg followed.

Lorri saw her grandfather talking to Rigg on Sunday morning, but even when they came toward the pew, she decided not to stare.

Rigg didn't appear to have anyone to sit with, and she thought her grandfather very gracious to include him, but Lorri was determined not to read anything into it.

Had she but known it, Rigg was on the end — on the far side of the admiral — hoping Lorri was getting some type of message. He wasn't sure of anything just yet, but it certainly seemed that the admiral did not object to his presence. He didn't want to play games with Lorri's heart, but if getting close to her family was what it took to get close to her, he would do it.

To his surprise he actually heard the sermon. It was easier not to have Lorri in his line of vision because she looked sensational in a green dress with lots of white trim. He was actually able to listen very well. It was also satisfying that Max wasted no time after the benediction. She scooted down the row to talk to him and even waved her friend, Arlene Andrews, over so they could meet.

Lorri didn't join them until it was nearly time to leave, but Rigg was okay with that. Little by little, whatever it took, Rigg had a challenge and a question ahead of him: Was there room for him in Lorri Archer's heart, and was she supposed to occupy his?

"Rumor has it that a certain good-looking sailor has been to visit you the last few weeks," Martha Beach teased Lorri when there was a lull in the day.

"Don't believe all the rumors you hear."

"So it's not true?"

"Well," Lorri drew out the word, "it might be."

The teacher laughed. "Too bad Violet is out sick. He won't have an excuse."

Lorri rolled her eyes at the teacher's tone and went back to putting vocabulary words on the board.

Several times during the day she'd been caught up with guilt. Was she sorry that Violet was sick or that the lieutenant wouldn't be coming? Each time she tried to remember the sick child and pray for her.

If the truth be told, she had grown very accustomed to seeing Lieutenant Riggs on Friday afternoons. It was the highlight of her day, and sometimes the highlight of her week. She wasn't exactly blue when it was time to see the children off, but it didn't hold the usual anticipation of most Fridays.

"Hello."

Lorri started when she heard the voice, not having seen him. The children were all gone, and he was waiting back by the classroom. For a moment Lorri stared at him.

"Violet was out sick today," she finally managed. "Did your brother not tell you?"

"Actually I did know that," Rigg said, hoping she would still ride home with him. "I didn't want you to get wet if it rained."

Lorri stepped out from under the over-hang of the building, her head going back to inspect a perfect sky — clear and blue, not a cloud in sight. When she looked back at the lieutenant, she barely kept from laughing.

"That was very thoughtful of you," Lorri just managed to say. "I didn't even bring my umbrella."

Rigg's smile now matched her own. "Whenever you're ready" was all he said.

This time they talked all the way home. Lorri learned of Rigg's duties at the base and that he would be done in late June.

"What will you do?" Lorri asked.

"Hopefully find a job. I was with a small architectural firm before enlisting, and I'll probably go back to that."

"To that line of work or to that firm?"

"That firm is in Santa Rosa. I'd like to stay in southern California if I can."

Lorri glanced over to find him watching her. Their eyes held. The light turned green, and the person in the car behind them tapped on his horn.

"You could get us into an accident," Rigg said, his foot going down on the gas.

"I could?"

"Certainly. It's quite obvious to me."

Lorri watched his profile, seeing that he wanted to smile.

"I think you're better behaved when your niece is along."

"Shh," he said softly. "It will be our little secret."

Again Lorri wanted to laugh. She felt that way a lot when he was around.

"So tell me," Rigg said. They were in the driveway, and Rigg had held Lorri's door open so she could get out. "Have you thought of any more questions you wanted to ask me?"

"Not really about the rescue, but I did think of one thing."

"Okay."

"The food on the boat was good, and I've always heard the opposite. Did Ellis fix special things for me?"

"Yes," Rigg replied drily, "I suspect he did go out of his way for you, but you need to remember that you were starving."

Lorri laughed. His tone and facial expressions had been hysterical.

"Oh, yes," he went on. "You can laugh. You didn't have to eat our usual fare for months on end."

"Come now." Lorri wasn't convinced. "It couldn't have been that bad."

Rigg's look was telling, and Lorri only laughed more.

The two heard the front door at the same

time. They looked up to see Ruth on the porch.

"I've got iced tea if you're interested," she called to them.

Lorri looked to Rigg, her brows raised in question.

"Lead the way," he said, and Lorri couldn't help but notice that her heart was as light as a balloon.

Nineteen

"That was fun," Max said at the end of the evening, Rigg having stayed for dinner.

Lorri didn't answer. Staring at seemingly nothing, she stood mute in the middle of the living room. She didn't even notice when her family came in, took seats all around her, and just watched her.

"What?" Lorri said, having finally noticed them.

"That's what we want to know," Dean said.

"I don't know what you mean."

"Sit down, Raine," Max invited, patting the sofa.

Lorri did sit by her sister and then looked back to Dean. Her eyes went to her mother, who was looking very satisfied, and then to Max, who was just barely holding a smile.

"All right," Lorri gave in. "I think I might like him."

That her family found this hysterical was all too apparent. They burst out laughing, leaving her to tolerate their mirth with a blushing face.

"What is so funny?" she demanded, waiting for them to catch their breath.

"You are," Ruth told her. "You nearly floated around this house tonight. You even stepped on Muffin's tail, and —"

Before Ruth could finish, Muffin came struggling into the room. She had captured one of Ruth's aprons and was dragging it in with her.

"Stop that, Muffin!" Ruth scolded. "Now look at that," she continued, disgusted. "There's cat hair on it, and I just finished the laundry."

Muffin had come close to Lorri and Max, knowing she was safer by their legs. She was, in fact, a very nice cat, but her propensity to attack and drag things around sometimes got her into trouble.

"We just wanted to know what you were thinking," Dean broke in, taking the conversation back to Lorri.

"Well, I was actually wondering what you were thinking, Grandpa. You and Lieutenant Riggs talked on Sunday and then again in the backyard tonight, and I just wondered if you're getting to know him a bit."

"Yes, I am. Sometimes we talk about the rescue, and he asks how you're doing with all of that. Other times we talk about his plans and things at the base."

"Can you tell us what *you* think of him, Dean?" Ruth asked.

"I think he's a fine young man. He didn't come right out and ask if he could court Lorri, but he did ask how we were all doing with Josie's loss, and then his questions zeroed in on Lorri."

"Well," Max declared suddenly, "I think Raine should marry him and be done with it."

"Max," Lorri said patiently, "there's a bit more to this than good looks and kindness."

"Well, you can see that there's more to the lieutenant than good looks and kindness, so you're all set."

Lorri looked to her mother, who knew that Max was mostly teasing, but if the truth be told, they all liked Lieutenant Donovan Riggs very much.

"Your turn, Lorri," she said gently. "How do you feel?"

"I think he's very special. In my mind I can see glimpses of the boat. He put Lionel in charge of me, but he took care of me too. And there was nothing romantic about it. He was just doing his job. And then when he saw me that first time at school, he wasn't expecting it, but he was still kind." Lorri looked at her family. "I like him. I like him a lot."

"Well, that's good," Dean declared, growing weary with the hour, "because I invited him to dinner again next Friday night."

Lorri laughed, her mouth opening in amazement. Ruth's mouth was open too, but Max looked like the cat who had just swallowed the canary.

"Don't forget," Max said as they all moved to go upstairs. "I was the first one to say that Raine should marry the man."

Max dodged the sofa pillow that flew at her, and everyone sought their beds.

Josephine Pearl Archer's twenty-seventh birthday would have been on April 10, 1946. Lorri took the day off from school, and Max stayed home as well. Dean did not go to the base, and Ruth had cleared her calendar.

Everyone said that first year was the hardest, but Lorri knew that this day would always be hard. Josie had loved her birthday. She had loved presents and surprises and was always pleased with the smallest gesture.

It was for this reason that Lorri picked flowers from the yard before going to the cemetery. She understood that Josie didn't need them, but they made her own heart feel better, and today she wanted that.

The four of them did not linger at the grave site. The day was nice, very sunny, but it was too sad, and Ruth said she was tired of crying. Dean suggested a drive to the coast. Everyone liked this idea, and they made a day of it.

Ruth was thankful for the distraction, but when the family arrived home, she found that Ken had written. She laid her things aside, sat at the kitchen table, and opened his letter.

Dear Dean, Ruth, Lorri, and Max,

How are you? You are in my thoughts this day since I know Josie must be on your minds. I am still not reconciled to never seeing her again, never making her my wife. I had never looked forward to anything more. I think that in time my heart will heal, but I don't know if I will ever love again. What I felt for Josie was not common. I do not expect anyone to ever compare.

I'm settled at Washington, having signed for another four years. I was not going to do this but now find myself rescued by the routine and familiarity. We have a country to rebuild, and I take that seriously. When I am in California, I will stop to see you. Until then, I hold you fondly in my heart.

Ken

Ruth folded the letter and held it. For a moment she let herself think about what it would have looked like to have Josie alive. She would likely have been married to Ken by now, living in a home of their own. It might not have been in southern California, but it certainly would have been closer than Australia.

But that was as far as Ruth could take it. Josie wasn't there. She and Ken would not marry, and Ken was, for the most part, out of their lives. Much as Ruth wanted to concoct another image, she couldn't do it.

Dean came into the room and saw Ruth at the table. He sat with her, and she handed him the letter, which he read in silence. Dean had not shed a tear all day, but Ruth saw him reach for his handkerchief.

"Dean," Ruth said at last, "can we cement those plans for the fall? Can we put it on the calendar and go to Minnesota?"

"We can do that, Ruth."

"I want to see my father before it's too late."

"We'll do that, honey. You pick the days, and we'll go."

341

They looked at each other for a moment.

"I never pictured her gone," Ruth admitted. "I had to bury my mother, and I thought the girls would all bury me."

Dean didn't have any words to offer. He wanted to make everything right for her, but he couldn't. They both remembered this day so many years ago. They both recalled the tiny girl born to parents who couldn't wait to hold her.

"I'd better work on dinner." Ruth began to rise, at the moment looking older than her age.

"I think we can just pick through the icebox and eat leftovers," Dean suggested; they had already eaten lunch out. "We'll just tell the girls they'll have to fend for themselves."

Ruth agreed, and it ended up being the perfect plan. Max was not hungry at all, and Lorri wanted very little. The four of them ended up gathering around the radio to listen to evening news and then a comedy show that made them laugh for a while. No one argued when Dean said they should make it an early night.

"Janice is expecting again," Cora told Ruth at Bible study. "They called just last night."

"Oh, Cora, that's wonderful. How is she feeling?"

"Good — better than last time."

"How are you doing?"

"I've cried a lot, but they've been good tears. I don't know why Janice lost the first baby, but I let it get my attention, Ruth. I've had an unthankful, complaining spirit about a lot of things. It was good for me to be reminded of my heart's condition."

Ruth hugged her friend. "You're so good for me, Cora."

"That's what I think of you."

"What do you mean?"

"I mean, you've never once complained, Ruth. All these months, and you've accepted what God has for you. There isn't another woman in this church I love or admire more."

Ruth smiled at her. So often she felt weak and unable to go on. Did she tell Cora how frail she could be?

"What are you thinking?" Cora asked.

"Why is it that when someone compliments us, all we can do is remember our mistakes?"

"I don't know. Were you thinking of mistakes?"

Ruth nodded.

"Well, don't do that. Tell me how Lorri is doing with *the dreamboat*, as Arlene puts it."

"Is that what she calls him?"

"Yes. She's got names picked out for their children and knows what color their house should be."

Ruth loved this. "Has Arlene considered writing romances? She might be very good."

It was time for Bible study to begin. The women needed to compose themselves, and it was no easy task. Each time they thought of Arlene, they wanted to laugh all over again.

"I thought of another question," Lorri said to Rigg as he worked over the grill. Dean was running late, and Ruth had put him to work.

"Okay, shoot."

"Were you angry at me when I met those other sailors on the beach?"

"Angry at you? Not at all, but I could have strung each one of them up." Rigg flipped a burger and flipped it back. "Did you think I was angry at you?"

"I didn't know what to think. It was all so strange and unsettling."

"Strange and unsettling is too kind. It was foolhardy and ridiculous. Had I been on the scene, it would have looked quite different."

"Why is that?"

"My rank," he said simply, and Lorri only nodded. She watched him work for a time.

"Lieutenant?" she started.

"Lieutenant," he repeated. "Lieutenant." He turned his head to really see her. "I do have a name you know."

"Do you now?" Lorri asked, her voice light. She wanted to tease him.

"Yes, ma'am. My family calls me Donovan, and everyone else calls me Rigg." He looked her in the eye. "Do you suppose you could try one of those?"

"I'll think about it, sailor," she said, not able to hide her smile.

Rigg's eyes narrowed as he watched her, thinking she had no idea how tempting she was to kiss.

Lorri's mind didn't go to kissing, but she was more aware of his interest than he realized. She picked up the meat platter and went inside to wash it off, fully aware that he watched her every move. Not until she was shutting the screen door did she let her eyes meet his, a full blown smile coming into view.

Rigg stared down at the grill, not seeing hamburgers at all. He wanted to take this girl home and introduce her to his family. He wanted to see her or talk to her every day. He knew her family liked him, but he was still trying to read her.

"Are they burning?" Max asked, having just come from inside.

"I don't think so," Rigg said to cover, realizing he hadn't paid attention at all.

"Flip that one," Max pointed and Rigg obeyed. "Ooh, just right."

"It sounds to me like you want to take over," Rigg challenged.

"Not a chance."

"Why is that?"

"If they burn, you're in trouble, not me."

"Thanks," he said sarcastically and got a smile much like Lorri's.

"So tell me the name of your boyfriend," Rigg said, watching Max's face.

"I swore off boys months ago."

"Is that right?"

"Yes, it's much easier."

Rigg looked at her beautiful face, pulled-back hair, rolled-up jeans, and oversized shirt and said, "Something tells me the boys don't find it so easy."

"Now you sound like Johnny."

"Is he someone special?"

"He wants to be, but it's all wrong."

"What's all wrong?"

"His family went to our church a long time ago, so I think he *might* be a believer, but he doesn't take Christianity seriously, and there have been too many girls already."

"You need to meet my brother, Mitch."

"Why is that?"

"He does take his Christianity seriously, *and* he's a gentleman."

"Let me guess: He lives in Santa Rosa?"

Her tone made Rigg laugh, and Dean chose that moment to join them.

"How's it coming?" he asked, giving Max a quick kiss and offering his hand to Rigg.

"I think I want you to be the judge, sir," Rigg said, gladly surrendering the spatula, afraid he would ruin all the meat.

"It looks good. Tell your mother, Max. We're almost there."

Shortages on wheat meant there were no buns, but they feasted on plain hamburgers and salads, with ice cream for dessert. They ate at the dining room table, and there was no shortage of laughter.

"I was hoping that Miss Archer would not find out why we were named *Every Storm*," Rigg said at one point.

"Why were you?" Max asked.

"Because every storm that hit the Pacific landed on our boat."

Smiles met this announcement, so the lieutenant went on.

"It was the night before we made port. A storm came in that tried to blow us out of the ocean. Up until that time, Miss Archer had done remarkably well, showing no signs of seasickness, but not this night.

"I went to the cabin to check on her and she was ready to sell her soul. She promised not to go into the water or disappear again and even to give my bunk back to me if I would just put her off that rocking boat."

Lorri groaned and everyone laughed.

"Why did you go into the water?" Max asked.

"Let's just say I had an urge to swim."

"You didn't care for that, Lieutenant?" Ruth asked.

"She gave me no warning," he said calmly. "My boat was in need of repair, and I had a rather frail female civilian on my hands. I came down the beach to find her in the water."

"What did you do?" Max needed to know.

"I asked her to come out, or rather, ordered her."

"Your voice was less calm that day," Lorri took pleasure in reminding him.

"So was yours," he shot right back, taking just as much delight.

Lorri's mouth opened. "I forgot that I argued with you."

"Lorraine!" Her mother sounded mildly shocked.

"I did, Mother." Lorri was still horrified

with the memory. "I'd forgotten all about that."

"The men loved it," Rigg told them.

"They did?" Lorri questioned, looking confused.

'Oh, yes. It went all over the boat that you had stood up to me. They were ready to keep you as a mascot for the rest of the war."

Not until Rigg said this did he remember to look at the admiral. He was glad to see a smile in those wise, older eyes.

"That," Rigg finished, "was before they learned you were an admiral's granddaughter."

Dean had a good chuckle over this last bit of information. It was still a little hard for him to picture his Lorri on a PT boat, but it delivered her back safely, and that was all that mattered.

"Were you ever assigned to a PT boat, Grandpa?" Max wanted to know.

"Transported on them," Dean replied, and then regaled them with some stories about his own ocean adventures. Some of his tales made Rigg's adventures seem tame.

"How was your week?" Lorri asked Rigg as they worked on the dishes later that evening.

"It was fine — busy, but I like that. How about yours?"

"Josie's birthday was Wednesday," Lorri said, the event still very much on her mind.

"Was that hard?"

"Yes, but then I knew it would be. The hardest part was thinking about my mother. Josie and I had been together in the past years; Mother and Josie hadn't."

"I wish I had known your sister," Rigg said, carefully drying a plate.

"Look at Max if you want to see her. She wasn't as talkative or inquisitive, but now that Max is older, they could have been twins."

The kitchen was silent for a time, but then Rigg plunged in, heart pounding, hoping it wasn't too soon.

"I was thinking it might be fun to go to dinner some night. Do you think you might be free next Saturday?"

"I think so," Lorri told him, feeling breathless with surprise and excitement.

"Do you want to let me know?"

Lorri nodded. "I'll check with Mother to make sure she doesn't have plans."

Before they knew it, the dishes were done. Lorri couldn't remember it ever going so fast. Max was waiting for them in the family room and wanted to play a game. Lorri and

Rigg agreed but should have known better. Max won three games in a row. For some reason, Lorri and Rigg found concentration a little bit taxing.

Rigg felt he was making progress. This Sunday when he sat with the Archers, Dean moved down the pew a ways, and Max came to sit by him. Lorri was still on the other side of her mother, but she was slightly closer. What he didn't bank on was Max's curiosity.

"So were you born in Santa Rosa or in southern California?" she asked.

"Santa Rosa."

"Were your brothers born there?"

"Yes."

His short answers didn't give her much encouragement, but Max was not easily put off.

"Do you hope to live in southern California for a long time?"

Rigg couldn't stop a smile.

"I hope so. Where do you hope to live?"

"Right here," Max said simply, and then opened her mouth to have another go.

Rigg's shoulders shook with silent laughter as the music leader stepped behind the pulpit and Max was forced to close her mouth.

"I'm not done with you," she whispered, fighting a smile.

"Thanks for the warning."

But Ruth had other plans. As soon as the service was over, she sent Max on an errand. This was not lost on Rigg, who also noticed that Ruth slipped away, leaving Lorri free for conversation.

"I'll have Miss Archer home early" were Rigg's last words at the front door on Saturday night.

Lorri didn't comment at that moment, but just as soon as she could manage it, she called him lieutenant, putting a slight emphasis on the word.

"Lieutenant?" Rigg asked, having put Lorri in on the passenger side and climbed behind the wheel.

"Miss Archer?" Lorri shot right back, her voice carrying no heat.

Rigg sighed. "I don't mind telling you that your grandfather scares me to death."

"Grandpa? Why?"

"I'm a lowly lieutenant; he's an admiral."

"Not for much longer. You'll be a civilian in June, and he'll be one in August."

They were headed down the street now, and Rigg was in a quandary. He knew he couldn't explain the rest of his thought process. He was working hard not to have impure thoughts about Lorri Archer, but men still knew the way other men thought. At times he would catch the admiral's gaze on him and feel caught, even when he'd done nothing!

"So my grandfather is the reason you have to call me Miss Archer?"

"I'm just trying to be respectful. I don't want to overstep."

"If you were overstepping, I wouldn't be on this date."

Rigg glanced at her. "Is that how it works?"

"Both my mother and grandfather have to approve. I'm sure you understand."

"Yes, I do, but I still get pretty nervous around him. I can't tell what he's thinking."

"He's not going to be quiet and let me walk out the door with a man he doesn't trust. You can trust *me* on that."

Rigg nodded. This was not the way he thought the evening would start, but maybe it was for the best. He glanced at Lorri's profile, wondering what she was thinking. "What would you like me to call you?" he finally asked.

Lorri looked at him, smiling a little. "My name," she said simply.

"Ah, but you have several. I've heard Lorraine come out of your mother's mouth, usually when she's scolding you. I know that your grandfather calls you Lorri, and Max calls you Raine. As you can see, I'm at a loss."

Lorri smiled over his dilemma and suggested this, "I'll tell you what: You decide what you want to call me tonight, and I'll decide if you're Donovan or Rigg."

"Not sailor? I rather liked that."

Lorri felt her face heat, glad that the interior of the car was growing dim. They rode in silence until they arrived at the restaurant, when Rigg decided he wanted the details out of the way. While they waited for the maître d' to come for them, he bent to where Lorri stood in front of him and spoke into her ear.

"Lorraine," he said softly.

Lorri turned her head just enough to look up at him, not even working to hide the emotions she felt.

"Is that going to be all right?" Rigg asked, his voice still low.

"If Rigg is all right with you," Lorri just managed, rather lost in his eyes.

"It's fine," Rigg got out before the maître d' came for them.

It was the start of a perfect evening.

Twenty

Lorri let herself quietly into the house but noticed right away that a light burned in the living room. She was glad to see it was her grandfather. His glasses perched on his nose, he sat with a book and looked up when she came in.

"Hi," Lorri said, bending to kiss his cheek and then sitting on the closest chair.

"Hi, yourself. How was your evening?"

Lorri smiled, her look dreamy. "It was wonderful. He's so nice, Grandpa."

Dean smiled at her.

Lorri's eyes suddenly darted to him. "He's afraid of you!"

That Dean was not surprised or dismayed by this announcement was immediately clear.

Lorri's mouth opened. "You don't mind, do you?"

Dean was still smiling when he answered. "Tell me something, Lorri. Whose car will Rigg be more careful with, mine or his?"

"Yours."

"That's right. It's not all bad that he remembers there's a man waiting at home for the car to be returned in perfect order."

"I'm not a car, Grandpa."

"No, but you get my point, don't you?"

"Yes. And you don't need to worry. He was a perfect gentleman."

"Good. I expect nothing less, but he's still a man, and men have areas of temptation, women being the strongest one."

"Why is that?" Lorri asked.

Dean shrugged. "It's the way God made us. We can't have excuses, but it's best to know our own weaknesses."

"When I was on the PT boat," Lorri told him, "I never went into the crew's quarters. But one day I glanced in the door. There were a lot of pin-ups."

Dean shook his head. "Some men surround themselves with those pictures and then wonder why they can't stay faithful to their wives."

"There was nothing like that in Rigg's cabin."

"That doesn't surprise me. He's different."

Lorri sighed again and Dean watched her. It wasn't hard to imagine how tempting Rigg would find his beautiful grand-daughter, and he debated whether or not he should question her about Rigg's conduct. He knew she was not a kid anymore, but that didn't change his responsibility and concern.

"Did you feel safe with Rigg?"

"Yes, very."

"He didn't touch you or say anything im-proper?"

"No, nothing like that."

"I'm glad to hear it."

"I'm going to bed now. Are you coming up?"

"Max is out with Arlene. I'll wait for her."

"Goodnight, Grandpa."

"Goodnight, honey."

Not until Lorri left the room did Dean re-alize he'd forgotten to ask one thing: Did she and the lieutenant have another date on the calendar?

Lorri's birthday is in two weeks. We're going to The Cove for dinner. Can you join us?

Rigg recalled those words from Ruth Ar-cher as he parked his car on the street and headed to the front door on the third of May. He and Lorri had been on another date, and he had even been invited for Sunday dinner — all of which he took as a positive sign about the future.

Rigg rang the doorbell and waited, pleased when Lorri answered.

"Rigg, hi!" she exclaimed, as surprised as she was supposed to be. "Come in."

"Thank you."

"I wish I didn't have to tell you this, but we're not going to be home this evening. We're going to The Cove."

"Yes, I know," Rigg said simply. "Happy birthday," he added, bringing the flowers from behind his back.

"Thank you," Lorri said, stunned at his gesture. Then she caught on. "You're going with us, aren't you?"

"That's the plan."

Lorri laughed. "Let me put these in water."

Lorri wasn't gone from the room five minutes when Max joined him.

"Hello, Lieutenant," she said, smiling her Lorri smile. "How are you?"

"I'm fine, Max. Yourself?"

Max was all ready to answer, but Lorri came back. Unfortunately she was trailed by Muffin, who had taken another captive.

"Muffin!" Max suddenly hissed, and Lorri looked behind her. In the cat's mouth and trailing down the length of her body was a brassiere. Lorri scooped the cat up and shot from the room. Max turned to Rigg, who was doing everything in his power not to laugh.

"We'll be right back," she said, scooting after her sister.

When they returned, Ruth and Dean were already waiting with Rigg, who still looked amused. Max bit her lip to keep from laughing, but Lorri was having none of it. She didn't plan to look at Donovan Riggs ever again.

"Are you going to spend the entire evening avoiding my eyes?" Rigg said to her profile. The reservations at the restaurant had been overlooked somehow, and they were having to wait a few moments for a table.

"I'm so embarrassed," Lorri admitted, still not looking at him.

"Don't you think it was a little funny?"

"I would have thought it very funny if you hadn't been standing in my living room."

Lorri felt the bench shake as silent laughter overcame him, the laughter he had wanted to release as soon as she'd spotted the cat.

"I hope," Lorri told him, trying to sound

angry, "that if I ever meet your family, they tell me something that turns *your* face red."

"Speaking of which," Rigg replied, trying not to laugh anymore, "I'm headed home in two weeks. Would you like to go with me?"

"Home as in Santa Rosa?"

"That's right."

Lorri worried her lip. "You can't get there and back in one day, can you?"

"No, we would stay with my parents, who have plenty of room."

Lorri only nodded.

"Is there a problem?"

"Not exactly. It's just that I haven't been away from Mother since I arrived home. There's been no reason."

"Until now," Rigg said, not catching how serious the suggestion was for Lorri. "I've written about you to my folks, and they would like to meet you."

"What did you write exactly?"

"That I'm seeing someone."

"I would like to meet your parents," Lorri said, not having fully worked out her thoughts.

"So do I take that as a yes?"

The face she turned to him bothered his heart. Her eyes, suddenly huge and vulnerable, reminded him of her condition on the island.

"Why don't I check with you later," Rigg suggested.

"I don't know if I can," Lorri said, panic overtaking her without warning.

"It's all right," Rigg said reassuringly, never dreaming his invitation would be this upsetting. "We'll talk about it another time."

"I'm sorry," Lorri began, but Rigg only shook his head.

"It's fine. Don't worry about it."

"Lorri?" her mother said when she saw her daughter's face. She glanced at Rigg, who looked apologetic. "What's the matter?" Ruth asked.

"Nothing," Lorri told her. "I just panicked over something. It was silly of me."

Ruth didn't want to, but she let it drop. Max and Dean had returned from seeing to the reservations, and they were soon seated at their table. As soon as they ordered, however, Lorri excused herself. Ruth waited only that long to check with Rigg.

"Can you tell me what happened?"

"I asked her to come home to Santa Rosa with me in two weeks to meet my folks. She said she hasn't been away from you since she got home." Rigg looked as helpless as he felt. "I didn't realize it would upset her. I'm sorry."

Ruth looked to Dean, all sorts of questions in her eyes.

"It's all right," Dean said to everyone. He knew something had gone on in his absence. "We're still in new territory here. Lorri does very well, but she's still the same person who had a terrible ordeal less than a year ago. It's impossible to know how everything's going to work out."

There was no further conversation on the matter until Lorri came back. All eyes on the table watched her, and she knew what the conversation had been. She turned to Rigg.

"Did you tell them how silly I was?"

"Nothing like that. Your mother just checked with me, and I explained."

Lorri's eyes went to Ruth.

"I don't know what came over me. I'm sorry."

"Don't worry about it."

Lorri did her best to do just that. And in truth, the evening was not spoiled. Not until she climbed into bed did she remember Rigg asking her to go home with him. She sighed when she thought about how she had behaved. She doubted if he would ever ask again.

Rigg was at the Archers' front door as soon as he dared Saturday morning. People were up and dressed but moving slowly. He asked to talk to Lorri, and they went into the living room.

"Bring your whole family," he began. "Come to Santa Rosa with me and bring your grandfather, mother, and sister."

Lorri was unbelievably touched. "You would do that? Invite everyone just so I would go?"

"I want you to meet my family. It's a bonus if your family can meet them too."

Lorri sat for a moment.

"I'll be nervous. I'll make a fool of myself and embarrass you."

"That's not going to happen."

"Why are you never nervous?"

"Who told you I was never nervous?"

"I can see it," Lorri explained, thinking it so obvious. "You're always in charge and composed."

Rigg shook his head, his eyes going heavenward.

"Okay, let's take this apart piece by piece. I'm so calm and in charge that I have to have my niece along in order to come and see you. Then I try a new church and find you there. Do I come up and speak to you? No. I keep coming because I enjoy the church and can see you, but come up and talk to you? Never."

Lorri's mouth had started to curl into a smile. She had not seen him like this before. He was exasperated and seemed desperate for her to believe him.

"You would dare laugh at my pain?" he asked, bringing a full smile to Lorri's lips.

Rigg watched her, not wanting to push but anxious to know what she thought of the idea.

"Lorraine," he finally said. "What do you think?"

"I think I should check with my family."

"Okay," Rigg agreed, but Lorri sat there. Rigg stared at her, trying not to laugh.

"Oh!" she suddenly started. "I could do that right now."

Rigg remained seated, and Lorri shot to her feet and found her family in the kitchen. Only five minutes passed before Rigg was joined by the whole gang.

"I have to be at the base that weekend," Dean launched right in. "But I think Ruth and the girls should go."

"All right." Rigg was ready to agree to anything.

"Will your mother welcome a whole houseful of people, Rigg?" Ruth asked on the practical side.

"As a matter of fact, she'll be fine."

"We don't want to put anyone out of his

room," Ruth began to object, but Rigg brushed it aside.

The five of them spoke about the trip for a few more minutes and the time they would leave, but not long after, Lorri and Rigg were alone in the living room again.

"I might need to warn you about my brother," Rigg began. "He's still in high school."

"Is that a problem?"

"Not for me, but it might be for Max."

Lorri looked confused.

"There's no way she's going to go unnoticed, Lorraine."

Lorri smiled, liking the fact that her sister was so lovely.

"She's beautiful, isn't she?"

"Yes, she is," Rigg had to agree. "But then I've noticed that beauty runs in your family."

"That was a nice thing to say."

"It's no effort to be nice to you," Rigg told her, still watching her face and seeing a small blush cover her cheeks.

"I'll still be nervous," Lorri felt it only fair to tell him.

"That's all right. I'm nervous every time I stand at your front door."

Lorri was still amazed by this. He hid it so well. Having ideas and giving orders just seemed to come so easily.

Rigg said he had things to do, and Lorri did as well, but she gave him coffee, and they talked for two hours at the kitchen table. When Rigg finally took his leave, Lorri couldn't remember a thing she had on her list.

Rigg's car was comfortable. Lorri had given her mother the front seat, and she and Max had taken over in the back.

"Where are the cookies?" Max asked almost as soon as they hit the road, bringing a laugh from her mother.

"Max, we just started."

"I'm hungry. Am I the only one?"

The rearview mirror was set in such a way that Rigg could see Lorri's eyes. He glanced up and caught her gaze, and Lorri smiled at him.

"Okay," Max said, disgusted with the lot. "I can see that this is not going to be the least bit fair. Raine and Rigg are going to make eyes at each other the whole time, and Mother isn't going to feed me!"

Everyone in the car laughed until Lorri made a suggestion.

"Why don't you ask Rigg to tell you a little more about Mitch."

Max didn't mention cookies for the next two hours.

Max had skipped her afternoon classes, but the late departure still made for a late arrival in Santa Rosa. Nevertheless, Rigg's family was waiting: his father, Del Riggs, his mother, Virginia, and his brother, Mitch.

Rigg hugged his parents before starting the introductions. From there Virginia took over.

"Come in and have something to eat," she invited graciously. "I won't even ask you to sit because that's what you've been doing for hours."

"Can we help with something?" Ruth offered.

"No, I have it all ready. Just come to the table and fill your plate."

They were tired, but it felt good to no longer be moving, and Lorri wasn't as nervous as she expected. Rigg, however, had been right: His brother had not taken his eyes from Max.

"Will he stare like that all weekend?" Lorri asked quietly when he came close.

"He might."

Lorri looked tolerant. "I find it hard to believe that you don't have pretty girls in Santa Rosa."

"Not that look like you two," he said, adding a wink.

It was happening again. He was looking at

her, and she was having a hard time looking away.

"Are you hungry?" he asked, needing to be rescued as much as she.

"Maybe a little."

"Come into the kitchen and get something."

They found Virginia in the kitchen.

"How are you, Lorraine? That trip can be so long."

"I'm doing pretty well. It's very kind of you to have us, Mrs. Riggs."

"Everyone calls me Virginia, and I hope you will too."

Lorri smiled at her, wanting them to be friends.

"Go ahead and eat."

"She'll try to feed you all weekend," Rigg teased his mother. "She isn't happy unless we're eating."

"Go on, Donovan. Don't you listen to him, Lorraine."

In the living room, Max and Ruth were getting to know Mr. Riggs.

"Donovan tells us your father-in-law is an admiral."

"Yes," Ruth answered. "Soon to be retired. He had duties at the base this weekend, or he would have joined us."

"We'll have to meet him another time.

Tell me, Max, what subjects do you like in school?"

"Art and math."

Virginia came in at that point with coffee, and Ruth was glad to have it. The women took no time in hitting it off, and Mitch wasted not a second in capturing Max's attention. Lorri and Rigg were still in the kitchen, and Del was left somewhat on his own, something that didn't bother him in the least. He was very happy to sit and listen to the people he was sure would soon be a part of the family.

"Horses?" Lorri asked on Saturday morning, looking at the animals they were approaching in the paddock, deep in the backyard. "Your family has horses?"

"Why so surprised?"

Lorri looked at him.

"I just never imagined you on a horse. PT boats don't really lend themselves to that pastoral theme."

Rigg smiled but still offered, "How about a ride?"

Lorri stopped in her tracks. "I think your mother wanted to show me some pictures in the photo album."

Rigg laughed but didn't let her get away. He took her hand and led her to the railings.

Clicks made somewhere in his mouth brought two horses running. Lorri almost did some running herself, but Rigg's arm gently brought her back.

"They're very tame, and I would never let you be hurt."

"They're huge!" she said, staying still only because his arm was keeping her in place.

"Hey, girl," Rigg said to the mare that came right to him. Rigg brought sugar from the pocket of his shirt, and Lorri watched in amazement as the horses enthusiastically went for it.

They stood for a little while at the fence, the horses eventually seeing that Rigg was out of sugar and going on their way.

"Was that Max?" Lorri turned and suddenly noticed her sister; she was headed into another building.

"I think Mitch is showing her the car he's working on. Do you want to see it?"

"Sure."

They walked that way, and without permission Rigg took her hand again. Lorri didn't mind. Larger than her own, his hand was warm, his hold undemanding.

"Okay," Mitch was saying to Max, the car not part of the conversation at all. "Here's Donovan and Lorraine. I'll bet your sister is going horseback riding."

"Uh, Mitch," Rigg tried to cut in.

"Go ahead, Lorraine," Mitch didn't hear a thing. "Tell Max that you're not afraid to get on a horse."

Lorri could only stare at him, her mouth opening in surprise. It took a moment for Mitch to realize she wasn't speaking and to see that his brother was calmly shaking his head no.

"You can't be serious!" Mitch said, thinking he had it all wrapped up.

That Max thought this hysterical was only too obvious. She covered her mouth and turned around, but her amusement was all too clear.

"Come on," Rigg invited. "Something tells me Mom will have breakfast ready. We'd better head to the house."

Mitch's eyes, so like Rigg's, told Max she was not forgiven. Max tried to look repentant but couldn't quite manage it. Lorri eventually joined her, and they laughed all the way back to the house.

"More toast, Mrs. Archer?" Virginia offered.

"Thank you," Ruth said, taking one from the plate. "Your home is wonderful. It's so warm and inviting."

Virginia looked around as though seeing

it for the first time. "It's not new, but it has that homey feel."

Ruth looked around as well, but Virginia had something to say to Ruth, something personal.

"Donovan told us about your daughter. I'm so sorry to hear that, Mrs. Archer."

"I hope you'll call me Ruth, and thank you." She sighed a little. "I don't know if I'll ever get used to the idea."

"How long has it been?"

"That's a complicated question. Josie actually died on June 1 of last year, but we didn't know there was a problem until a few days later. The telegram telling me that Josie was gone and Lorri was alive arrived on August 2. Up until that moment, I chose to believe that both my daughters would come home to me."

"We never think it's going to happen to us, do we?" Virginia asked. "My mother suddenly dropped dead in her kitchen one day. My father died 48 hours later. I walked around in a fog for more than a year."

"How painful for you."

"It was. At the time I didn't know how I was going to keep on, but God is always bigger than the pain."

"That's certainly true," Ruth agreed, just as they heard the door. Rigg, Lorri, Mitch, and Max came in, smelling like the out-of-doors and looking for food. Del arrived also, and the feast began.

"That's a sweet girl you've got there, Donovan," his father said to him late Saturday night. "You'd better keep her."

"I'm working on it."

"How is she doing, Donovan? I mean, really?" This came from his mother.

"She's doing well, but the loss is huge. She wasn't willing to leave home this weekend, to be separated from her mother. I thought I would have to drop the entire suggestion until I realized they could all come."

"And she was fine with that?"

"Yes. At first I thought Mrs. Archer might be struggling with her being away, but it's Lorraine who can't do the leaving right now."

"Did she say why?"

"Not specifically, but she told me she was utterly desperate to see her mother while on the island. It meant more to her than eating. I wonder if it's just too soon."

Rigg was enjoying this chance to visit alone with his folks, but he had to drive back to southern California the next day after lunch and knew he'd better get some rest.

"I'm for bed," he said, kissing his mother and hugging Del.

Del and Virginia were tired as well, but they continued to talk long after Rigg was asleep.

"I liked your family," Lorri told Rigg on the way home. It was late, and even though they were almost home, Ruth and Max dozed in the backseat.

"They liked you too."

"Did they? I'm glad."

"You sound like you doubted."

"No, not really. I'm just pleased."

"What did you think of Santa Rosa?"

"It's a beautiful town. It must have been fun growing up there."

"It was," Rigg told her just as she yawned. Conversation drifted off. The car pulled up at the Archer home some 20 minutes later. The family thanked Rigg and let Dean carry their bags inside. They had much to tell him, but it would have to wait until morning.

Twenty-One

Dean did not rush off on Monday morning. Max told him all about her weekend, how much fun she had with Mitch Riggs, and how nice the Riggs family turned out to be. After Max left, Dean stayed to talk with Ruth and Lorri.

"Did Rigg seem more relaxed to you this weekend than he usually is?" Lorri asked once they'd given Dean a run-down and were settled in with coffee and toast.

"I think he was," Ruth replied, having also noticed it. "It must be because he was in his own home. That's bound to have an effect."

Lorri nodded thoughtfully, but before too long she turned, a rather serious frown directed at Dean.

"Lorri, why are you frowning at your grandfather?"

"He knows why."

Dean's head went back when he laughed.

"It's not funny, Grandpa. You scare the man to death!"

"I'm not trying to scare him, Lorri, honestly."

Lorri was still frowning, and try as he might, Dean could not stop laughing.

"Will someone tell me what's going on?" Ruth requested.

Lorri told her mother about the way Rigg feared Dean. Ruth looked surprised.

"He never indicates that he's afraid," Ruth argued.

"I couldn't tell before he said something to me, but now I notice the way he'll slip and call me Miss Archer." Lorri sent another frown. "It's because Grandpa scares him."

Lorri's ire was amusing. Ruth could finally see why Dean wanted to laugh.

"What do you want me to do?" Dean asked, laughter still lurking.

"I don't know." Lorri sounded aggrieved, and even Ruth's hand came to her mouth.

"What's funny?" Lorri asked, not very angry at all.

"I don't know if I can explain it. It's not like you to be so protective, so it's a little humorous."

Lorri sighed, not sure she found it so amusing.

"I am protective of Rigg. I just realized that."

"Then he's a very blessed man," her grandfather said, all humor gone.

"You don't disapprove, do you, Grandpa?"

"If I did, you would have known it a long time ago."

Lorri nodded. Rigg might be nervous around Dean Archer, but there was no reason. It looked as though it might be something Rigg would have to work through on his own.

"My brother and sister-in-law want to know whether you can join them for lunch on Sunday," Rigg told Lorri when he picked up Violet on Friday afternoon.

"Will you be there?" she asked, teasing him a little.

"No," he teased right back. "They want to give you the third degree and don't want me around."

"Oh, I don't know if I can agree to that. I might end up as nervous around them as you are around Grandpa."

"I thought I was hiding that better."

Lorri looked sympathetic. "Does he still scare you?"

"A little. It's probably his rank more than anything else."

"Are you coming to our house?" Violet suddenly asked.

"I believe I am. Won't we have fun?"

"I have a brother. He's little."

"What's his name?"

"William. We call him Billy sometimes."

"Nicknames are fun."

"What's a nickname?"

"Well, like when you call William, Billy, or when your uncle calls you Vi. It's not your full name, but it's still part of your name, or sometimes it's a fun, silly name. My name is Lorraine, but most everyone calls me Lorri."

"I call you Miss Archer."

"Yes, you do, because you're a very good girl."

Violet managed to look shy and pleased all at the same time. Lorri invited her to help with the classrooms, and they were done in record time.

Rigg stood back and let them talk, staying quiet in the car when Violet continued to question Lorri. It was not how Rigg wanted to spend the few minutes he had with her on Friday afternoons but felt he had no choice. He dropped Lorri off and comforted himself with the fact that he would see her Sunday, and not just for church. They could spend the afternoon together at Jim and Dorothy's.

Max could hardly believe her eyes. They still had five minutes until the service started, so she walked to the back pew, her eyes on the serious face of Johnny King.

"Hello, Johnny."

"Hello, Max," he returned, all swagger and bravado gone.

"Are you all right?"

Johnny looked ahead for a moment, his eyes pained. Max hesitated in indecision, but went ahead and spoke.

"Do you mind if I pray for you, Johnny?"

"No," his voice had grown hoarse. "I don't mind at all."

Max gave him an understanding smile and moved to sit with her family. Each one of them, Rigg included, saw the tears in her eyes, but the music was starting and questions would have to wait.

Lorri felt her heart pound. She didn't know why. She had already met most of Rigg's family, and they had been wonderful. But for some reason Rigg's brother and wife, Violet's family, seemed like the last hurdle. If they liked her, that meant she had passed.

Lorri told herself to quit being silly, but when Rigg stopped the car in front of a small bungalow, her heart continued to pound.

"That was Johnny King from your class, wasn't it?" Ruth asked when the family sat down to lunch.

"Yes."

"I haven't seen him in ages."

"I think he stopped coming about two years ago."

"Do you know why?"

"No, and I don't know why he was there today, but he looked so upset." Tears had come to Max's voice again, but she continued. "I told him I would pray for him, but he didn't want to talk. He's never not wanted to talk to me."

"Is this the boy who has been interested in you all year?" Dean wished to know.

Max nodded, not sure what to think.

"Did any of the men speak to him, Dean?" Ruth asked.

"I don't know, but I can find out tonight."

Max didn't know why, but she prayed that Johnny would be there. If he needed help, he needed to come back as often as he could.

"That was delicious," Jim told his wife, sitting back, full and satisfied.

"Thank you. Shall we wait on dessert?"

"I think that's a good idea. Besides, if Violet can't give Lorri a tour of the house soon, she's going to expire in her seat."

All adults laughed and looked to the little girl with compassion. She had been so excited to show Lorri around, but her mother had put the meal on as soon as Rigg and his guest arrived. As it was, Violet ate very little of her food, over-the-moon with excitement to have one of her teachers visiting her house.

Just as soon as Lorri thought it time, she told Violet she was ready for a tour. They naturally started in the little girl's bedroom. Dorothy trailed, loving the commentary from her daughter, and when Violet got distracted, the women visited.

"Your home is wonderful," Lorri told her sincerely.

"Thank you. We are really enjoying it."

"It's so warm and cozy."

"That's just what we were going for. Jim's folks' place is warm and cozy, and that's what I wanted."

"Yes, it is. I enjoyed their house very much."

"Virginia wrote and said that Mitch could talk about no one but your sister."

Lorri laughed, and Rigg chose that moment to seek the women out.

"I was telling Lorri that Mitch is a bit taken with Max."

Rigg smiled. "I told you," he said to Lorri.

Violet arrived back at their feet just then, William in her arms. Lorri asked if she could hold him, and for the rest of the afternoon, they were inseparable. Violet stayed close as well, but William had clearly fallen in love.

"Your family is so nice," Lorri told Rigg in the car.

"They're all just like me," he told her, his voice making it seem like a simple matter.

"Are they as modest as you are?"

Rigg managed a very pious look. "No one is that modest."

Lorri told herself not to laugh; it would only encourage him.

"I almost forgot. There's something I need to ask you. Do you suppose you could take a long lunch sometime this week and come to the base? Before I'm done I'd like for you to see some of the men. They ask about you."

"I would enjoy that," Lorri said in complete sincerity, thinking the timing was perfect. Next week she took over full-time for Mrs. Carter. "What day should I come?"

"Any day would work. Do you want to give me a definite answer now or check with your grandfather?"

Lorri shook her head. "I don't need to ask

him. Most sailors have a thankless job. If I want to see my rescuers again, he won't object."

"So you'll let me know the day?"

"Yes."

They fell silent for a moment, and then Lorri said, "I had a good time today. I enjoy your family."

Rigg smiled. "William was certainly taken with you." He paused. "Not that I blame him."

Lorri smiled but didn't look his way. Rigg's eyes were over the steering wheel, not looking at her either, but the awareness was there. It had been there almost from the first moment they'd seen each other at the school.

Your letter made my day, Ruth's father wrote the last week in May. *You and Dean come anytime you can. I don't get out as much these days, and there isn't anything on my calendar that can't be changed. You haven't seen the fall colors in many years, and that's sure to be a treat.*

Ruth didn't know why, but the words made her cry. She missed her father, missed him more with the passage of time. He was a great communicator, writing faithfully over the years, but not seeing him, not being close enough to hug him, was taking a toll on her heart. She also pined for her hometown, the precious people there, and the house where she grew up.

Ruth turned to the kitchen calendar and studied the weeks. Late September should work. That would put them in Minnesota in early October. Ruth took a pencil and wrote in the date. The colors would be beautiful.

Lorri Archer had been on U.S. naval bases since before she could walk, but not in recent years. She had been a young teen the last time she visited. And she was learning something in a hurry: Coming onto the base as a woman in her midtwenties was a completely different affair.

Jeeps slowed to a crawl. Sailors in a hurry suddenly had no place to go. Lorri didn't make eye contact with anyone but kept moving toward the building where she was supposed to find Rigg's office. She could feel eyes on her from every direction, and it was a tremendous relief to gain the building and slip inside.

A sailor stood when she stepped up to his desk, his look respectful as he offered to help her.

"Would you please tell Lieutenant Riggs that Miss Archer is here."

"Certainly, ma'am. Feel free to take a seat while you wait."

Lorri thanked him and did sit down, but the wait was far from taxing. The sailor returned, Rigg on his heels. He smiled at the sight of Lorri.

"Come on back to my office," he invited as he led the way.

"Did you get stared at?"

"Yes," Lorri said, looking down at herself with a frown.

"You look too good in that dress."

"I was going for severe."

Rigg shook his head in pity. Navy was her color, and her figure was too shapely to be ignored. Lorri looked up to find his eyes full of amusement.

"It didn't work, did it?" she asked.

"No, and since my men saw you looking distinctly different than you do right now, the staring is going to continue."

Lorri nodded, sure she knew what he meant but not prepared for the real thing. She walked into the mess hall and found the men all waiting for her at a table. They were astounded. Hugh Westland needed a few moments to find his voice, as did most of the others. Lionel was the only man who greeted her as though nothing had changed.

"It's good to see you, Miss Lorri."

"It's good to see you, Lionel," Lorri warmly returned, shaking his hand in the process. "I'm so glad you're home safe. I don't know if I ever thanked you for everything."

"You did, Miss Lorri, many times."

Lorri moved to speak to the others, but Hugh was catching Rigg's ear.

"You could have warned us," he accused.

Rigg smiled. "It's more fun this way."

Hugh shook his head a little. "I don't think I realized just how starved she was. I assumed she was a very thin woman to begin with."

For a moment Rigg was swept back. He could see how easily that would be to imagine. The pathetic little person they rescued — pale and skinny — was difficult to conjure up while in the presence of the current Lorri Archer, who exuded good health and well being.

The time went by fast. Lorri listened to stories of how the war had ended for the *Every Storm* as well as to the men's future plans. She also answered questions about her own life and her teaching. Most of the men were not afraid to tell her they were sorry for her loss, and Lorri wondered how many details of their personal lives they were omitting. Hugh had recent information about Harlan Ellis, and Lorri was glad to hear that he was home and recovering well.

She found it a little hard to leave them, but Rigg rescued her with the reminder that they all had to get back to work. Click had given her an envelope of pictures, which she tucked into her purse before Rigg saw her to the car.

"Would it be all right if I stop by tonight?" Rigg asked after he opened Lorri's door.

"Certainly. Would you like to come for dinner?"

"It will probably be afterward if that's all right."

"It's fine. Any time is fine."

Rigg thanked her for coming and smiled his warm, kind smile at her, but Lorri left with a feeling of unease. She didn't think tonight's visit was for pleasure. She tried not to worry about it the rest of the afternoon.

Ruth came from upstairs to find Lorri at the kitchen table, surprised that she hadn't heard her come in. It was on the tip of Ruth's tongue to ask about her trip to the base, but something in her daughter's posture stopped her.

Ruth came forward to see pictures set out on the table. About ten photos in all, they were the focus of Lorri's gaze. Her face was closed and very pale. Ruth sat down slowly, picking up a photo that showed the remains of the plane.

"Oh, my," she whispered. "Where did these come from?"

"A man I only know as Click. He always had a camera with him, but I have no memory of his taking most of these photos."

Ruth looked at Lorri lined up with the men, so thin and emaciated that Ruth's hand shook. She looked like a prisoner of war.

"You posed for this one."

Lorri looked at it. "That was at Seaford, just before I left the boat to see Grandpa."

"And did you see all these men today?"

"Some of them. This man," Lorri said as she pointed, "has cancer; he wasn't there. This is Ensign Westland — he was Rigg's second-in-command. And this is Lionel. He took care of me."

Lorri and Ruth looked at each other.

"Are you glad you have these, or are they too upsetting?"

"They're upsetting, but I'll treasure them, Mother. Look right here," Lorri picked up a picture of the clearing. "Just past these trees is where Josie is buried."

Tears came to Ruth's eyes, but they

weren't sad tears. It was like receiving a gift. Simple black-and-white photos that let her see a glimpse into her daughter's life.

"Are you going to write to Click?"

"I believe I will."

"Please add my thanks, Lorri. Please make sure he knows how much this means."

"I can't find work here in Harmony Hills or anywhere in southern California," Rigg told Lorri as they sat alone in the backyard that evening. "I've been writing letters for weeks, and no one is hiring architects right now."

"I knew you'd been applying," Lorri said, trying to ignore the sinking in her heart.

"I felt I had no choice," Rigg went on, "but to contact my old firm in Santa Rosa." He paused, his eyes meeting hers. "They have an opening. They want me back."

Lorri licked lips that had suddenly gone dry and found that her mouth was dry too. He was leaving. He couldn't find work here, so he was going to leave.

"What will you do?" Lorri asked in a voice that sounded completely normal.

"I've written and asked them to give me a few weeks. They agreed. If nothing down here comes up in that time, I'll take the offer."

Lorri nodded. "I think you're wise, Rigg. Jobs are not easy to come by right now."

Rigg looked at her, seeing that she was not as calm as she sounded.

"Santa Rosa is a long way from here," he said.

Lorri nodded a little. "It certainly is."

Lorri could feel his eyes on her and turned her head to look at him. For a time they only watched each other. Lorri read helplessness in his gaze and felt she needed to offer words of comfort.

"I really do understand, Rigg."

"Do you?" he asked quietly. "I wish I did."

To that Lorri added nothing. They stared at each other a bit longer before turning their gaze to the yard. At the moment there didn't seem to be anything else to say.

Graduation day, June 14, 1946, was upon the Archer family without warning. Standing in the living room, cap and gown in place, Max smiled for the picture her mother tried to take.

"I think the light is too bright from the window," Ruth said, staring down at the camera. "Let's close the curtain."

"I'm getting hot," Max complained.

Lorri closed the curtain and then checked her sister's hair.

"This hat looks awful, doesn't it?"

"It's a cap, and yes it does," Lorri replied.

Max didn't expect this. She burst out laughing just as her mother snapped the shutter.

"Raine!" she protested. "She got me with my mouth wide open."

"Well, then it will really look like you."

Again Max was taken off guard and laughed. Dean came in, a box in his hand, and waited for the women to turn.

"Well," he said to Max, "you look almost ready."

"What's missing?" Max asked.

Dean gave her the box. Inside was a beautiful iris corsage. Max gave him a huge hug and went to the mirror to put it on.

"That was sweet," Ruth told him.

"I'm a sweet guy," Dean teased.

"Have you seen the other *sweet guy* that usually hangs around here?" Ruth asked dryly. "We're going to be late."

The doorbell rang on cue. Rigg was in a suit, ready for this grand occasion. In his hand was a gift.

"Gifts now or later?" he asked Max once he'd bent to kiss her cheek.

"We're a little late, so it had better be later. But," she stopped him before he could get too far, "you can tell me what it is."

"Not a chance" was all he was able to get out before Dean hustled them all to the car. Rigg sat in the back with Lorri and Max, pushing thoughts of his departure from his mind. Instead, he concentrated on Max.

"How's the job hunt going?" he asked her. Max had decided against school right away opting to work for a time.

"I've got one at Brennan's if I want it."

"You don't sound like you do."

"I'm still hoping to get in at one of the hospitals. That's the only way I'm going to know if I'm cut out for nursing." She sounded discouraged. "Brennan's wasn't exactly what I had in mind."

She was quiet for the rest of the trip. Once they were there, last-minute hugs were given before Max scooted away to join her classmates.

Rigg and Lorri were side by side for the ceremony. The speeches were too long, as usual, but once the grads started across the platform, Max's name was the third one called. Ruth held up nicely, but Lorri found tears pouring down her face.

"Are you thinking of Josie?" Rigg whispered to her.

"Yes, and it's so silly. How can I feel sorry for her missing this when she has heaven?"

Rigg took her hand, knowing he didn't need to answer.

"You look great," Johnny told Max when it was all over. They had done it — they had graduated from high school.

"So do you," Max said warmly, smiling up at him. "How are you doing?"

"Better," he told her, knowing that the changes in him were confusing to her. He had gone from speaking to her every day to speaking to no one. Now he was smiling again, in church each Sunday but not falling all over her every time they met. "I was looking for happiness in all the wrong spots," Johnny explained for the first time. "I thought if I just had a girl who loved me, I wouldn't feel so lousy. It took a long time to find out I was wrong."

"My grandpa says you're meeting with Pastor Higgins."

"Every week."

"How is that going?"

"It's going well. I thought I knew a lot about the Bible, but I don't. I thought just believing was enough, but it's only the beginning. There's a whole life to be lived in submission to God, and I don't do well with that sort of thing."

"It's nice that we don't have to go through

it alone," Max said, thinking of the way God's Spirit lived inside of each believer.

"Yes, it is."

Johnny's family had arrived.

"I'll let you go," Max said with a hand to his arm before starting away.

"Max," Johnny stopped her. "Can I stop and see you sometime?"

"Yes, Johnny," she was able to say for the first time. "I'd like that."

Not ten steps later, Max's family found her. They hugged her with great enthusiasm, assuming that the tears in her eyes were all about graduation.

Twenty-Two

The Fourth of July, 1946, was on a Thursday. Americans everywhere celebrated the nation's one hundred and seventieth birthday, and the Archers were no different, working all morning on the food they would take to the church picnic that afternoon.

Lorri was kept especially busy. Rigg was done with the military. His belongings were packed, and he was leaving for Santa Rosa in the morning. His job with Bankman and Associates would start on Monday. Lorri was pleased for him, but her heart still hadn't taken it in. He was leaving. She didn't know how she would stand it, so she tried not to think about it.

"How are those potatoes coming?" Ruth asked, peering into the pot.

"Just about ready," Lorri told her. "I hope

you know that every woman in the church will bring potato salad."

"That's why we're not taking it," Ruth said, pleased with her planning. "I'm always exhausted after the Fourth of July, so that salad is for tomorrow. We're taking the fruit salad Max is working on."

Lorri laughed at her mother's satisfied tone.

"What else are we taking?" Max asked.

"Two pies, and those little rolls with ham and cheese."

"Oh, my favorite," Max said dramatically.

"Hey, Muffin," Lorri said sweetly to the cat that curled around her legs. "Are you behaving yourself?"

"She doesn't know how," Ruth said wryly, having wrestled a sock from her just that morning.

"She thinks she's a great hunter," Max declared. "She would have made a good lion."

"If lions lived on socks and underslips," Ruth put in.

"And bras!" Max added.

"Oh, that was awful!" Lorri groaned. "I may never get over it."

"You're going to marry the man, Raine, and then it won't matter."

"I think you forgot that he's leaving, Max."

"God can work these things out, Raine; just you wait and see."

Lorri tossed her sister a tolerant glance, but if the truth be told, she had done far more worrying than praying lately. With the school year ended, she was out of a job, and there was way too much time to sit around and worry about Rigg's departure. Lorri knew better but wasn't finding it easy to trust these days.

When the eggs and potatoes were done, Lorri pushed her thoughts aside to make the salad, once again choosing to ignore the situation rather than deal with it.

"Hey, Max."

Max wondered at the way her heart thudded at the sound of his voice. She turned to find Johnny behind her. They hadn't spoken since graduation, and she had not assumed he would be here this day.

"Hi, Johnny. How are you?"

"Fine. Yourself?"

"Fine."

"How's the job going?"

"It's all right — better than I thought it would be. How's your job?"

"It gets pretty hot on the job site during these months, but the pay is good, and I need the money for school."

Max was about to ask Johnny something else when she spotted someone behind him.

"Johnny, is your family here?"

Johnny's face lit with pleasure he did nothing to hide.

"They are here."

"Johnny," Max had to ask, "why did you stop coming to church a few years ago?"

"Because my parents never changed. They made my sister and me attend church with them each week and sit through sermons we found boring, but all they did at home was fight and spend too much money. I didn't see the point, so I started refusing to go. Then my sister stayed home with me, and eventually my whole family gave up."

Max nodded with compassion, seeing how easily it could happen. She had more questions for Johnny, but Arlene was coming.

"Maybe I'll see you later," Johnny said, turning back toward his family just after Arlene arrived and greeted him.

The two girls looked at each other, questions in Arlene's eyes, but Max gave a small shake of her head, telling her friend she couldn't talk about it right then.

Rigg and Lorri had driven separately from the family. The picnic complete, the fireworks over, Rigg drove Lorri home in silence. He found himself wishing he'd not already started to pack the car — it only reminded them — but knew it would not change the inevitable. Rigg pulled into the driveway, and they stood and talked for the last time.

"It was a fun day," Lorri started.

"Yes, it was," Rigg agreed, thinking she had never been sweeter or looked lovelier.

"What would you have done in Santa Rosa today?"

"Probably the same thing — picnic with the church family."

Lorri could only nod, her throat suddenly tight. She had so much to say but forced herself to be brief.

"I'll miss you, Donovan Riggs, but I wish you the best, and I want you to take good care of yourself."

"I'll see you again," he said to her, having heard this note of finality in her voice before. "I *will* see you again, Lorraine."

Trying to picture weeks and months without him, Lorri nodded and wasn't able to stop the tears that flooded her eyes.

Rigg suddenly put his arms around her, holding her close to his chest, and Lorri hugged him right back.

"I'll write you," he whispered, bending close to her ear.

"I'll write back," Lorri promised.

Rigg couldn't take it any longer. He released her gently and slipped back into the car. Lorri stood on the driveway and waved as the car pulled away, her heart frozen in her chest.

How could You do this? Ruth asked of God late that night. Alone in the living room, she sat on the sofa, trying to make sense of God's will. *She's lost so much — we all have — and now You've taken Rigg away,* Ruth accused. *I don't understand; I just feel pain.*

Ruth buried her face in the sleeve of her bathrobe to muffle her sobs, sure she was not going to survive this test. Rigg had come into their lives. They had all grown to love him. And Ruth thought if she lived to be a hundred she would never forget Lorri's face when she'd come into the house. Dry-eyed and in a state of shock, she had told everyone goodnight and gone up to her room.

Ruth thought it would have been easier if she'd cried. She had checked on her when she went to bed, but even though Lorri was awake and still dry-eyed, she didn't want to talk.

Sleep had been hours away for Ruth. She had tossed and turned far into the night before giving up and going downstairs.

Grabbing her Bible, but not really knowing why, Ruth acknowledged her anger at God. She didn't want to hear anything He had to say.

This attitude, however, did not last. In her heart Ruth knew her only solace was God's comfort. She cried for a time but eventually opened to Psalm 27. As she read with sudden hunger, many verses jumped out at her.

"Hear, O Lord, when I cry with my voice; have mercy also upon me, and answer me. When thou saidst, Seek ye my face, my heart said unto thee, Thy face, Lord, will I seek. Hide not thy face far from me; put not thy servant away in anger. Thou hast been my help; leave me not, neither forsake me, O God of my salvation. . . . I had fainted, unless I had believed to see the goodness of the Lord in the land of the living. Wait on the Lord; be of good courage, and he shall strengthen thine heart. Wait, I say, on the Lord."

Oh, Father, Ruth was forced to pray, completely humbled by the words. *I blamed You and was angry, and I'm sorry. I lost my trust. I was sure You had failed. I'm sorry. I have no excuse except for wanting my way. I thought Rigg was the one, but You know best. Help me not to lose heart again. Help me to remember Your faithfulness so my own will be sound.*

Ruth was suddenly spent. Having come full circle from anger to repentance, she didn't have the physical will or strength to stand. Clicking off the light and pulling her robe around her a little more, she slept on the sofa this night.

The last person Max expected to see in the women's department of Brennan's an hour before closing time was Johnny King, but he was there, his younger sister in tow. His sister began to look at dresses almost immediately, but Johnny stood, clearly uncomfortable in his surroundings.

"May I help you?" Max offered his sister. She knew her name was Evelyn.

Evelyn looked suddenly shy, and Johnny spoke up.

"My sister needs a dress for an outing she has on Friday. My mother couldn't come."

Max couldn't stop the amusement that lit her eyes. His tone had been so resigned, and he looked as though he would rather be anywhere but there.

"You're enjoying this," Johnny said, relaxing a little when Max was herself.

"Not at all," she lied, a smile peeking through. "What color do you like, Evelyn?" Max suddenly turned professional, and Evelyn, after some moments of shy interaction, selected three dresses to try: two yellow and one blue in lush summer prints. Following along slowly, Johnny stood outside the changing room trying to pretend he wasn't there. Max was having none of it.

"Is Evelyn supposed to let you see the dress, or is she deciding on her own?"

"I'm not sure."

"Does she have a price limit?"

"I don't know."

"Were you supposed to bring your brain into the store with you, or did you leave that in the car?"

Johnny finally caught on to what she was doing and even laughed a little.

"You are an evil woman, Maxine Archer."

"Are you just now figuring that out?"

"Men are not supposed to be in this section," Johnny pointed out.

"That's not true. A lot of men shop with their wives."

Johnny's face changed in a heartbeat. Pure, unadulterated interest filled his face, and he did nothing to hide it. His eyes held onto Max's until her cheeks began to flush.

"I need to check on your sister," Max managed, but her voice carried very little conviction. She turned for the dressing room, able to feel Johnny's gaze on her at all times.

Evelyn had found a dress. The blue one fit her well, was perfect with her fair hair, and was even within the price range her mother had said she could spend. Johnny had little else to say through the encounter, but Max was wholly aware of him. How could she not be? After her comment concerning husbands and wives, his eyes had barely left her.

"Oh, my," Lorri said when Ruth handed her the letter and she saw the postmark. "He must have written as soon as he arrived."

"He must have," Ruth agreed, but Lorri just stood there, the letter in hand. "Are you going to read it?"

Lorri looked at her mother. "There's something I have to do first."

Ruth watched as Lorri placed the letter on the table and then walked up the stairs. She knew her daughter had been in agony for the last several days and suspected that it looked much like her own struggle. Ruth sat at the table and prayed, asking God to help Lorri make peace with Him.

I don't know what the letter says, but I can't keep fighting You. I've been so angry and hurt, and I've blamed You for everything. I'm sorry, Lorri prayed from the floor next to her bed.

What a miserable marriage it would be if Rigg's not the one. I don't know why I insist on having my way. If he's the one, then You've planned a way, Lord. You always plan the way.

Lorri cried for a time, but they were tears of relief. She was done ignoring the pain and being unthankful. God understood that she was hurting, but the anger had to go. She didn't expect to have a headache when she read Rigg's letter, but the pain was a good one. This time it meant she was right before God.

"Okay, I have something to tell you," Max said before they started, "but you can't tease me or tell anyone."

"When do I ever tell?" Arlene wished to know.

"Okay," Max agreed, "you don't, but you can't tease me either."

"I won't. Go ahead."

Max bit her lip but still admitted, "I think I'm falling for Johnny King."

The stunned look on her best friend's face was hysterical, but Max wasn't in the mood to laugh. Arlene searched her friend's eyes and saw that she was serious, more serious than she'd seen her in a long time. Arlene's heart filled with compassion, and she simply put her arms around Max and hugged her.

"Do you hate me?" Max asked, and Arlene pulled back.

"Why would I hate you?" Arlene demanded.

"I don't know!" Max wailed in confusion. "I spent the whole year putting him off and now I tell you this."

"So what changed?"

Max looked as amazed as she felt. "I just didn't expect him to ever take his faith seriously, and every time he comes into church with that Bible in his hand, I just about die."

"What kind of die? Happy die, or upset die?"

"Happy die," Max confessed. "He's still fun and charming, but there's a peace about him now, like he knows he doesn't have to prove himself any longer."

"What does your family think?"

"You're the first one I've told."

Arlene smiled, seeing what Max had not realized.

"Your children will be beautiful. I hope you realize that," she said.

"Arlene Andrews!" Max exclaimed, shocked. "What a thing to say."

"He's the one, Max. I'm sure of it."

Max suddenly heard herself. Didn't she say that to Lorri about Rigg on a regular basis? And what did it do to Lorri's heart?

Right now her own was trying to leap from her chest.

"So what now?"

"Nothing," Max said. "I have no idea how he feels."

Arlene sat back, looking as satisfied as Max had ever seen her.

"What does that look mean?"

"Only that it's a matter of time. I'm sure of it."

Max grew serious again.

"Arlene, are you really all right with this? Do you think Johnny could change that much?"

"What I think is that God can do anything. And if Johnny keeps on the way he's going, I can't think of why anyone would object."

"I'm glad you said that," Max replied, hearing more than the words. "I've got to give it time. I can't rush this."

"And wasn't it your grandpa who told you Johnny's having Bible study with Pastor? So you know he's aware of the situation."

"Right, right," Max agreed, trying to catch her breath, the possibilities flying through her mind.

"Are you finally ready?" Arlene teased.

"Yes," Max said, positioning herself in the chair, magazine in hand.

"Show me the picture again," Arlene requested.

Max held up the page full of models from the Sears catalog and pointed. Arlene took a moment to study the woman's image and then picked up the scissors. Max Archer was getting a haircut.

Well, what do you expect, Maxine Archer? that woman asked herself in disgust, the church service just starting. *You're not here to worship God and learn; you came to show off your new haircut to Johnny King, and he's not even here today!*

This scolding complete, Max bent her head with the rest of the congregation, but she didn't hear Pastor Higgins' prayer. She was too busy confessing her self-interest and asking God for an improvement on the day, especially concerning her attitude.

Santa Rosa

Rigg smiled over every line of Lorri's letter. She confessed how angry she'd been with God about his leaving and how she even had a headache when she read his letter but still loved it. He laughed outright when she described some of Muffin's latest escapades but was mostly remembering the night Muffin had arrived in the living room with an unmentionable article of clothing dangling from her teeth.

The letter read, Rigg sat at the kitchen table and sighed. *I've got to go back and ask her to marry me, Lord. I love her, and I know she loves me. My family loves her. Her family loves me; I can see it every time we're together.*

Rigg ordered his thoughts for several more moments before settling in to write another letter. He would write Lorri as well but not just yet. This time he had business with the admiral and Lorri Archer's mother.

Max wrapped the two blouses carefully for the waiting woman, glad she would be headed on her way. The woman had been almost impossible to please and Max feared she would find some reason to complain to the manager.

Max was just about finished when she spotted him. With no mother or sister to give him an excuse, Johnny was standing at the edge of the department, his eyes on her. The tissue paper almost tore in Max's hands, but she forced herself to concentrate and finish.

"There you are, Mrs. Duncan. I hope you enjoy them."

"For that price, I ought to."

Max didn't try to comment. She let the

woman move off and then straightened the work area, wondering at the sudden shaking of her hands.

"Hello," Johnny said, coming across the room faster than she figured possible.

"Hi, Johnny," Max said with relief, glad to see a friendly face. "How are you?"

"I'm fine, but I can see you've been busy."

Max's brow creased with confusion until Johnny reached out and touched the ends of her shorter hair.

"Oh, my hair." Max was suddenly embarrassed. "I'd forgotten for a minute."

Johnny just stared at her, and Max's heart sank. She could tell he didn't like it.

"You know, Max," he said quietly, "you were already more than a little distracting. I don't think it's fair that you do things to make it worse."

Max's shoulders sagged with relief and she smiled up at him.

"You didn't think I'd like it, did you?" he asked.

"Well, I wasn't sure. You didn't look too pleased."

Johnny didn't verbally comment but he still communicated: His smile was warm and familiar, and for a moment Max forgot where she was.

"I can't have visitors while I'm working,"

she remembered, coming back to earth with a thud.

"All right. I'll just wander around until you're off."

Her confused look told him every normal thought had flown from his head and he hadn't explained his presence.

"I stopped by your house," he said, "but your grandfather said you were working. I told him I'd bring you home."

"Oh, okay. The employee exit is on the east side of the building. I'll come out as soon as I can."

"No hurry," Johnny told her, moving calmly on his way.

Watching him, Max wished there was something calm about her just now. Her heart felt like a trip-hammer. She was only too glad that no other customers came in before the store closed. Fueled by extra adrenalin, she left the department in perfect order and was out the door in record time. Johnny was standing nearby, and there was still plenty of light to find him.

"Long day?" he asked.

"Not too bad. The woman you saw wasn't very pleased, but then she never is."

"So most of your customers are regulars?" Johnny asked, holding the door for Max to slip inside.

"For the most part, but we get plenty of new faces all the time."

In silence Johnny maneuvered the car from the parking lot and onto the street. Max felt nervous, and in an effort to cover it said the first thing that came to mind.

"I didn't see you on Sunday, did I?"

"No, my family took a little weekend trip."

"Oh, how nice. Where did you go?"

"My uncle has a lake house. We went there."

"Sounds fun."

"It was. It never has been in the past, but this year it was great."

"Why was it different?"

"Because we're different," Johnny said without conceit. "My dad didn't understand that he was to be leading the family. My mom didn't get that either. It didn't go very well with it the other way around."

"I don't think I've ever met your parents, but they sound like wonderful people."

"What do you mean?"

"It's not easy to be told you're wrong, and change is hard, but now they've found out they need to grow and they're working on it. That's pretty special."

"Yeah, I guess it is. Even my sister is doing well. She loves that dress you helped her buy."

"It looked nice on her."

"I'll tell her you said that," Johnny put in and then laughed a little. "She'll want her hair cut as soon as she sees yours."

Max's hand went to her now shoulder-length locks.

"Why is that?"

"She thinks everything about you is perfect." They were now in the Archers' driveway, and Johnny turned to look at her, his eyes far too serious. "She's just finding out what I've known all along."

When Max didn't have a snappy reply, Johnny climbed from the car. He opened Max's door before informing her that her mother had invited him for pie.

"Apple pie," he told her as they walked to the door. "I just might offer to drive you home more often."

Max laughed with more than just humor; she was relieved. He sounded like the fun-loving Johnny she knew. Her heart was already trying to gallop ahead of her. If Johnny kept talking the way he had in the car, there would be no stopping it.

Twenty-Three

August was hot. Lorri knew the earlier she got into the yard to water, the better it would be. Not bothering to do anything more than pull on a pair of shorts and an ancient blouse, she headed out to soak the yard, singing quietly all the while.

Activity went on in the house behind her, but she didn't notice, not even when someone came from inside, sat on one of the patio chairs, and waited for her to finish. It didn't take long. Lorri turned off the water, coiled the hose and started inside. She stopped when she saw Rigg. Even when he stood to his feet, she stayed still on the grass.

Rigg was a man of tremendous patience, something for which he had never been more thankful. Knowing how patient he would need to be in the coming days and weeks, he now waited for Lorri to speak or move toward him. She finally did walk his way, never once taking her eyes from his.

"I missed you" were the first words out of her mouth, her hands coming out to touch him. "I missed you so much."

"I missed you too, every moment." Rigg had taken her hands in his.

Lorri continued to look up at him. It was so clear to her now. She loved him. She loved him with every fiber of her being.

"Are you here for the weekend?" Lorri asked, trying to think clearly.

"Yes, staying at Jim's."

"When do you have to head back?"

"Tomorrow, sometime after lunch."

"So we have all day?"

"All day."

Lorri smiled and Rigg laughed a little.

"In fact, we're going out to dinner tonight," Rigg told her. "Just the two of us."

"I would like that."

"I think your mother is making breakfast. Shall we go in?"

Lorri nodded, not able to stop looking at him. Her heart had come to a place of resignation, a place of low expectations. She had not expected him to keep in touch for too much longer. She thought the letters would become fewer and fewer and then end altogether. A visit from him had never crossed her mind.

"How about some coffee?" Ruth offered, trying not to weep over the look on her daughter's face. This had been a hard secret to keep. Rigg's coming and his intentions while there had been known to them for a while now. But Ruth also knew her daughter. And with that knowledge she realized that things might not end the way everyone hoped.

"Hi, Rigg!" Max suddenly said, coming into the room wearing her bathrobe. "I didn't know you were here."

"I just arrived," he said, giving her a hug.

Dean was working on eggs and bacon, and Ruth was taking muffins from the oven. In a short time, they feasted, Dean asking God to bless them all through the weekend and give Rigg safety in his travels.

"What will you do today?" Dean asked of the young couple.

Lorri had no plans and looked to Rigg.

"The coast?" Rigg asked Lorri. "Since it's so warm?"

"Sure. Which beach?"

"I think Sand Hill. How does that sound?"

"I'll pack a picnic."

And just that simply, the day was full. They ran away like children, sat on the beach, got too much sun, and dozed and talked all day. And the talk only continued when they changed for dinner and went out for the evening.

The coastal restaurant Rigg had picked was dark and romantic. Lorri loved the atmosphere and the chance to dress up. The meal had been delicious, but now they just sat and talked, tall glasses of tea in front of them.

"I think your nose is sunburned," Rigg told her in the candlelight.

"It probably is," she agreed, touching the offending facial feature. "Do you ever burn?"

"Not easily. Some of the men on the boat did. It wasn't overly fun."

"Do you miss military life at all?"

"No. I like order, but I have that in my life, so I'm fine without having to salute anyone."

Lorri laughed, but something was on her mind, and she wanted to talk about it. She saw no other way but to start.

"My imagination ran wild when you were gone," she admitted.

"What did you imagine?"

"That you would meet a nice girl in Santa Rosa and forget all about Lorri Archer."

"That's not going to happen."

"But I wouldn't blame you if it did

happen. Long distance relationships are so hard."

"Not when you really care."

Rigg put his hand on the table, palm up. Lorri put her hand in his.

They stared at each other for some moments before Rigg asked, "Do you mind if we skip dessert and go for a walk?"

"Not at all."

Rigg took care of the bill a short time later, and the couple found themselves walking along the beach, Rigg's hand holding hers. Sand crowded into Lorri's sandals, but she barely noticed. It felt so wonderful to be with him, to have him hold her hand.

Rigg suddenly stopped and brought her to rest in front of him, his hands on her shoulders.

"You need to understand that I came this weekend for one reason: to tell you that I love you and want you to marry me."

"Oh, Rigg," Lorri breathed. "I love you so much."

Her hand came out to rest on the front of his jacket, and she could feel the thundering of his heart. It was on her lips to say yes, that she would marry him any time he wanted, when she suddenly came back to earth.

Her head shaking a little as she worked not to panic, Lorri said. "I don't know if I can."

"Can you tell me why?"

As kind and patient as his voice was, Lorri suddenly felt cold, her heart squeezing with pain.

"I'm so insecure, Rigg."

"No, you're not."

Lorri shook her head. She had no choice but to tell him.

"I don't think I can do it, Rigg. I don't think I can live so far from my family. I'm sorry. I'm so sorry I'm not the woman you thought I was."

Rigg put his arms around her, searching desperately for words that would comfort her. For a time he only held her.

"Have I ever rushed you?" he asked at last.

"No."

"Have I ever made you do something you didn't want to do?"

"No."

Rigg moved back enough to see her face.

"I'm not going to start now."

Lorri didn't see where it came from, but suddenly it was there. A ring with a diamond. A perfect gold circle with a small diamond mounted on top.

Amazed by its beauty, Lorri was in her own world for a moment. But it wasn't long before she turned pain-filled eyes to Rigg.

"Don't say anything," Rigg stopped her. "I just wanted you to know I have this. It's not to hurt you or force you to say yes. I'll just keep it, and when you want it, you can have it."

"Oh, Rigg," Lorri said, dying a little over his gentleness. "I wish you could love someone other than me."

Rigg laughed. Lorri didn't expect that. Neither did she expect him to wrap his arms around her and give her a huge hug.

Lorri felt amazed. She was devastated to learn this truth about herself — that she couldn't move away from her family — but Rigg acted as though it were a perfectly normal reaction.

"Shall we walk some more?"

Lorri gawked at him.

"Okay, let me get this straight. You just proposed; I have to say no; and you want to go for a walk?"

The back of Rigg's hand came up to stroke her cheek as he asked, "How should it go? Do I storm off the beach because you need more time? Do I plead with you to marry me now? Do I give up my job and just hope for something in southern California?"

Rigg waited, but Lorri had no answer.

"I didn't know how else to do this, love. I wanted you to know how serious I was, but

I'm also a very patient man. Somehow, some way, we'll be together. We'll live as husband and wife and have a whole bunch of little Riggs and little Lorris. And we'll remember this conversation on the beach and the fact that more time was needed, but that's all it will be: a memory."

"I love you so much," Lorri said, thinking there was no one else in the world quite like him.

"And I love you. That's why I know this is going to work. We just have to give it more time."

"You mean give *me* more time," Lorri said, feeling disgruntled with herself.

"Lorri, I'm not the one who lived in Australia for more than four years and was then forced to say goodbye to my sister. It's not surprising that you don't want to live far from home right now."

Lorri realized, not for the first time, that she was harder on herself than anyone else was. She wanted to say yes to Rigg, but she couldn't. Not right now.

"And you'll wait?" Lorri asked him again.

Rigg bent and pressed a soft kiss to her mouth. He moved back just enough to look into her eyes.

"Yes."

Lorri threw her arms around the man she loved. She squeezed his neck so hard that he laughed with what air he had left.

"I'm ready to finish that walk now," Lorri told him, looking up into his face.

"And when you're ready for the rest?"

"I'll let you know."

A huge smile coming to his face, Rigg claimed her hand once again, and they continued down the beach.

"He's picked me up every Friday night for four weeks, Grandpa," Max tried to explain. "I just know that one of these days he's going to ask me on a date."

"And you're not sure if you should go?"

"I want to, but you've never said how you feel about Johnny. I mean, you seem to have a good time with him when he's here, but I can't tell exactly."

"I like Johnny, but that doesn't change the fact that you're both 18."

"He's 19, but I see what you mean."

"Do you? It's easy when you have an older sister in love to feel like you're ready for love yourself."

Max hadn't thought about it in those terms. She was a romantic at heart, and over the years Johnny King had said some very romantic things to her. She would have denied that it turned her head, but now she wasn't so sure.

"What do they call it?" Max thought out loud. "Being in love with being in love."

"I don't think you're that shallow, not in the least, but you and Johnny are young. I just want you to move very slowly, and dating won't let you do that. Keep getting to know each other in group situations where you're not paired off."

"So he can keep picking me up, but you'd rather I not go on a date with him?"

"Yes. If it comes up and he has a hard time with the idea, I'd be glad to explain it to him."

Max smiled. "I don't think he would mind that. Rigg would have been terrified."

Dean had a smile of his own. "You're probably right, but don't forget, Johnny's never had to salute me."

The two of them laughed over this for a time before Dean suggested ice cream. It was much too close to dinner — Ruth was sure to scold if they were discovered — but this time they didn't let that stop them.

Lorri stood at Josie's grave, not really needing to talk to her sister but wanting to face some of her fears and thinking this might be just the place. Her mother and grandfather were coming behind her, moving a little more slowly to give her time.

It didn't seem like 14 months ago that she died. Today it seemed like years. Lorri looked up at her grandfather, still in the distance, thinking that he wasn't a young man anymore. He was fit, in perfect health, actually, but not young. Lorri's eyes swung to her mother and knew she was healthy as well.

What am I so afraid of? she asked God. *Why can't I go on with my life? A man waits for me in Santa Rosa. He loves me, but I'm trapped here like a child holding onto my mother's apron. If I lived in southern California, I wouldn't see my family every day. They could still die at any moment, no matter where I lived.*

Lorri looked down at the grave and read her sister's name. Ken Showers had thought he would marry Josie. It had been his plan for years, but it was not to be. Would he change anything? Had he known it was not to be, would he still have asked?

Lorri knew that Ken would have asked anyway. He would have asked because he loved her and was ready to marry her whenever they had the chance. Just like Rigg. Even knowing she would say no, Rigg had proposed and bought a ring, and then told her he would wait.

"What a fool you are, Lorri," she whispered to herself, resolve filling her as she decided she didn't want to be foolish any longer.

"I'm going to Santa Rosa this weekend. I'm taking the bus," Lorri told Dean and Ruth as soon as they arrived home.

"Are you sure, Lorri?" Dean checked. "I can take you."

"No, I've been dependent long enough."

"You haven't, not at all," her mother argued.

"Well, I have been about some things, and I do want to marry Rigg. I want it with all my heart."

"I need to tell you something. I wish I'd told you before," Dean said, his voice thick. "I spoke to Rigg early on. I wanted you to be able to talk to someone about the island, and I told him just that. I put pressure on him to find a way, and when your mother asked him to dinner that first night, it seemed to be perfect.

"I thought he might be the one, Lorri. Maybe I shouldn't have interfered without telling you, but I didn't want you to be embarrassed. I only wanted you to have someone who had been there to talk to."

Tears had filled his eyes, and Lorri went

to him. "Thank you for telling me. I'm glad I didn't know."

Ruth was the next to hug her. She didn't let herself think about how far away her daughter would be living. It was closer than Australia, and she and Rigg needed each other.

"Mrs. Riggs," Lorri said into the phone the next morning. "It's Lorraine Archer. Am I getting you at a bad time?"

"Not at all, Lorraine. How are you?"

"I'm fine. I was wondering if I could be so presumptuous as to invite myself for the weekend."

Virginia Riggs had all she could do not to squeal with delight but simply said, "We would love to have you."

"If you're sure it will work, I'll come on Thursday and stay until Sunday. I'm not telling Rigg I'm coming."

"Well, you can trust me to keep a secret, and you come any day you like."

"All right. I'll be on the early bus and with you before dinner."

"Del will be there to pick you up, and I'll come up with some plan so that Rigg comes for dinner and doesn't know why."

"Okay," Lorri said on a laugh, loving her conspiratorial tone. "I'll see you Thursday."

Lorri hung up the phone, her heart pounding. There was some fear, but her excitement was greater. She was going to Santa Rosa. She was going to tell Rigg that she would marry him.

"What time I am afraid, I will trust in thee." Lorri recited Psalm 56:3 to herself, still working hard not to be a fool.

Santa Rosa

"Hello, Lorraine." Del Riggs greeted her warmly, even giving her a hug.

"Hello, Mr. Riggs. Thank you for picking me up."

"The pleasure is all mine. Is this your only bag?"

"Yes. I didn't even try to bring a dress as I have to be back on the bus right away Sunday morning."

"Let me take that for you. How was the trip?"

"It was fine. I read most of the way."

"You don't get sick?"

"No, but my sister does, and it's not very fun."

Lorri was calming more with each minute. She didn't know these people very well, but she shouldn't have worried. They must have approved of Rigg's proposal, and she knew what a wonderful son they had raised.

"Is Max with you?" were the first words from Mitch's mouth when she stepped through the door.

"No, not this time."

"Tell her she should have come."

"Oh, go on, Mitch," his mother teased, "and let me hug this girl. It's so good to see you, Lorraine."

Lorri hugged Virginia back, so thankful that she'd taken this step.

"Now, why don't you take your bag up to the room you had before and then come down and help Mitch set the table. You've timed this just right, you know. Donovan will be here in about 30 minutes."

Lorri smiled and headed upstairs, so excited she could hardly stand it. She had actually done it, actually pulled off the surprise.

Rigg had a headache. His mother was expecting him for dinner, but tonight he was just not up to it. He stood next to the phone in the kitchen, one hand rubbing his temple, and dialed his folks' number.

"Hello," Virginia said into the receiver.

"Hey, Mom, I don't think I'm going to make it."

"Are you not feeling well, Donovan?"

"Just a headache. I think I'd better stay home."

"Why don't you come by long enough to fill a plate?"

"No, I think —"

"Lorraine, why don't we put that milk pitcher on the table now," Virginia said, barely moving the phone from her face. "What were you saying, dear?"

"Mother," Rigg's voice had dropped. "Who were you just talking to?"

"Me?" Virginia could have accepted the Academy Award then and there. "I wasn't talking to anyone."

The silence lasted only a moment.

"I'll be right over," Rigg said into the phone, not even giving his mother a chance to say goodbye.

Virginia had just replaced the receiver when Lorri poked her head around the corner.

"Did you say something to me, Mrs. Riggs?"

"No, dear. I was just on the phone."

Virginia smiled when Lorri nodded and went back to setting the table. Right now she thought she could smile for the rest of her life.

Much as Rigg's heart told him to run, he walked. He knew his mother would not play games with him. If Lorri wasn't there, she would have admitted it to him, but Rigg couldn't quite get his mind around the fact that he was going to see her in just a moment.

Slipping in the back door as he always did, Rigg stepped into the dining room and found her setting the table with his brother. Mitch was the first to spot him. He set down the cup he was holding and waited. Lorri saw that action and looked up.

"Hi," she said, loving that she was in the same room with him.

"Hello, yourself," Rigg said, just wanting to drink in the sight of her. He glanced around but didn't see her family. "How did you get here?"

"The bus."

"Is Max here with you?"

"No." Lorri began to smile.

"Your mother?"

"No."

Rigg could feel his heart beginning to pound.

"You came alone?"

Lorri just nodded, and Rigg came toward her, took her hand, and led her toward the back hall where he'd just come in.

"If you'll excuse us for just a moment," he said to his family, who had all stood watching with unabashed curiosity. Once in the hall, he turned and took Lorri in his arms.

"Please tell me you're here to say yes to my question."

"I am," Lorri told him and watched Rigg's eyes shut, his forehead coming to rest on hers.

Lorri smiled up at him and waited for him to look at her.

"I love you so much," he said.

"I love you too." They had said it in letters; it felt so good to say it again in person. "I came on the bus to tell you."

Rigg wanted nothing more than to kiss her, but his family was waiting. Still holding her hand, Rigg went back to the dining room.

"Dad, Mom, Mitch, I want you to meet the future Mrs. Donovan Riggs."

As might have been expected, dinner was a little late.

Twenty-Four

"When will you marry me?" Rigg asked. He and Lorri had offered to do the dishes. It gave them a chance to be alone.

"Well, I'm going to Minnesota with Grandpa and my mother at the end of September. We'll be gone for about three weeks. I can marry you any time after that."

Rigg smiled at her pragmatic tone, but he actually had tougher questions he needed to have answered.

"What changed for you? Why did you come?"

Lorri dried a dish and thought about how to answer.

"I was afraid, but I couldn't see that. I thought I just needed to be near my family because of all the changes in the last year, but it was fear."

"Of what?"

"Fear that they'll die when I'm away, like Josie did for them. Fear that I won't see them again on this earth."

"Is the fear gone now?"

"Not all of it, but I'm fighting it. I'm trying not to let it control me."

Rigg didn't want to keep his distance any longer. He came close enough to kiss her but just looked into her eyes.

"I was coming to see you this weekend. Did I tell you that?"

"No, but I hadn't seen you since the weekend you proposed, and I thought you might come down. I was afraid we'd pass each other on the road. That's why I came on a Thursday."

"I'm not going to want to go to work tomorrow."

"But we have all day Saturday."

"And Sunday."

"No, Rigg, I have to be on the morning bus in order to get home by evening."

Rigg shook his head. "I'll take you home."

Lorri frowned. "Do you have Monday off?"

"No, but we'll leave early like the bus would have; we'll make much better time than the bus does; and I'll get back when I get back."

"That's an awful lot of driving."

Rigg got a little closer. "Ask me if I mind."

Lorri smiled, and Rigg wasn't willing to wait any more. He kissed her. Not a long, passionate kiss, but one that still left them a little breathless.

"What day did you say you would marry me?" Rigg asked comically, giving Lorri the giggles.

Del was headed to the kitchen from the living room. He wanted a glass of water, but the sound of Lorri's quiet laughter stopped him. They had so little time together before Lorri would have to go back. Del knew the drink could wait.

"Okay, have you got the calendar?" Rigg asked. It was early Sunday morning, and they had been on the road for all of ten minutes.

"I have it."

"Okay, mark the dates you're gone on your trip."

Lorri turned to the end of September and circled the date her mother had written on the calendar at home. She paged ahead three weeks later and circled that day.

"When will you be back?"

"Around the twentieth of October."

"Okay. How much time will you need after that?"

"For what?"

"Oh, you know, finding a dress and such."

"My mother will make my dress."

"Does she sew that well?"

"She sews so well that you don't realize she's made many of the things we wear."

"I had no idea."

Lorri only smiled but didn't look back at the calendar. Rigg knew he was excited to find a date and wondered why she wasn't. He asked her.

"I am excited," she told him, "but it's just occurred to me that I don't know all that goes into this. I want things to be simple. Is that going to be all right with you?"

"Are you asking me about simple? I'm the one who wanted to suggest elopement to you all weekend."

Lorri loved this. She laughed and looked over at him behind the wheel. Rigg glanced her way several times.

"Don't you want to scoot over here and sit in the middle of the seat?"

"I do, as a matter of fact," Lorri told him but held her place.

Rigg had to smile. "You're a smart girl, Lorraine Archer."

"I might be, but I think mostly you've just remembered that my grandpa was an admiral."

It was Rigg's turn to laugh, and Lorri hoped they would do just that all the way home.

The family was very pleased to see Lorri earlier than expected, a ring on her hand and Rigg in the bargain. Lorri, however, knew that Rigg had to get back on the road and didn't take long to call a business meeting — wedding business.

"So what's a good time, Mother?" she asked the woman she thought would have all the answers to such things. "How much time do we need after the trip?"

"Well, do you want something fancy and grand?"

"No," Rigg and Lorri said together, causing Dean to chuckle.

"Have you considered eloping?" Dean asked, and it was Ruth's turn to say no.

"We want something simple," Lorri told her. "I don't want a fancy gown or an elaborate reception."

Ruth studied the calendar. Figuring they would return around October 20, she added about six weeks.

"How does November 30 sound? It's a Saturday." Rigg and Lorri studied the calendar with her. They smiled at each other before Lorri drew a heart in the square.

Coleman, Minnesota

"How are you doing?" Paul Stewart asked his daughter when they had a few moments alone. "How is life without Jo?"

"Most of the time I do well, but some days I can't take it in. She was gone for so many years that I can convince myself she's still in Australia."

"Max looks like her."

"Yes. Max is even prettier than Josie was, but the resemblance is certainly there."

"It's no surprise that your girls are beautiful," he told her, eyes full of love.

Ruth smiled at him. "I'm so sorry it took so long to get back here, Dad."

Paul dismissed her words with a shake of his head. "You're here now, and that's all that matters."

Ruth loved him for understanding, but her heart was also resolved. Her father was not getting any younger. Even if she had to come alone on the train, she would not wait this long between visits again.

Harmony Hills, California

"How was your trip? When did you get back?" Johnny asked Max the next time he saw her at church. It had felt as though she'd been gone forever, but he didn't add that.

"We got back yesterday, and it was wonderful. The colors of the trees were amazing, and my Grandpa Stewart was so much fun. It was great to see him."

"And did you have to quit work, or did they give you the time off?"

"They gave me the time. They were very fair about it."

Max remembered back to her decision to accompany her family to Minnesota. She knew they would probably never go as a family again, and she didn't want to miss it, even if it meant quitting her job. Brennan's had not forced her into that. The time off was not paid time, but she still had her job when she returned.

"So it's back to the old grindstone in the morning?"

"Yes. How are your classes going?"

"Pretty well. It's still school, and you know that's not my favorite place."

"Yes, but when you're finished you'll be an engineer, doing what you love."

Johnny smiled at her enthusiasm but then remembered that she wasn't doing what she wanted to do.

"What about you? Any word from the hospitals?"

"I haven't checked back with anyone lately. I think I've given up."

"That's not like you."

"How do you know that?"

"You were in the top five of the class, Max."

"Maybe I'm just naturally brilliant."

"Well, there's never been any doubt of that."

He'd done it again. Just when she least expected it, his tone had grown warm and serious, with no teasing light in his eyes. And the worst part was, she never knew how to respond, so once again Max looked at Johnny in helpless silence until he rescued her.

"I'm glad you're back," he said simply, his tone light again, his head tipped to one side in a way she found adorable.

"Thank you. It's nice to be back. Oh! I almost forgot," Max reached for her purse, dug around a bit, and handed him a postcard. It was all filled out but with no address.

"Thank you," Johnny said sincerely, effectively masking the way this made him feel.

"I didn't have your address with me."

Johnny studied the red, orange, and yellow leaves in a copse of maple trees and knew she'd seen these. He thought about how much fun it would be to see them together. Johnny felt a yearning so strong inside of him he couldn't speak for a moment.

"Oh, there's the music. I'd better get to my seat," Max said.

"Okay," Johnny agreed, feeling rescued.

He went to sit with his family, smiling at his mother when she sent him a small wink. She knew his feelings for Max Archer. From that point he did his best to listen to the sermon and not think about the postcard he had tucked into the back of his Bible.

"Admiral," Pastor Higgins said, catching Dean before he could leave. "Have you got a few minutes?"

"Certainly."

The men moved off to a corner of the foyer, giving them enough space to be private.

"I want to talk to you about John King," the pastor began. "It's probably no secret to you that he cares for Max."

"No, no secret there. He's been at the house enough for me to have figured that out."

"I assume if you had objections at this point, you would have said so by now."

"I do not object to his getting to know Max, but you almost make it sound like I've missed something."

"Not at all, but he wants you to know that

he's not playing games. He just doesn't know how to tell you that."

Dean nodded, trying to think this through. He and Ruth both liked Johnny and could see why Max did too.

"Does he still meet with you?"

"Every week, as do his folks and sister."

"All together or separately?"

"I see John on his own."

"How would you say the family is doing?"

"Very well. Working hard."

"And how would you say Johnny is doing?"

The pastor's mouth quirked. "If my own Charlotte were 18 instead of 13, I'd be steering her in John's direction."

Dean nodded, very pleased to hear this.

"Tell him to call me, or if he'd rather, he can write and tell me his thoughts."

"I'll do that. I think he'll be very encouraged that you're giving him a chance."

"I take it he hasn't had many of those."

"That family has had its share of problems, mostly brought on by themselves, but one of the things he talks about the most is that Max has always shown him respect. Even when she spent the whole school year turning down his advances, she did so with kindness. It was her witness before him that showed him he had to get back to the church

441

family and find his place before God."

"Is it all right if I tell Max that?"

"I'm sure it is. John may have already done so."

The conversation over, Dean thanked Pastor Higgins and went to find his family, already planning to speak to Max as soon as they arrived home.

"He said that?" Ruth asked of Dean when Max seemed stunned into silence. "He said Max was an example to him?"

"That's right." Dean looked to his grand-daughter, who had tears in her eyes. "What's wrong, Max?"

His tone — somewhere between compassion and commanding — was too much for her. Every thought and feeling she'd had for weeks seemed to burst out of her.

"I'm just so confused! I mean, I think I care for him, but you're just going to tell me I'm too young. I swore off boys and put him off all year, but now he comes each week to church and I see him with his family. He comes to see me at work, and he's so sweet. He looks at me in that special way."

Ruth and Dean watched as she dissolved into heart-wrenching cries, her head buried in her arms. Lorri heard her from the other room and came to the kitchen. She stood in silence, her heart tearing to see her sister in pain.

"It's all right, Max," Ruth comforted, having drawn close. "Don't cry anymore. It's all right. We're not going to dismiss your feelings because of your age."

She tried to stop crying, but it wasn't working. Dean still tried to speak to her.

"How long have you felt this way, honey? Is it something I said?"

"I guess so. I mean, we are young, and Johnny has never said that he loves me, but I do care for him, and I think that's where love starts."

Ruth stroked her hair and her arm, very shook by her daughter's response. Max was their little rock — the strong, resilient one. She always had the positive attitude and seemed to bounce back faster than her sisters. Ruth had no idea she had struggled with any of these issues.

"First of all," Dean began, passing his handkerchief to her, "I need to tell you that your mother is right. I don't think any less of your feelings because of your age."

Max's head had come up, but she was still moping.

"If you recall, I married your grandmother when she was 18, and I was two months past my nineteenth birthday."

"I'd forgotten about that."

Dean's mouth quirked. "I want to see you giving this time, but not because of your age. A marriage is first and foremost a fellowship between two faithful people. You and Johnny must prove you can be faithful to God, so you can have a fellowship that's pleasing to Him. Your age is not the issue, even though I reminded you that you're young. More time is the issue."

"He hasn't asked me to marry him, Grandpa," Max felt a need to remind him.

"No, but if you keep on as you have been, you know it will come."

Max had a whopper of a headache by then, and the conversation didn't last much longer, but her grandfather's words lingered in her mind: faithfulness, a fellowship, and an inevitable proposal from Johnny King.

Rigg could not stay away even though the hour was early. It felt like a year since he'd last seen Lorri, and much as he wanted to knock on the door, things looked quiet. For this reason he slipped in through the side gate and got comfortable in the yard, enjoying it even when Muffin found his lap, an immediate rumble starting in the cat's chest.

Dean was the first to spot him. That man

came to the yard, two mugs of coffee in hand.

"How was your trip?" Rigg asked of the retired admiral.

"Wonderful. We should have gone many years ago."

"How is Mr. Stewart?"

"Doing well. He and Ruth have always gotten on famously, and they entertained us with family stories for days. I had forgotten what a character he is. Max is just like him."

Rigg took a pull from his coffee cup and just listened as Dean shared the things they had seen and done. He had received postcards from Lorri, but he knew there was only so much you could fit into that space.

"Well, now," Dean suddenly said, his head turning to look in the kitchen window. "I think someone is up who might want to see you."

Dean left the yard on that note, and by the time Rigg got to his feet, Lorri was there. Rigg took her in his arms and held on tight.

"I missed you," she said, stretching on tiptoe to hug his neck. Rigg's arms were around her, and as far as he was concerned, there was no reason to ever let go.

"Five weeks from today you won't have to miss me anymore."

Lorri stepped back and smiled at him. Rigg gave her a swift kiss.

"Have you had breakfast?" Lorri asked.

"No, but there's something I want to tell you first."

Lorri took her grandfather's chair, and Rigg sat beside her.

"Bankman and Associates is opening an office in Shore Hills."

Lorri blinked. "Shore Hills, California?"

"Yes."

"As in 15 miles from here?"

"That's the one."

"What did you tell them?"

"I told them to count me in."

"Rigg," Lorri said, instantly beginning to worry. "Are you sure you want this? Are you sure you want to live outside of Santa Rosa?"

"I'm the one who looked for work down here for months before throwing in the towel."

"But wasn't that because you wanted to be close to me?"

"Yes, but the truth is that I like both cities and the churches in each one, so if you have a preference, we can live here."

"You don't mind?"

"Not at all."

"I still feel like a compromise is needed here."

"Okay," Rigg said slowly, not sure what he was agreeing to.

"I think we should retire to Santa Rosa."

Rigg laughed until he had tears in his eyes. With the interruption of the war, he'd only just started his career, and his bride-to-be was already talking about retirement.

"I don't think it's funny," Lorri told him seriously, watching his hysterics and trying not to allow even a smile. "We need to have a plan."

"I'm 27," he reminded her.

"Well," she conceded, "maybe it's a bit premature."

"A bit?"

Lorri looked exasperated and ready to tell him as much, but Ruth put her head out the door and said that breakfast was on.

"Well, Mother certainly rescued you," Lorri told him. "You need to be pinched."

"Do I get to pinch back?"

Lorri saw the look in his eyes and wagged a finger at him, her eyes telling him no. Nevertheless, she took no chances. She let Rigg go ahead of her into the house, not sure he was entirely trustworthy at the moment.

"I got your letter," Dean said to Johnny, catching him right after the service. "Thank you very much."

"Was I clear, Mr. Archer? I don't want to step out of line."

"Very clear, and I wasn't the least bit concerned of that. I think the idea of you and Max getting to know each other is a very good one."

Much as this affected the rhythm of Johnny's heart, he still calmly asked, "Do you know if Max is all right with that idea?"

Dean couldn't help but smile. "She was rather set against seeing anyone during her senior year, wasn't she?"

Johnny relaxed a little and gave a comical shake of his head.

"She was smart to hold me off at that time, but I didn't think anyone could have such resolve."

Dean smiled with pride.

"Maybe we'll see you Friday night," Dean told him, offering his hand.

Johnny gladly shook it, not even waiting until they'd left the church parking lot to tell his family what the admiral had said.

"You're looking rather distracted," Lorri teased Max at the end of the week. Johnny had just left.

"I am," Max teased right back. "I can't decide between waffles or pancakes for breakfast. I don't know if I'll be able to sleep."

Lorri laughed, grabbed Max's arm, and pulled her down to sit close to her on the sofa.

"I think he likes you," Lorri said.

"Why do you say that?" Max asked, sounding more than a little pleased.

"Well, how many weeks does this make that he's brought you home, and he doesn't just drop you off but comes inside, plays with your dog, talks to your family, and couldn't be more charming if he tried."

Max looked over at her sister.

"You make it sound like it's a big put-on."

"Not at all, Max. I didn't mean to. Johnny is a great guy. I'm just teasing you over the fact that he's having a hard time hiding how he feels."

"Do you think he can see how I feel?"

"I think so. You're a little cautious, but you haven't shown him the door."

"I got so used to rejecting him that it became a habit."

"I hope you know, Max, that that still has to be talked about," her sister advised, all at once serious. "If he's had girlfriends, you'd better make sure he's now ready to be a one-woman man."

"Grandpa said the same thing."

"I'll pray for you, Max."

"Thanks, Raine."

Not long into the silence that followed, Lorri sighed.

"Do you miss Rigg?" Max asked.

"All the time."

"It's not long now," she comforted her older sibling. "Just three weeks from tomorrow, and you won't have to miss him anymore."

Lorri sighed again. "Now I'll be the one who won't be able to sleep."

"You're up early," Ruth said to Dean when she went downstairs a few days before the wedding. "Are you feeling all right?"

"I'm fine. Buddy wanted out, and I didn't go back to sleep."

Ruth wanted tea this morning. She brewed a cup and then joined Dean over the newspaper.

"Did you see this ad?" Ruth suddenly asked. "The Simmons Company is making electric blankets. How does that work?"

"I don't know. It doesn't sound too safe."

"I think I will stick with the cotton and wool blankets we have," Ruth told him, going back to the printed page.

"Do you think Rigg and Lorri have enough blankets? Santa Rosa gets cold at night."

Ruth looked at her father-in-law. It wasn't like him to even think of such things.

"Are you worrying about them?"

He made a face. "Maybe a little."

"You'll like Rigg's family. They're wonderful."

"So you think about the distance too?"

"I do, Dean, but not with a heavy heart. I know it will be hard, but we've had her for more than a year, and Santa Rosa is easier to reach than Australia."

"Not to mention, they'll be moving back down here sometime next summer," Dean added.

"I keep reminding myself of that very thing."

No other words were shared, although Lorri's departure was still on their minds. By mutual, unspoken consent they went back to the morning paper.

Twenty-Five

November 30, 1946

"Oh, Raine," Max said when she went to the small room off the church foyer and saw her sister. "You look beautiful."

"Is the dress all right? Not too plain?"

"No, it's perfect, especially with Mother's pearls. She did a great job."

Lorri looked excited, but in truth she was very nervous. The idea of walking down the aisle in front of all those people made her knees shake.

"Don't be nervous," Max said, reading the look just as Dean knocked on the door and Max let him in.

Lorri's heart thudded when her grandfather said they were ready. She tried to calm down, but it didn't work. Not even the sight of Rigg in his suit, smiling up the aisle at her, their families and friends all around, could calm her down. Her voice quivered through the whole service. Rigg's own voice was deep and somber, and then it was over. They were husband and wife.

Lorri relaxed at the reception. Her husband holding her hand, she laughed, visited with everyone there, and loved knowing that Rigg was hers for keeps. Nevertheless, she had no desire to linger. When Rigg told her it was time to go, she said her goodbyes and thankfully left with her husband.

"Thank you, Mrs. King," Ruth said to Johnny's mother when she stayed to help with the cleanup. "Max was in charge of that, but she's a little sidetracked right now."

"I think we can blame Johnny for that," Mrs. King joked, and after a glance at the couple sitting alone and talking at one of the tables, they continued to work, leaving the young couple to themselves.

"That was a nice wedding," Johnny told Max over at the table, his hand fiddling with the flowers that had served as a centerpiece.

"It was, wasn't it?"

"And they met on an island in the Pacific, right?"

"Yes, the crew of Rigg's PT boat rescued Lorri."

"Wow," Johnny said with a shake of his

head. "That's amazing. Did they know then that they cared for each other?"

"Lorri said it was nothing like that. Rigg just made sure she was safe, and that was all. They didn't see each other for months, but when they did —" Max shook her head, leaving the sentence hang.

"Love at first sight?"

"I don't believe in love at first sight, but there was interest at first sight, that's for certain."

"Now, why doesn't that surprise me?" Johnny's voice told her he would not let that one go by.

"What?" she asked, pretending not to understand.

"The girl who swore off boys doesn't believe in love at first sight. I'm shocked."

"Do you?" she challenged him.

Johnny put his head back, as though in deep thought, and Max covered her mouth to keep from laughing. She knew she was being teased and flirted with all at the same time.

"It's not that hard of a question, John," she pointed out when he didn't speak.

"What did you call me?"

Max blinked at the change in him. "I don't know. I think John."

The eyes that watched her had turned intense. Max waited, hoping he would say what was wrong.

"Could it be," he began slowly, "that you don't think of me as a little boy anymore?"

"I've never thought that," Max said without hesitation. "Johnny's just your name. It's what I call you; it doesn't mean that I still think you're in the fifth grade."

"Then there's hope," he said.

"Hope for what?"

John realized he'd already said too much. He didn't know how to get himself out of this, so he simply reached up and tucked a stray curl behind Max's ear.

"I'd better help put tables away," he said, coming to his feet.

Max held her place and looked up at him.

"Don't look at me like that, Max. I shouldn't have said what I said. It's not time yet."

Max nodded but still wasn't altogether clear on what he meant. She did realize, however, that they both needed to be rescued. Max went to help Mrs. King and her mother, and John went toward his father and the admiral.

Rigg and Lorri were spending their honeymoon in a cottage on the beach. They drove for nearly two hours, and by then the sun was sinking fast and the night was growing cold.

Rigg used the key for the cottage, found the light, and held the door so his wife could make a run for the bathroom, a room that took a moment to find. He teased her for not having remembered such things before they left the reception, but she only laughed and said there was no time to lose.

On his own, Rigg didn't waste any time. The Campbells, the family who had let them use the small beach house, had left everything in immaculate order. They'd even laid paper and kindling for a fire. By the time Lorri came from the bathroom, Rigg had a nice blaze going and was seated on the sofa, his feet stretched toward the warmth.

Coming from the bathroom and seeing the arm Rigg held out toward her, Lorri joined him, fitting nicely against his side and putting her head on his shoulder.

"We did it," she said. "We got married."

"Yes, we did." There was no missing the smile in his voice. Rigg shifted so he could look down into his wife's face.

"You're so beautiful."

"I'm glad you think so."

"I definitely think so."

Lorri smiled just before he kissed her.

The first kiss led to another, and then another. It didn't take long before the fire wasn't the only warm thing in the room.

The new year dawned, and it occurred to Max that life in 1947 had returned to a place she'd been before. With Rigg and Lorri living in Santa Rosa, Max was once again an only child, but life around the house was a little different this time: There was no school, Max continued to work five days a week at Brennan's, and Lorri was close enough to visit and to have her visit them. And then there was John King and his family.

Max had been invited to their home on several occasions, and people were starting to form conclusions. Max's own heart was anything but cold to John King, but neither was it as settled as others seemed to think.

There were issues that the couple had yet to talk about, but Max had determined to let John lead on any discussion. The time came in early March. It was a Saturday, and the two had gone for a walk to the park. John walked them to an empty bench.

"Have you been meaning to ask me about the girls I've dated?" he asked with little prelude at all. "Or have you hinted and I missed it?"

"No, I didn't hint. I was pretty sure you knew that it bothered me and assumed you would bring it up."

John nodded, his eyes on the children who played on the swing set. He'd been talking to his father and Pastor about this subject but putting it off with Max. He wanted to marry Max Archer — he wanted it with all his heart — but even though he knew this might stand between them, it had to come out on the table.

"I have no excuses, Max, but I want to tell you everything I'm thinking, even if it sounds like an excuse."

"Okay," Max agreed, more open-minded than John realized.

"I was one of those typical high school boys who didn't think the future mattered. Rarely did I consider that my actions of the moment would affect the rest of my life." John turned his head to look at Max. He found her listening with full attention.

"I was sought after," he said with embarrassment. "The girls seemed to like me. I would ask them out, and they would go. Not you, but anyone else I asked. Sometimes we would date several times, even go together for months." John swallowed, hating to admit the rest. "If they would let me kiss them, I would. I assumed they wanted it as much as I did, and I never even tried to hold back."

"Was there more than kissing?" Max asked when he stopped for a moment.

"No," he said quietly, still not about to be anything but ashamed. "I wanted more. My mind went further, which is just as bad, but it stopped with kissing and hugging."

Max didn't know where the tears came from. They were for both of them. This was no secret to her, but it hurt to hear it from John's mouth, and to see his pain and regret over the past.

"I'm sorry," John said, his own eyes moist. "I think you deserve better than me, Max, but that doesn't change the fact that I still want to be the one. I can't picture my life with anyone but you."

"Oh, John," Max said as she reached for his hand. "I don't want this to keep us apart, but it's hard to know you kissed those girls. I'm afraid that you'll think of one of those other girls and not me."

John shook his head and knew he was going to have to tell all.

"That's the horrible part about it, Max: You were all those girls."

Max stared at him.

"Not in my senior year," John continued. "I waited for you that whole year, but in my

459

junior year, when I began to date, I went out with those girls only because you had no interest in me. I used them to get you out of my mind."

Max's mouth opened a little. She hadn't known this. She hadn't even suspected.

"Pretty bad, huh?"

"I had no idea," Max admitted.

John's eyes went back to the children. He felt as though his heart was being torn in half. All these months he'd been allowed to get close. He realized today might be the end.

His eyes went to their hands, just now realizing that Max had reached for him. Her hand was smaller than his, softer too. Touching her for one of the first times gave him hope.

"I'm a different person now, Max. I'm sure my list of faults is long, but I'm working hard to be faithful to God so you'll know I'll be faithful to you."

"I know you'll be faithful," Max told him. "I can't say that I'm never going to think of those other girls, but I believe you've put that behind you."

John nodded, relief filling him. He knew this wasn't the end of the discussion, but at least it was out in the open.

"Do you think about kissing me?"

John had not seen this coming. His head whipped around, and for a moment his face showed all the astonishment he felt.

"I'm sorry." Max was instantly contrite, panicked even, and stole her hand back in a hurry.

John laughed a little and gently reached for her hand again. He held it on the bench between them, but it didn't help Max's wide-eyed look.

"It's okay," John tried to reassure her.

"I didn't mean to ask that."

"It's all right. I don't mind."

Max looked at him, pale with embarrassment. John's face was calm and patient, but Max was still mortified.

"Do you want me to answer you?"

"I don't know," Max said honestly.

"What does your heart tell you?"

His words — tenderly asked — melted everything inside of her. She looked into the eyes that she'd come to love in the last months, eyes that always looked at her with respect and caring and something she'd never wanted to face until today: love.

"My heart tells me you're wonderful," Max said, not bothering with the original question.

John smiled at her, knowing that some day he could tell her what it cost him to keep his distance. He stood to his feet but kept Max's hand in his own. He held her hand all the way back to the Archer house, his heart and head telling him for the first time that he would have a future with this girl.

Rigg followed his wife up to the driveway of the Archer home, asking himself whether this was a good idea. Their first child was due at any moment, but when he mentioned staying home from Dean's birthday party, Lorri had looked crushed. They were actually closer to the hospital at the Archers' than they were at home, but his wife looked ready to pop, and the whole thing was making him very nervous.

"Do you know," Lorri began, peering down at the steps, "that I can't see my own feet these days, let alone where the steps are."

Rigg put his hand out. "Humor me then and let me help you."

Lorri took his hand and didn't bother to hide her amusement.

"You never did tell me why you thought we should stay home."

Rigg stopped, not reaching for the door handle as he had planned. He looked at his wife. Right now she had energy and was ready for anything, but it wouldn't last. He'd watched her do this every day for weeks.

"Being here will wear you out," Rigg said simply, knowing he could be honest with her. "And that's no way to start labor."

"We don't know that it will be today."

"Listen to me, love," Rigg said, still patient but wanting to make his point. "You've been saying that to me for a week. One of these days it's going to be *the day*, and you'll wish you'd taken it easy."

Lorri frowned at him but still said, "You're probably right."

Her frown always made him want to laugh. She tried to be fierce but wasn't at all good at it.

"Shall we go in?" he asked. "Or do you need to frown a little more?"

"I just might." She was still working to be tough.

"You can save it for later," Rigg said, his arm around her, a kiss going to her temple. "I'm sure to be in trouble again when I suggest you take a nap."

Lorri opened her mouth to get after him, but he smiled and opened the door, effectively cutting off anything she might have said.

The family came to hug her, and Rigg

stood back and watched, raising his brows in pure amusement when she looked his way, almost making her laugh.

"Is Lorri all right? I mean, should they be here?" Cora asked of Ruth when they had a moment. Ruth laughed a little.

"I'm not sure Rigg is all that thrilled with the idea, but I suspect Lorri desperately wanted to get out. He's going to get her to lie down in a little while."

Cora glanced over her shoulder and watched Lorri sink into a chair, relief on her face.

"If he came for her now, I think she'd go."

Ruth looked too. The women exchanged a glance but decided to leave it up to the Riggs.

"Why don't you and I take a trip upstairs?" Rigg asked, not waiting for an answer. "I think lying down might be a good idea."

"I don't think I'm tired yet," Lorri said, her words coming after a moment's thought.

Rigg wanted to laugh. She was blinking owlishly at him, and her movements were slow and deliberate. She hadn't noticed it, but there had been a collective sigh as he'd taken her from the group of men and women working on dishes.

"Look at this," Rigg said, doing his best to sound surprised once they reached Lorri's old room. "A nightgown, and right on your bed."

Lorri laughed a little. "I think I've been plotted against."

"Not at all," Rigg replied, working buttons and ignoring every protest in an effort to get her to lie down. Clad in the comfortable old gown her mother had unearthed, she made a trip across the hall to the bathroom. Rigg hovered near the door and urged her into bed as soon as she was done. Lorri finally stretched out, more comfortable than she'd been in hours, her eyes closing fast.

"Rigg?" she said softly.

"Right here, love."

Lorri's hand came out, but she didn't say anything else. Rigg held her hand in both of his until she was sound asleep.

The living room was actually quiet. Rigg and Lorri had gone upstairs, and the rest of the adults were in the kitchen and family room. This was the reason that Max invited John to sit down when he arrived, opting for a few minutes of peace.

"How are you?" he asked, thinking she looked good enough to eat.

"I'm fine. How are you?"

"Fine." He held a card out to her. "This is for your grandfather."

Max took it. "I'll put it with the others," she said, but she didn't look in any hurry to move.

"We have snacks if you're hungry," she offered.

"I'm fine, but thanks for offering."

Silence fell, something that had become unusual between them. Max wasn't sure what he was thinking, and John wanted to take his cue from her because she seemed distracted.

"How is your sister doing?" John finally asked.

"She's here — upstairs lying down. I think the baby might come soon."

"Are you all right with that?"

Max looked caught. How had he guessed that she was troubled?

"Did you suddenly become a mind reader?" she asked, trying to put him off.

"Where you're concerned? Always."

Max glanced around the room, not wanting to admit her true feelings.

"What's going on?" John pressed.

"I just don't want anything to happen to her. I've been worrying about that lately."

"Does she know that? Have you told your mother?"

"No. It seems too silly in this day of modern medicine, and I know I'm not supposed to worry for any reason."

"You've already lost one sister, and you don't want to lose another."

Relief flooded Max's face. "I didn't think anyone would understand."

John reached for her hand and held it.

"My mother told me that Evelyn and I are not really hers to keep, but that we belong to the Lord. Should the Lord want us, He has the right to take us, since we belong to Him." John hesitated. Max was listening to each word. "I think it must be the same with sisters, Max. You can't hold on to Lorri too tightly. She doesn't belong to you. If I had to make a guess," John put in right away, "I would say she's going to be fine, but either way, she belongs to Jesus Christ."

Max nodded, thankful for the reminder. The admiral showed up just a few minutes later, and John was able to personally deliver the card and birthday greeting. Dean could see that Max had been crying, but he didn't intrude, knowing that if she wanted to tell him she would. And besides, John was there with her. Dean knew there was no reason to worry.

467

★ ★ ★

"I think I hear movement upstairs," Dean quietly told Rigg just 30 minutes after Lorri fell asleep.

"Is Max or Ruth up there?"

"No."

Rigg took the stairs two at a time and came to his wife's door just as it closed. He knocked softly and slipped inside. What he saw stopped all the words he'd been ready to say.

With only a towel wrapped around her, Lorri Riggs stood in the middle of the room, the bedding on the floor.

"My water broke," she said simply.

"We have to get to the hospital immediately," Rigg commanded, sounding as though he were aboard the *Every Storm*.

"Not wearing a towel," Lorri said pointedly as she began to look for her clothing. Rigg had hung everything in the closet and now helped her redress.

"Did you get any sleep at all?"

"I think so."

But to Rigg's ears she sounded tired. It was not what he wanted for her, but clearly the choices were over. Most of the house knew what was happening before they could get out the door, and Ruth was there, hugging her daughter goodbye and telling her they would come soon.

468

Rigg gently tucked his precious bundle into the car, and off they went to the hospital. It was time to have a baby.

Everyone told him that for a first baby, the timing had been amazing, but the five hours Rigg had been forced to sit in the waiting room and wonder about his wife had been nothing but miserable.

He followed a white-garbed nurse down to his wife's room, finally able to see her. The room was dimly lit, but Rigg had no trouble spotting Lorri in the bed. He pulled a chair close and leaned to touch her.

"Hi," she said, eyes peeking open to see the face she loved.

"Hi, yourself," he said and kissed her. "You're a mommy."

"Isn't she beautiful?"

"Yes! What else would she be?"

Lorri laughed, a tired, relieved laugh.

"I thought we were having a boy," Rigg said.

"We don't have any girls' names picked out," Lorri responded, trying to concentrate when all she wanted to do was sleep.

"I have one."

Lorri looked at him.

"Josie."

"Oh, Rigg." Lorri wasn't sure. "Do you think it will be all right?"

"I think it will be wonderful, but I can ask your family first."

"Do that, Rigg." Lorri relaxed, knowing he would take care of everything. "Check with them, please."

"Okay, I will. Go to sleep now. I'll be here when you wake."

Lorri nodded, not able to fight it any longer. Rigg stayed close, watching her drop off before he closed his eyes to pray.

Thank You for this wonderful woman You have given me and this daughter that You've now given us. Help us to be faithful, Lord; help us to show her the way.

"Hello, Mr. King," Max said from their doorstep much later that day. "I know it's getting late, but I wondered if John is still up."

"Of course, Max." Mark King was delighted to see her. "Come right in. John," he called to his son. "Max is here."

John needed no other urging. He was in the living room in the next few seconds, his father leaving the young couple on their own.

"Hi."

"My sister had a baby," Max told him,

barely holding her tears. "She's fine and the baby is fine. I needed to tell someone."

John moved forward and put his arms around her, holding her close.

"I was scared," Max confessed. "Even at the hospital, I was scared. I didn't want to be, but I was."

"You weathered the storm."

Max moved her head back to see him. "The boat that rescued my sister was the *Every Storm*. I don't know if I've told you that."

John only nodded.

"Every storm we've ever been in, God has rescued us, John. Every time, the ultimate Rescuer has been there. I just realized it."

John smiled into her eyes before saying, "I prayed for you. I prayed for all of you."

"Thank you."

John continued to look down into her face. That she would come to him like this was huge. He knew she was the one, and it seemed she knew it as well.

"One of these days, Max, I'm going to be asking. One of these days, I'm going to be coming after you."

Max smiled. "Well, then it's a good thing that I'm not going anywhere."

John's smile matched her own as he pulled her back into his arms for another hug.

Epilogue

Ruth sat on the floor of the living room, five-month-old Josie in front of her, trying to sit up. She smiled with delight over anything Grandma did, a small laugh escaping when Ruth placed her in her lap and kissed her soft neck.

"I found them," Lorri called, coming from upstairs, photo albums in her arms. She joined her mother on the floor and took her daughter into her lap as soon as Josie reached for her.

"We're going to look at pictures, Jo," Lorri said to her daughter. "Look, this is your Aunt Josie. You were named after her."

"Isn't that a cute photo of the two of you," Ruth said, leaning close and remembering having a baby and a toddler who looked so much alike at that age that anyone could have picked them out of a crowd.

"Oh, and here's one of Max. Wasn't she adorable?"

"Where do you suppose they are right now?" Ruth asked, thinking of John and her youngest daughter on their honeymoon, a driving trip up the California coast.

"I don't know," Lorri said with a smile in her voice. "But something tells me they're having fun."

"Well, now," John said, looking down at the flat tire on their car. "This is fun."

His tone made his wife of three days laugh.

"You can laugh, Maxine King, but I'm the guy who's going to have to crawl around and get filthy in an attempt to fix this."

Still wanting to chuckle, Max offered, "Would a kiss help?"

"Just one?" John asked with a smile, already leaning toward her.

The flat tire forgotten for a time, the two stood next to the car and kissed. Not until a passing motorist was heard did they break apart, only to discover that it was a truck, a gas station advertised on his door.

"Can I help you folks?" the man asked as he parked his vehicle. In very short time Mr. and Mrs. King were back on the road.

"I don't think you got dirty at all," Max

told him, wind from the open window blowing her hair.

"Then why are you sitting all the way over there?" John asked.

Max slid across the seat, and settled right next to her husband, who smiled at her.

"My mother still sits next to my father in the car," John said, satisfaction filling his voice. "And they've been married for 24 years."

"Shall I plan to do that?"

"I think you should."

Sighing with contentment, Max snuggled a little closer, planning to run with that idea for the next 60 years.

About the Author

LORI WICK is one of the most versatile Christian fiction writers in the market today. Her works include pioneer fiction, a series set in Victorian England, and contemporary novels. Lori's books (more than 4 million copies in print) continue to delight readers and top the Christian bestselling fiction list. Lori and her husband, Bob, live in Wisconsin with "the three coolest kids in the world."